Give Them All My Love

Catherine
Cavender
From Carolyn

GIVE THEM ALL MY LOVE

Gillian Tindall

HUTCHINSON

LONDON SYDNEY AUCKLAND JOHANNESBURG

This edition first published in Great Britain
by Hutchinson, an imprint of Century Hutchinson Ltd,
Brookmount House, 62–65 Chandos Place,
London WC2N 4NW

Century Hutchinson (Australia) Pty Ltd
89–91 Albion Street, Surry Hills, NSW 2010

Century Hutchinson New Zealand Ltd
PO Box 40–086, Glenfield, Auckland 10, New Zealand

Century Hutchinson South Africa (Pty) Ltd
PO Box 337, Bergvlei, 2102 South Africa

British Library Cataloguing in Publication Data

Tindall, Gillian,
    Give them all my love.
    I. Title
    823'.914 [F]

    ISBN 0–09–173919–5

Photoset by Deltatype Lecru, Ellesmere Port, Cheshire
Printed and bound in Great Britain by
Butler & Tanner Ltd, Frome and London

After

So I lie here alone. At last.

But not lonely. Even without the face appearing at irregular intervals at the small grille in the door, I feel that I am accompanied, looked after. People who are stronger than I (though I never really believed in them till now) are taking charge of me, perhaps for ever. In my present state I am almost glad of that. It is like being a boy again. Freedom, of a sort.

No, I know it is not really like that. And tomorrow, perhaps, I shall feel differently. Tomorrow, perhaps, I shall feel again. And hate again. And fear again. But here, now, as I lie on this thin mattress, on this flat shelf, seeing only the yellowish walls near at hand, the white bulb high up out of reach in its wire-mesh cage, I do not believe, much, in tomorrow. It is as if, in the early morning brightness of today, I disposed of tomorrow. All the tomorrows. What a deliverance.

It is as if I myself had died. Or, no – for my body is still docilely functioning, heart beating, lungs inflating; I sweated a lot, first thing, in spite of the frost, and now I feel cooler, almost cold; I emptied my bladder a little while ago in the dank, disinfectant-smelling recess provided, I even ate some of the thick soup and bread I was given at the end of the day – no, it is, rather, as if my death had not yet happened but were a foregone conclusion, something so certain that I exist in a tranquil place beyond hope, the calm man under sentence of certain execution.

With part of my mind I know that this is a day-dream – another one. It is the night-before-the-end fantasy, an old friend familiar from adolescence. When I was young and full of hope, I nevertheless used to find it pleasant at times to picture how valiantly *I* would face a firing squad. If the war would last till I was eighteen, and by some fluke my

1

schoolboy French became so good that I would be picked by the Intelligence service for a dangerous and secret mission in occupied Europe . . .

The same dream was surely lodged in the mind of the boy that Jacquou knew, the boy that Jacquou . . . On his unremarkable face I saw, and see in my mind now, the very expression I would wish to have worn at his age: noble, courageous, unregenerate. The fact that he was not actually a hero dying a hero's death no longer seems of any significance. He thought he was.

It occurs to me only now, when I am alone at last, that my schoolboy fantasy of the dangerous, secret mission did not fade, as I had assumed, into adult common sense, but has remained concealed with me all the years in between. Why else do I now feel so calm, so much myself, in a word so *happy*? I did what I had to do, having arrived at the point at which I seemed to have no choice. A moral imperative, of a kind. But perhaps I have achieved more even than I thought I was achieving: the realization of a lifelong dream.

The further dream, of the execution squad, will not be achieved. I know that really. It is forty years since the war, and neither in France nor in England do men any longer kill other men in the name of the Law. No, I shall not enact that ultimate teenage fantasy, in either its British or its French version. I think I rather prefer the latter, perhaps because of the general prejudice in favour of France that has run through my life – or perhaps, more simply, because the element of uncertainty in it seems to fit best with my present situation. In Britain, the practice used to be to tell the condemned man his date of death well in advance, so that he could count off the days on a calendar and have the satisfaction of knowing that he was pitied and admired by his warders as The Day, the only day that would ever count, the one he would barely see, came steadily nearer. A crowd would even assemble on The Day before the prison gate: his anticipation was shared, social. In France, however, the tradition was to spare the prisoner both conceit and horror by keeping him in decent ignorance – as all other men and women are ignorant – of the exact date of his death. For the

2

condemned French murderer every night on which he lay down to sleep on his narrow shelf might be his last. He never knew, till it happened, on which morning he would be called out of sleep in the dark by a hand on his shoulder, other human presences abruptly in his cell: '*Maintenant, X, il faut que tu aies du courage –* '

I imagine that the continual possibility of such a waking, postponed every morning upon natural waking but renewed every night as he closed his eyes, and every night statistically a little more likely, made the condemned man dream obsessionally that that very thing was occurring. So that when the morning came when at last it really did happen, he, mazed from sleep and from echoing tunnels of dreams, was no longer quite certain any more if he was waking or sleeping, as he was hurried through the last few yards of his life, out into the prison compound before dawn.

To know. To understand with absolute certainty that a particular event is going to occur. To feel, whether or not you do it or have it done to you, that it *will take place*. And yet to have taken the final steps towards it so often both in clear fantasy and in confused dream that, when at last it happens – you are not even totally sure that it has happened after all.

Has it happened? Did I do it?

I lie here and ask myself. And tell myself that the very fact that I lie here. . . ? But I ask the question, all the same.

When I was, I suppose, in my early forties, the sort of age at which a man is conscious for the first time of not being 'young' any more, I began to have a dream which has re-occurred at intervals over the years since. In essence, it is this: I am no longer young, various disasters have happened, and I look back with yearning nostalgia and regret to the unattainable past. Then the dream appears to break up; I 'wake' and realize with relief and gratitude that it has been 'only a dream': I am still a young man, full of vigour, with all my life before me.

It is then that I wake up in reality.

It is a bitter dream. I have not, I think, had it for several

3

years now, perhaps because in the recent time my dreaming self has not been so easily fooled and has instead been busy with other obsessional projects. But it does just occur to me now to wonder if I might be stuck in some newer version of this same dream?

I don't think so. Really, not. Yes, I know that, in spite of the way I feel now, tomorrow will still come. And then, or the next day, or next week, there will be another cell, other corridors: other faces outside this grille or a similar one, other and even known strangers standing in the heavy, swung-open door, hesitant, concerned or disapproving greeting on their faces. What, you here, Tom? You, Mr Ferrier? *You*? But none of that matters. Just so long as I do not wake up into yesterday.

Meanwhile I lie here, my arms behind my head, conscious of the shelf against my back, my head at rest. I've gone, it's over: what a good feeling. A great weight lifted. Give them all my love. For years, constricted with sorrow, I could not say that, could hardly feel it. But now that my mission has been accomplished, my responsibility discharged, I am freed. Give my love to all of them, alive and dead. And all of my love. That's so easily said, now.

PART I

I remember a time, perhaps five years after it happened. Long enough to have got over it. In any sense in which you can get over it.

I was sitting in Court. I should explain that this does not just describe my physical situation but an occupation, a status if you like. I am a magistrate, a Justice of the Peace, and have been for many years. I was first appointed when I was a headmaster, the kind of person who traditionally sits on the Bench, and I went on doing it, as and when time permitted, after I became an HMI.

Occasionally people have asked me 'why' I do it. Sometimes there is an edge of aggression in their voices, a hint of 'judge not that ye be not judged' (not that people like that know the Bible these days, but the dissenting impulse remains). More often, the question seems to be humble, faintly admiring, as if the questioner is ready to hear that I have some overall moral mission to Society.

Usually I respond to either approach by saying that if the Bench were to be occupied only by people utterly convinced of their own rightness, then the quality of justice would be pretty odd. Having thus avoided answering and created a general impression of down-to-earth responsibility, I can usually move on to another subject. What I don't say – what in fact I did not notice myself till I had been a JP for a number of years – is that there is a wonderful irresponsibility in the administration of the Law. A procession of people – or rather, a permutation of about a dozen prototypes – appears in sequence in the dock. Across the space between, you gaze at this successive variation on the usual man or woman in the usual place, take some sort of decision, often a partial or temporizing one, and away the glum face goes, to be replaced by another, and then another, till the day draws to its close, and you have a vague, comfortable sense of having once more imposed some order on life or at least done what you were asked to do. In a busy London Court you will rarely see any of these particular defendants again: more crucially, it will not be *your* job to lock them up or to pursue them for the fine or bully and wheedle them into keeping Probation Orders. The long-term responsibilities of real life will not be yours as you cheerfully clatter down the stairs to the retiring room. For judges, indeed, there is rarely tomorrow.

Which is just as well. For I have come to see that, for most of the persistent offenders who make up the staple of the Courts' work, there is simply no appropriate, fair or useful means of disposal. Fines are hardly significant to those congenitally on the dole. As a last resort you can always send them to prison, but if a recent prison sentence has obviously had no redeeming or intimidating effect it is hard to justify another except as retribution, and that is a taboo word in polite Court circles. A pity, I have come to think. We might at least discuss the idea openly.

The defendant I am recalling now was hardly distinctive. There are any number of him. And quite a few of her. This one was called Amanda, which is why her name on the charge sheet evoked a fleeting echo of something very far in the past, an echo that then became a chain of memory. And then far more.

She was a persistent shop-lifter, which is the only crime for which women regularly appear, but I think there were other charges on her record too, including some sort of assault and also a history of drugs. There was, as far as I remember, the usual saga of ineffective or broken Probation Orders; and there was also a suspended sentence knocking around. A Bench on another day had found her guilty of the latest offences of theft and had managed, in the traditional way, to put off deciding what was to be done *this* time by ordering up-to-date Social Enquiry reports. We happened to be the Bench on which those reports landed, as in Pass the Parcel, and we would now have to be seen to act on them.

Amanda was twenty-one. (I remember this with

precision, because her name, combined with another circumstance, made me pause a moment to work something out.) The reports, when we settled down in the Court's uneasy quiet to read them, sketched a background that was not entirely typical of such cases. Many Amandas (who are not, by the way, usually called Amanda) have reports which tell a long tale of ineffective families, of spells in and out of care, of criminal and drunken fathers or stepfathers, of hints of incest or battery, thereby opening at least a decent loophole for the merciful belief that they are as much victims as offenders. But this Amanda came from a middle-class home. Not wealthy, it would seem (so no opening here for those other folk-figures dear to social workers, the worldly and heartless parents with more money than time for the children). She came from what sounded like a pleasant suburban environment. Father a civil servant. Mother a part-time teacher. One elder sister. Stealing from a grandmother at twelve. A history of school truancy. Left at sixteen halfway through the O-level year. And then the progression of offences, the 'bad company', the flight from home, the 'efforts to help her'. 'Her mother feels . . .', 'her father is very concerned that . . .' Her Psychiatric Social Worker. Her Probation Officer. The doctor in charge at the Drugs Dependency Unit. The full supporting cast.

All right, after all my years in schools, I know that such a simple description of an apparently satisfactory home background may conceal depths of family neurosis and collusion. But the fact is that even this particular Probation Officer (whose name I knew and whose over-optimistic reporting style I recognized) had not been able to point to anything in the family environment that might be the 'key' to her client's persistent criminality. Oh, there was one thing there, but the PO did not make anything of it. Brushed it aside at the beginning, indeed, and did not refer to it again, as if it had no possible relevance to the present. Amanda was not her parents' born child, but was adopted by them soon after she was born.

This was the point that, because of the coincidence of

7

name, made me pause, remember something that had, till then, dropped clear out of my mind. I did a small sum. But of course at any time of life one tends to telescope the years: *this* Amanda was far too young, about ten years too young, to be the baby whom I had once, briefly, with a young man's awkwardness, held in my arms. She had no name then, that baby, but she was dispatched to another country, to an unknown but reportedly eager adoptive family, and the one thing I did ever hear of her was that they had called her Amanda. 'Deserving of love'. Clearly, a most suitable family.

So, as I sat in Court waiting in assumed impassivity for my two colleagues to finish reading their copies of the report, my mind went back to that other Amanda, so long obliterated from memory, and I hoped that the character traits she had inherited from her own natural parents had equipped her for a better life than this Amanda was leading. Probation Officers and their kind barely seem to have heard of inherited characteristics. A rather sizeable blind spot, in my view, but perhaps, given the discouraging nature of their calling, they cannot allow themselves to believe in anything further that smacks of fate and hopelessness.

I looked across at this Amanda, sitting sullenly in the place where she had so often been before. All Courts are the same Court, and crime a narrow life, on the whole. Pale-skinned, dark-haired, a little plump and pasty. Tight jeans, boots, a bright jacket, earrings, bitten nails. Twenty-one. Much the age that the mother of that other baby Amanda had been when I knew her, and could from her looks have been her sister. Anyone's sister, anyone's daughter. Twenty-one. Like mine. But mine would have been older now.

I had been getting on better, I had thought, the last year or two. Whatever 'better' means. But at that moment, waiting in the enclosed Court, with a winter afternoon darkening across the ancient glass in the roof, my colleagues rustling paper and an usher coughing in a suppressed way, the old bitterness returned to me in a secret, acrid rush, like an unpleasant taste in the mouth: the unassimilable core of

8

feeling, the weight within – *Why does this one live, stealing and lying, taking drugs, turning her back on everyone who tries to help her, on care and love and life itself, while mine, who loved life so, lies dead? Dead today, tomorrow and for ever and ever, just as dead as she was on that first day, the first day of the rest of my life.*

The papers were laid down. The young legal-aid lawyer rose to speak, as he was bound to, exhaustion lying like a fine skin over his boy's face. 'You may well feel . . . Cannot pretend . . . far be it from me . . . Would however make the point . . . relatively small amount . . . hardly the most dangerous criminal . . . given her age . . . her age . . . Wishes to make a fresh start . . . Her Probation Officer . . . help . . . problems . . . Hospital unit ready to accept her . . . problems . . . needs . . . problems . . . can only be exacerbated by a custodial sentence . . . Would ask you to consider one final chance . . . will not take up any more of your time . . . A new life?'

As if he had disconcerted even himself by this last suggestion, he sat down abruptly. 'The Bench will retire,' I said. We bundled out, in the usual genteel muddle of papers, 'after *you*' gestures and – Mrs Levy – tripping high heels. I suppose the public in the Court envisage us retiring to leather chairs in the proper secluded chamber, but actually at that Court we usually sit on the stairs, because it is more convenient and saves time.

'I'm going for a pee,' I said.

When I got back, I could tell that Mrs Levy had been wistfully discussing with our other colleague, a newish young man with a local government background, the possibility of doing what the lawyer had implausibly suggested. There wasn't a hope, not with the breach of Probation and the suspended sentence there already: she knew that really, but Mrs Levy is one of those justices who believe in going through all the motions of 'considering all the options' even when there aren't really any options there any longer. The young man, however, was looking vaguely recalcitrant.

'Don't see how we can possibly let her off again, with her record,' he said.

'Oh, but further Probation wouldn't really be letting her off – '

'Oh, come on! She'd think it was, and she'd be right. She'd laugh at us. She'd probably go out shop-lifting again to celebrate.'

'But we've been told that the Drugs Dependency Unit are prepared – '

I let the matter be kicked around for a few minutes for the look of the thing. The new boy was a bit too sure of himself, and I thought he ought to be made to argue the point. But fairly soon I'd had enough.

'Look,' I said, 'let's not pretend to predict or talk in terms of what effect we may have on her, because the fact is, as you both well know, anything a Court can or can't do has very little discernible effect on someone like this and that's where the problem lies. If there was the sort of cause-and-effect logic in these cases that each of you is suggesting, then this particular girl would never have clocked up such a criminal record at all. Why her? Why not hundreds of others? It's unanswerable. But meanwhile there really aren't any grounds left for burdening the Probation Service with her. Even they admit that. It's a waste of their time and resources. All this standard stuff about a "final chance" – look at her list of previous, she's *had* her final chances, several of them. And there isn't going to be a new life for her – not yet, anyway, not a sign of it. In years and years maybe, when the whole mixture has changed, if she lives that long . . . But for the moment she's had it.'

Mrs Levy gave me a reproachful look. She does not approve of intemperate cynicism, particularly before junior members of the Bench, and I have to admit that, in calmer retrospect, I don't blame her. She is really a nice, thoughtful woman, Cora Levy, and entirely sane except for a minor obsession about the evils of alcohol. But that afternoon I did not mind upsetting her. Crushed by my own inner weight, I wanted to.

'Just had it,' I repeated sadistically. 'Some situations are not retrievable. Some *people* are not retrievable – or not by anything we can do here. I think we should face that.'

10

There was a silence, there on the draughty stairs. The old-fashioned lavatory cistern was still refilling itself noisily on the floor below. I think I had managed to shock even the other man, slightly. He cleared his throat and said;

'Well I do agree that prison is the only place for her this time, if the Law isn't to seem an ass.'

Mrs Levy sighed, but then said brightly after a moment:

'I suppose there's this to be said for prison, that it'll get her off drugs. That's something positive, isn't it?'

Neither of us replied.

We argued a little more about the length of the sentence, but I forget now what we decided. I suddenly felt very tired.

Many, many years before it happened, years indeed before my own child was even born or I understood about such things, I was living in Paris as a young post-graduate student and I knew a couple who gave their child away. Much later, I was to feel shocked – no, beyond shocked, simply disbelieving – that I myself had played a subordinate, matter-of-fact role in this domestic tragedy. And after that, I think, I suppressed the whole thing.

That day, as I drove home from the Court in heavy traffic, recalling it all again as I had not done for so long, I was haunted by the sense of fearful import which can accompany elation or depression but goes into abeyance on the plains of ordinary living. I even found myself wondering if my thoughtless involvement then in what may have been a substantial wrong could have constituted some sort of first step in a complex sequence of cause and effect that had led me, half a lifetime later, to my own bereavement. Or no, not anything quite as marked as cause and effect – in my best bullying–realist tone I had just told Cora Levy and young Wilkinson that I did not believe in all that – but an obscure patterning, harder to establish but still more inexorable: a dark ebb-tide of fortune. If I had never met – never known – never been in Paris at all . . . Obsessional but essentially circular train of thought. I am now as I am because of the life I have led. I *am* my life, nothing else.

There must, once, have been key choices and decisions.

11

Mustn't there? I know that when I was a Head and talked routinely to leaving sixth formers of their 'choice' of career, I used as a matter of course the language of self-determination. It was indeed the language in which I was reared by my good, enlightened, unselfish parents who wanted only the best for me. In the home on the Cadbury estate in which I grew up, the presiding spirits were J. H. Muirhead and Joseph Chamberlain, the ethos that of the Birmingham Midland Institute: the civic pride of self-made men, technocracy leavened by a spiritual vision, the legacy of Methodism plus the expanding motor industry. And, preceding Methodism, an older tradition of high-minded dissent: my ancestors were Huguenot refugees, Protestants from south-west France. They were silversmiths and weavers who settled in the Midlands at the beginning of the eighteenth century with their modest home-industry skills; their descendants saw the place transformed into the industrial nexus of the world.

A scholarship at eleven to King Edward's School . . . a growing aptitude and taste for work . . . the friendship and influence of good teachers . . . a place secured at university . . . Paradoxically, the moment of choice and decision that had been an essential part of my parents' dream for me never quite seemed to occur. At every well-mapped stage the next step seemed clear. Even Army service, that classic intervention which altered the course of some young men's lives for ever, just seemed to me like more of the same competitive endeavour in a different guise. Unlike many boys from sheltering lower-middle-class homes, I did not mind the coarse life of barracks. Nobody bullied *me*, which at the time I liked to imagine was due to the force of my personality but which probably owed as much to the fact that I am built like a brick shithouse – as the crudest of my uncles used to say. I am not especially tall, not quite six foot, and, dressed, I look unremarkable, but I am very solid and even now, approaching sixty, I am stronger than most other people. I like to think my distant forebears were too, for 'Ferrier' is the old French term for blacksmith – a shoe-er of horses: becoming silver-workers was presumably a later refinement. In any case, by and by the Army gave me a commission: I was the 'right sort'. I was sent to Germany in 1946, and there, as an officer in a victorious army of occupation, of course I thrived.

So, I went on to Oxford to read History, my 'best' subject. So, towards the end of my third year, my tutor suggested that a post-graduate degree at the Sorbonne might, since I seemed particularly interested in France, be a logical 'next step'. Flattered by his confidence in me, I cheerfully agreed that a couple of years in Paris doing a thesis on some aspect of modern French history, and being an assistant in a Lycée part-time to help support myself, would suit me nicely. So, was the die already cast by then?

Of course, what I mainly wanted was to get out of England for a bit. It was 1951, and I was typical of those who had grown up since the war and for whom the Utopian hopes of 1945 already seemed a little embarrassing, as belonging to another, more innocent era. Limited as our experience of foreign travel still was, even we had become aware of the peculiar and seemingly interminable dowdiness of post-war Britain, officially sanctioned as 'austerity'. A brief holiday in Paris the previous year had introduced me to that city, a prelude to a lifetime's relationship with it. It was still physically the Paris that had been liberated in 1944, a capital in which quantities of people still lived with single water-taps at the back of greasy-cobbled courtyards; yet it made every British city including London seem ill-lit, provincial, populated by dull people in hand-knitted cardigans reading inane tabloid papers and eating cheap sweets. I still liked my compatriots, but I was ashamed of them. I was also inclined to the contemptuous belief, derived from the limited experience I had now acquired, that whereas on the Continent sex was rightly regarded as important, in England people tended to prefer hot-water bottles and sentimental films.

So, in the autumn of that year, I found myself occupying my own domain on the seventh floor of an antiquated building (*Gaz à tout étage*) overlooking a lighted boulevard. It was a tiny, brick-floored room tucked away like a rat's nest behind the building's fortress-like façade, and it was reached by a scrofulous service staircase and a windowless corridor as in a bad dream, but I like that room almost better than any other I have ever lain in. I was often lonely in it (a fact I concealed successfully much of the time even from myself); my new life was not easy, strung out as it was between the medieval aloofness of the crowded Sorbonne and the demands of a classroom full of sharp-eyed Parisian adolescents, but as I clung grimly onto the French language and to my own self-esteem, stunning myself every night with quantities of the cheapest food and wine, I dimly perceived that I was living through what might be some of the most important days of my life.

I was simply an early swallow in what would, as the fifties advanced, swell to a great flock. Within a few years, growing prosperity all over the western world would bring rolling into Paris a great army of young men and girls to whom foreign travel seemed almost a birthright, a democratic generation too young to remember the war clearly and careless of its old alliances. This army would create its own international city within the décor of the old streets. But the trickle of foreign students and adventurers who had found their way there by 1951 were attracted to it not by any promise of affluence but by its obsolescent culture of poverty, within which they could scrape a living like urban gipsies.

Such a one was Evan. Evan Brown. That was his unsuitably nondescript name.

An adventurer, Evan. A sharp-eyed boy from a back street in some Welsh town (Cardiff?), who'd had the acumen to turn his provincial origins to good account. Half professional Welshman, half cosmopolitan polyglot – for somewhere in his self-educating wanderings he'd picked up convincing French, the clever bastard. He was clever, you had to hand it to him: in no time, it seemed, he'd learnt his way about the Left Bank, spoke of Sartre and Greco, was on terms (if you believed him) with the American jazz musicians who lived in the Hôtel de la Louisiane. He was a painter, naturally, but unlike every other Paris dauber of conventional abstracts he had the shrewdness to paint neat little 'naïve' pictures that were then rather unusual: views of Wales like improbably ideal children's drawings, all bright blue skies and surprised sheep. He and his girl – Joyce, yes: her name, which had evaded me in the Courtroom, came back to me only then, driving heavily homeward to a London suburb through the rain – he and Joyce used to hawk the pictures round the larger cafés and sell them in Montmartre on Sundays. In spite (or because) of their Parisian know-how, they managed to give an impression of exotic rurality, in that time when men still used Brylcreme and women wore permanent waves and cheap-smart tailored suits. Evan wore corduroy trousers and a battered sheepskin jacket; Joyce grew her hair long with a crooked fringe, like Juliet Greco. Her dusty black clothes seemed a little large for her, thus subtly suggesting the cosmopolitan waif or urban refugee. I learnt by and by that it was Evan who had invented this style for her, and their joint appearance was picturesque, arresting: beatniks and hippies years before the words were invented, purveyors of the radical chic fantasy a generation before it became the cliché of mass fashion.

So, remembering Joyce with her own few words of broken French disarmingly cajoling purchasers in the Deux Magots, remembering too her sitting on the unmade bed in some minimal hotel talking insistently to me about Evan's talents, Evan's needs – remembering now all sorts of nostalgic and pointless details that, for years, had dropped right out of my mind – I eventually parked the car and went into my house. Ann had got home before me.

She wanted, as usual, to ask me questions about my day in Court. But I did not want to talk about that. Or about anything much. Ann observed me tactfully, and busied herself making a pot of tea.

We drank it, and then I made an effort and said:

'A case we had today . . . Never mind what, a girl, it doesn't matter, that's not the point – reminded me of a couple I once knew who gave their baby away.'

'You never told me about them.' Ann looked eager. She is really more interested in people than in anything else, though she tries, poor girl, she does try, to 'share my interests' in other ways.

'I never told you about them because I'd forgotten all about them myself. It must be – oh, thirty years ago that I knew them. In Paris.'

As always when anything touching on France comes up, Ann looked a little tense, but she said: 'Oh yes? Go on.'

'It was when I was doing my Great Work on the French Left,' I said, wishing already I had not embarked on this pointless tale, for what was I trying to convey? 'They were just an English couple hanging round the Latin Quarter scrounging a living. The chap was a sort of bogus painter.'

'Oh, one of them, *I* know,' said Ann, who doesn't. 'There were lots of those around, I expect?'

'Yes, but not quite like him,' I said irritably. 'The point is, he was using Art as an expedient. He had other irons in the fire – or would have. He wasn't a negligible person. Rather, somehow, voracious. He had to do everything everyone else did. Have what they had. Admirably ambitious, you could call him.' Just as when I used to speak of him long ago, I heard a careful if false note of fairness in my voice, of judicial pseudo-detachment. 'He'd already been involved in some fringe theatre group in London – as a scene-painter, I rather think, but he'd scraped acquaintance there – made friends, I should say – with actors and directors, and had plans for setting up some low-budget film company. Well, it was probably just pie in the sky, but that sort of scheme didn't cost the earth then as it would now. The cinema in France was becoming fashionable again, and Evan had a very good Geiger-counter for that . . .' Hauling my memory back again from the overgrown side-tracks down which it was wandering, I added, with an effort at briskness: 'His girl was quite different though, I think. She tried to be what he wanted – streetwise it would be called today. But really, I think, she was just a loving female wanting a home and a man who would stay in it. Poor cow.'

16

Some of the people I meet in the teaching world, particularly the younger ones, get annoyed these days when I make remarks like that. They feel their feminist principles are affronted by such truths – or they think they ought to feel that. But one of the good things about Ann is that she is far too honest for that sort of pretension. In fact she looked happier now at my feeble attempt to describe Joyce. She said softly:

'What happened?'

What indeed. I couldn't, really, understand it myself, much less explain the situation succinctly to Ann all these years later. There was some core of meaning here that was nagging at me but evading me. And, packed round that core, too much old, confused distress and resentment – long-dried griefs that were trivial in comparison with the other things that came later, but which, now that I recalled them, had left a scab of pain.

'Well – she was pregnant. And not for the first time, I think. I wouldn't really know . . .' Other details rose unpleasantly to the surface of my mind; I pushed them aside and continued doggedly. 'Anyway this time she was quite far on. People had illegal abortions all the time in France in those days, as there didn't seem to be any birth control, but it was too late for an abortion. Anyway she and Evan decided to have the baby adopted at birth.'

'But why? I mean, if they were together. Why couldn't they just have kept it? Why couldn't they actually have got married? Isn't that what people did in those days?'

'Yes, quite. That's been bothering me now too. I just can't quite work out how the case for not keeping the baby was argued. I seem to remember a lot of talk about it being "better for the baby" that way. And Joyce – that was the girl – was only eighteen or nineteen.'

'Masses of girls that age have babies and bring them up.' Ann sounded censorious, for her.

'Yes of course. But she was very much under Evan's influence – very much in love, I suppose I mean. And he was persuasive, a very strong character. When he didn't get his way he could also turn quite nasty.'

'How old was he?'

'Oh – my sort of age. Mid-twenties. Maybe a year or two older.'

'Tom, this is a dreadful story.'

'I know. That's the point of it, I expect.'

'He forced her – Joyce – to give up the baby *because* she loved him?'

'Something like that. Certainly she must have been afraid he'd push off if she tried to make a stand about the baby. And probably she was right.'

'How horrible.'

Of course I agreed, but her instant indignation made me perverse:

'Not necessarily, Ann, not necessarily. Perhaps he did have a point about it being better for the baby to be brought up in a proper family. Perhaps in insisting that, he was trying in his own way to be honest – to show that he knew Joyce and he weren't a permanent arrangement, whatever she might hope.'

'Did he tell you that?'

'Something like that, I think.' I really could not remember. Evan had always talked a lot.

'Well – he must have felt very guilty.' Ann readily decides that people must have felt guilty.

'But it turned out to be true. When I ran into Joyce after it was all over, about a year later, she was on her own.'

'Well, mightn't that have been partly *because* . . .' I saw her grapple with the concept of the self-fulfilling prophecy but give up. With one of her sudden shafts of acumen, she said:

'Did you – sort of help them?'

'Sort of.'

'I guessed you might have. Did you help them get the baby adopted?'

'Well, not personally. But I did happen to know one social worker in England – just someone I'd met when I was working at a vac. job, a survey, while I was at Oxford. So I sent Evan to her. In those days, when there were still a lot of babies around wanting "good homes" like kittens, the

18

whole procedure was quite amateurish still. Third party adoptions fixed up by well-meaning vicars and so forth.' Since Ann herself was a child in the 1950s, I tend to find myself instructing her in such things. She looked vaguely disbelieving.

'But this woman was a proper social worker?'

'More or less. I think she'd had some minimal training just after the war. She was,' I remarked at random as that name too came back to me, 'called Shirley Gilchrist.'

Ann clattered teacup down into its saucer:

'Tom – how extraordinary! But I know her. We met at that conference on school counselling I went to in Bristol two years ago. You did say Shirley Gilchrist? – oh it must be the same! A PSW?'

'Well if she is a Psychiatric Social Worker she must have done some more training since I knew her. But, yes, I suppose that's possible. I remember her as a fairly ardent Freudian.' Shirley had been in love with me, for a guilty, pleasurable six weeks on the survey job, but my baseness did not extend to telling Ann this.

'I'm sure it's the same. And I'll tell you who she's worked with – Melvyn Baines. They've done some research together. Published a book, on Family Therapy, I think.'

Ann brought this out with a faint note of triumph in her voice. She knows I dislike and distrust Melvyn Baines, who runs a Child Guidance outfit in the district where she herself is a deputy head teacher, but we don't talk about my views on him because she gets hurt if I speak my mind too clearly on certain subjects: this is one we've tacitly agreed not to explore. It was as if she supposed I would think better of Melvyn for having worked with my old acquaintance, whereas in fact the news had the opposite effect: it made me suspect that Shirley Gilchrist, whom I had known only as a young and vulnerable woman, had not improved with the years. Melvyn Baines goes in for a succession of adoring female collaborators, who become his disciples in the application of psychoanalytical theories to commonplace school problems.

'Oh heavens,' I was suddenly very sick of the whole

subject, adoption and all, and wanted to bury it again, probably for ever: 'I should think Shirley Gilchrist's knocking on a bit now to be in full-time employment.'

Ann looked distressed, not exactly at me, more on my behalf, as she tends to at any oblique reference to my own age, so I kindly added:

'She was quite a few years older than me, I seem to remember.'

Ann began to collect the tea-things together. But she could not resist asking:

'Was it all right? Did the baby settle down all right in the new home?'

We have no children, though at that time Ann was still hoping. Of course, at our joint ages, adoption was out of the question, which meant that (perhaps fortunately) we had never seriously discussed the subject. But I was aware that, in other circumstances, Ann's maternal heart might have turned towards adoption. This conversation about a couple she had never known held different, but painful, associations for her as well.

'I never asked for news of the baby,' I said, and she looked disappointed. 'In those days, you know, a curtain was supposed to descend.'

And anyway, by the time it was done, I was already anxious and half ashamed at my own interference in the sources of life, and did not much want to think about it any more. Which is no doubt one reason I never contacted Shirley Gilchrist again after she'd done me that practical favour, never thought of Evan or Joyce again after a year or two . . . Never, till that day.

But Ann still insisted:

' – And the girl. Joyce. You said you saw her again?'

'I ran into her once, yes. On the Metro. But that was all.'

'I wonder . . . I mean, I wonder what happened to her. If she married someone else, had more children. . . ?'

She wanted to be reassured, comforted, told Oh yes, I'm sure she did. But, though I sensed her distress, I would not yield to it. Unpleasant of me, I do know; Joyce may very well have found happiness. But something in me resists that

20

kind of appeal. I cannot give Ann facile comfort for the world's ills, I don't think I ever could have, even before . . . And I also resist, because I must, her stealthy desire, unrealized I think even by herself, to have control over the past, my past, by 'understanding', by 'knowing what happened'. It is the second-wife syndrome, I see that. I, in my turn, I think, understand the yearning, lonely nature of Ann's desire to possess that very large part of me she does not possess. But it is a desire I cannot possibly gratify and would not if I could.

When we had that conversation we had only been married a couple of years. She seemed particularly vulnerable around that time. It was as if the excitement of actually being married had dissipated itself, but out of it had not developed the emotional security and identification with me that she surely had the right to expect. (And no baby; she was having to face that: almost certainly no baby). I tried to be attentive and appreciative towards her efforts to make me a good, supportive, loving wife. Quite often I even felt appreciative. But at some level, beneath her innocence and optimism, Ann was not fooled, I think. She felt I was disappointed in her.

It was not exactly that, but I could not possibly have explained without hurting her further. It was rather that I had never expected all that much when I re-married anyway. There is a French saying – one of Jacquou's favourites – 'Women without long hair cannot do magic.' Of course I don't mean to apply that literally, though it is a fact that Ann has short, sleek hair and Simone's was long. So, for most of her years, was Marigold's. But it expresses what I feel about this marriage.

I had known Ann for several years as a good teacher, a wonderfully efficient and devoted administrator and a loyal and cheerful colleague on one of the numerous committees to do with education on which I then still sat. That sounds like an empty, public reference; she was also pretty – really quite pretty, in a clear-eyed, neat-waisted way; she was warm; she loved and admired me. She was well into her thirties and getting secretly desperate about the fact, so it didn't seem to matter much that she was, even so, young enough to be my daughter. My daughter. In fact I believe I thought, if I thought at all – a marriage is such a flamboyant, boat-burning act that real thought tends not to figure prominently in it – that the rather large gap in our ages would create a comfortable space in which I could continue to exist in my own selfish secret weighted way. It did not occur to me, as of course it should have done, that Ann herself would be perpetually, wordlessly striving to close this gap. She, poor girl, still expected magic from life, even if she could not do it.

Before we set up home together (in a small, pleasant house that was new to both of us, a place without ghosts or resonances), I suppose she gave her friends some account of me, those few who did not know me professionally already. What must she have said? I imagine her using that slightly special, hushed, set-apart-from-the-ordinary voice people use for such things, and saying rather quickly:

'His first wife was French. He met her when he was doing a post-graduate degree there. She died young, of cancer – oh, a good ten years ago now. I think it was in her family. He told me once that *her* mother'd died of the same thing at about the same age.'

And then, I suppose, even more briefly, she must have gone on to speak of Marigold. There are some things Ann cannot cope with at all. It seems to me that thoroughly nice people are prone to this moral failing. Even simple tragedy so offends the morale-boosting compound of faith, hope and charity on which they run, that they can't fit it into their own picture of life. And as for any hint of deliberate wrong-doing, of cruelty, or evil – well Ann, panic-stricken, reaches at once for the compensatory thought of 'guilt', as she did when I was telling her about Evan Brown.

But I am running too far ahead in time now. At the period of which I am speaking the possibility of evil as a factor had not yet presented itself.

Though I did not yet know it that afternoon, in fact something, some sequence of piecemeal revelation, had been coincidentally set in train. But it was like a timed device, burning away slowly on a long fuse, still in the dark.

It is impossible for me to imagine what my life would have been had I not met Simone: it is like trying to imagine myself with a different personality. We used to regard with a kind of amused disbelief the fact that we owed our meeting, indirectly, to my supervisor at the Sorbonne, a very intelligent but nasty and insecure man with a terrorized wife of his own and an obsession about rising prices.

At first, disconcerted by the vast, uncaring Sorbonne in which I found myself adrift, I had assumed that much of the blame for my discomfort lay with this supervising tutor, Professor Gombach. He was a man in his fifties whose health had been permanently damaged by experiences in the war of which I only learnt much later. He was paid disgracefully little, he was supposed to deliver many lectures every week in echoing eighteenth-century amphitheatres to huge crowds of restless youngsters only a tiny proportion of whom he would ever get to know personally. In addition there hung around – or had been hung around his neck by the chaotic university bureaucracy – an indefinite number of young men and women like me, both French and foreign, who were devoting half their time to teaching incompetently in Parisian schools. In the other half, supposedly, we were not only to absorb, by some undefined osmosis, 'a Sorbonne education', that asset famed since the Middle Ages and, in the 1950s, virtually unchanged since then; we were also to emerge at the end of several years clasping in our arms that weighty piece of original work known in England as a doctoral thesis and in France as a *licence*. No wonder Serge Gombach, like most of the professors, defended himself against us. If he had taken seriously his responsibilities to all those nominally in his care, he would have collapsed in a month.

If I eventually managed to make some sort of an ally of him, that was more by good luck and my own crude confidence born of innocence than because of my merits as a student. I was a hard worker, and I was genuinely quite interested in the roots of Socialism in France but, by French standards, I was woefully untrained in logic, philosophy, religion, mythology, high rhetorical style and indeed in everything but modern history – or rather, in the progress-of-mankind, Whig version of it then still imparted at the oldest British universities. But I had been used to a personal tutor who devoted an hour to me alone every week and seemed happy to receive me courteously at almost any other time – ('Ah, Mr Ferrier – a glass of sherry? Now, about that last essay of yours. It's good – really quite good'). So that when I called on Gombach in his Sorbonne office, and he was cold, sarcastic and evasive, I refused mentally to believe it.

I set to work to tell him my outline ideas for the thesis, trying to quell my bewilderment that he seemed so little interested. He, in turn, appeared surprised that I should bother him at this stage, in my shaky French, and was at no pains to hide the fact. By and by I managed at least to rouse a spark of intellectual irritation in him.

'You English are all the same,' he cried, 'you think that Socialism was invented by Marx, sitting in a London suburb, and was a product of your own early industrialization. You imagine that Britain taught the French, whereas the reality was otherwise. You must emancipate yourself, Monsieur, from your bourgeois Anglo-Saxon complacence, or you will never make an historian.'

I was in turn irritated and offended by his classification of me, as I was no doubt intended to be. But it gave me more of a clue to how his mind worked than I had gleaned from reading my way through his own doctoral work, a three-volume analysis of the thought and influence of Jaurès. I compared notes with a fellow student of his whom I had happily chanced to meet. She was a world-weary American girl several years older than myself with a post-graduate degree already from Johns Hopkins.

'He's a louse,' she pronounced, puffing smoke over her usual double black coffee. 'But he's kind of an innocent louse, if you know what I mean. He's supposed to be so advanced and radical and sceptic and all the rest of it – he takes himself for Jean-Paul Sartre, that's why he wears those silly black wool shirts with turned over collars, like a little school kid. But have you noticed how conventional and old-fashioned and shiny the suits he wears are? And those rimless glasses? And the way he keeps his handkerchief in his sleeve and smells of stale sweat and cheap toilet water, and calls one "Monsieur" and "Mademoiselle" all the time because he's terrified of informality, and says "*N'est-ce pas*" at the end of every other sentence? He's like someone in my first French primer, he's like French professors have always been. Did he tell you you were insular?'

' "Complacent" he said.'

'Same department. He thinks he dislikes the British for being "insular" but actually he dislikes them because that's what traditional Frenchmen have done for centuries. "*Perfide Albion*", you know.'

'Well, yes, but we are insular, actually.'

'Yes, but so's he. He's not modern at all, really. He's a nineteenth-century French anti-clericalist still waiting for the Red Dawn to appear. Secretly, he'd love to die on a barricade, but no one seems to be building them much these days, so he has to pretend he's above all that.'

'Someone did tell me he was deported during the war.'

'Well he's Jewish – or at least I suppose he must be with that name, but like most of the French Jews he's too craven to be open about the fact.' Her nostrils dilated scornfully. 'Jesus, this is a fetid little country, I'm beginning to think they deserved to be occupied in 1940, I really do! But actually the war – at least until he was deported – was Gombach's big moment. The one time I've known him be quite expansive was when I got him onto his days in the Resistance. You should try that, some time.'

'Yes I will, thanks. You seem to have discovered quite a lot about him.'

'Well I've been suffering him much longer than you have. But it's been uphill all the way because he hates young women – yes, didn't you realize? He hates us even more than he hates young men! He only really likes people who remember Verdun: that's very French too. They're a

25

gerontocracy. Look how old Pétain was when they put him in charge. Well into his eighties. Senile. But anyway, yes – Gombach's marginally better with men, or so Paul tells me. Also, he respects people who stand up to him. So you should try to cultivate him . . . Jeez, is that the time? I must rush, I'm late again and Paul will go into his "You Americans are all crazy" act. He only does it to be annoying – and he succeeds. 'Bye honey!'

She rushed, and I was left in the noisy café feeling rather wistful and that I should like to meet the then-unknown Paul. I should also rather have liked it had he not existed. Hermione (for that was her name) had a pinched young-old face and smoked too much, but I liked her better, at that point, than anyone else I had yet met in France.

I wondered inconclusively how I might cultivate Professor Gombach. My first cold, damp Parisian winter was drawing to its close when he disappeared one week. The door of his office remained locked without explanation, and was still locked the next week. Eventually the sweeper, an old, dirty and deaf Parisian whom I prized because he claimed to remember the Prussian siege of 1870, told me that 'That one had taken to his bed.'

'To his bed? Then he's ill. Ill,' I shouted in French. '*Ill!*'

'Oh, I wouldn't know about that. Ill! What's ill? Sir will have his little joke, I'm thinking. Likes of me haven't never had the pleasure of being ill. Ho no!' He banged his broom furiously along the wainscot.

There was influenza in Paris. I had felt wretched myself for several days the previous fortnight but, being too young, ignorant and basically healthy to recognize what was the matter with me, I had attempted to go on with my usual life. Fortunately kind Hermione had encountered me on my way to teach at the Lycée one morning, when I had a roaring fever that I had tried to stupefy with coffee and brandy. She had persuaded me I was unfit for work, led me back across Paris to my attic, telephoned the Lycée, brought me milk, aspirin, Vitamin C and paraffin, and visited me the following evening with other provisions accompanied by her Paul. It was the first time I had met

26

him, and I would not have chosen the circumstances to be thus, but (as Hermione said wryly) in spite of being French, conventionally handsome and living in the expensive Sixteenth district, Paul was kindness itself.

So I considered that I had some current understanding of 'ill' myself, and since I needed a note from Serge Gombach in order to consult a particular archive, I persuaded myself that he would appreciate a visit of sympathy from his most assiduous student. It was a rash decision. I did not then fully realize what a closed bastion is French family life, particularly among the class from which my professor came.

I had vaguely imagined Gombach in some pleasant flat on the Left Bank, perhaps overlooking the Luxembourg Gardens. Although I knew in theory that many Parisians lived in restricted and comfortless accommodation compared with their English equivalents, it was a shock to me to find my professor, this power figure with a name well known in academic circles, living in a high, peeling block behind the Gare de l'Est, a place that in London or Birmingham would have been classed as a near-slum. The single staircase was hardly better than the service one up to my own eyrie, and, unlike my own building, every floor in this one seemed uniformly poor. It reminded me of pictures of eastern European cities: perhaps, I thought, since Gombach was a member of the French Communist Party, he felt spiritually at home in such surroundings.

The door was eventually opened to me, with a reek of pickled cabbage, by a dumpy middle-aged women who had recently been crying. I began to wish I had not come, but it was too late to withdraw. The flat was tiny, and Gombach's irascible voice, half-strangulated as if with pain in his throat, could already be heard asking the meaning of this disturbance:

'Another of those people you encourage, Cecilie?'

'Not this time, Serge.' Cecilie was horribly meek as well as red-faced and damp. 'He says he's one of your pupils.' With timid incredulity.

The following ten minutes passed for me in a haze of

embarrassment. Cecilie did not know what to do with me; such a visit was clearly unprecedented. The sitting room was cold, she said nervously, and she seemed appalled at the thought of introducing me into the bedroom where her husband lay. I babbled that I did not want to disturb him – had just happened to be passing – that what I had wanted to ask the professor would keep for another day . . . But since both of them were evidently under the impression that I could not possibly be intruding in this way unless it were on a matter of some urgency, they conferred in anxious half-tones in the bedroom, while I loitered in the tiny hallway in the smell of old cabbage pretending not to listen. Presently I heard Gombach shout in a whisper:

'Well in that case bring him in here, you fool. Oh bring him *in* and stop dithering.' And Cecilie, gulping, ushered me into a room where Gombach, looking older and smaller than he did in his office, lay in a bed with yellowed sheets, the shutters drawn, in an atmosphere redolent of slop-pails, seldom-washed clothes, ice bags, rectal thermometers and other unmentionable intimacies of French illness. I hastened to apologize, once again.

So unnerved was I by this time, and so weak was Gombach's voice, that I had more or less achieved the note I had come for and was preparing to take my leave, when it dawned on me that he, this sick, bad-tempered domestic tyrant, was actually quite pleased at my visit.

'Sit down,' he said, gesturing at a spindly chair not meant for anyone of my build. 'Since you're here, you can take some notes for me for various people. That will at least save the postage. And you can tell me some more about your project at the Bibliothèque de l'Hôtel de Ville. I suppose you do realize that's a major archive for material on the Resistance? Though a lot of it's uncatalogued, so far.'

'Yes, Professor. That's why I wanted to use it. You see – ' Once embarked, I was off. He lay and listened without any great enthusiasm but without his usual air of sarcastic mockery – that automatic questioning, like a neurotic tic, which had earned him his sorry reputation for brilliance. Eventually, when I ran out of steam, he said:

28

'You ought to meet my old friend Jacques Mongeux. He can tell you more than I can about how the Resistance actually worked – I mean, the welding together of the elements, the committed Party members with the others . . . He was one of the few organizers who was there right at the beginning and was still there at the end.'

'A survivor, then?' I said, no doubt attempting something of Gombach's own habitual sharpness. But on this occasion he looked perversely disapproving, as if almost hurt by the implication of the word I had used.

'Jacques – Jacquou – was a hero of the Resistance,' he said heavily. 'A great man, and a modest one. You should go and talk to him. No, he's not in Paris, not Jacquou. He's a man of central France. We met here at the École Normale, but then he returned to teach history in his own part of the country. A beautiful part, all hills and streams . . . You should get out of Paris for a few days, anyway, you're free enough: I only wish *I* could. Stinking, crumbling, rotten place – a whole city, and most of it fit for nothing but to be pulled down. There are rats in this building, would you believe? Rats. In the middle of the twentieth century. Faugh! Have you seen pictures of the new architecture that's going up in places that were devastated in the war, like Cologne and Budapest? I tell you, sometimes I think the Nazis didn't do us any favour after all in refraining from burning Paris – ' As if this attempt at his usual manner had been too much for him in his present state, he embarked on an unrestrained fit of coughing. He looked so ill that I was afraid some seizure was about to follow. Cecilie obviously thought the same, for she came from her kitchen to hover in the doorway, but he waved her away furiously, flapping a dirty handkerchief at her as if she were an undesirable bird.

'Give me that pad of paper again,' he gasped at last. 'I'll write some messages for you to leave in pigeon holes in the Sorbonne. And I'll write Jacques Mongeux's address down for you too. Meanwhile take that magazine – yes, take it away with you, someone passed it onto me (I can't afford to buy such things) and I've finished with it. There's a piece in

29

it about the Swiss architect, Le Corbusier. Now *there's* one man with vision for you. Ah, if only this disgusting, obsolete Second Empire Paris could be replaced by his glass towers . . .'

Oddly, though Serge Gombach remained my supervisor for most of my time in Paris, this is the clearest memory I have of him. Later, no doubt, although I saw him regularly, I needed him less, had met more people both in and out of the university and had constructed my own existence. And when my thesis was finally taking shape as a great stack of cross-referenced papers, he fell ill again, more seriously this time, and it was a younger and less formidable colleague of his who shepherded me perfunctorily through the concluding stages. I left the Sorbonne without seeing Gombach again, and the next I heard of him he had retired prematurely, suffering with emphysema. The thought of him and his wife, confined together by his illness, with him ranting alternately about Socialist glass towers and the countryside he had known in the Resistance, gave me an unexpected pang.

They must both have been dead for decades now . . . Well of course they must be. Dead, and rotting away separately in one of those great, sad cemeteries on the outskirts of Paris, all rusting iron and dirty wax flowers. Come to that, almost all the people I knew when I was young are gone, including my parents. That is the common lot, the natural consequence of middle age. But one never quite gets used to it. You are young, or at any rate fairly young, for such a significant part of your life, that you never get entirely used to not being young any more. Or to the fact that the world and its inhabitants that you have lost will not, like the seasons and fruits, return.

Jacques Mongeux lived in the Creuse, a part of central France which takes its name from a substantial river. This rises among the limestone plateaux of the Massif Central, winds through sheep and cow pastures and then through deepening gorges, past ruined medieval strongholds, through a hydroelectric dam and a reservoir, past a dilapidated iron works or two and under bridges with Roman names. It joins forces with the Gartempe, and then the Vienne, and finally, among the flat lands and wide wheatfields and vineyards, it decants itself into the great, indifferent, sandy Loire on her way to the Atlantic Ocean.

Jacquou's home was one of the old mills along the river's middle reaches, where the flow of the water, channelled, is strong enough to turn the paddles of a wheel even in a dry summer, but where the gorges, with their rocky cliffs, lie some miles downstream.

'Creuse' means 'hollow', but with a more intense resonance than the English word. In the Department of the Creuse you are hidden away in a fold of land in the green heart of France.

I have come to Jacquou's mill so often over the years, both accompanied and alone, at every season and at almost every time of the day or night, that all my arrivals are in a way one arrival. I have come when the ditches are spotted with pale cowslips and the first wild cherry and hawthorn are whitening the black twigs of the wooded slope above, or when the river meadow is strident with buttercups and with the first lush grass of summer. I have come when the hedgerows are shaggy and dusty and the reduced water in the millpond is brown as beer, and I have come when the whitening on the branches is morning hoar-frost. There, near the unseen mountains, the heavy evening dew crystallizes on a cold night, decorating with its carapace every twig and leaf, every spider's web, every piece of the intricate millwheel's disused structure.

(Even the hardy late flowers, the chrysanthemums and marigolds, become limned with frost, as they were when I last saw them, and then, as the autumn sun climbs in the sky, this icing melts away, sometimes leaving the blossoms untouched. But the last time, the very last, that I was there, I did not have a chance to note which flowers were still living.)

So, my memory of the first time, the very first, that I came to Jacquou's mill is overlaid by so many others that I

31

can no longer be sure how it was. But I know I came on foot down the long, winding road from the village, as I had no car in those days; and my feeling is that, as I descended the road, catching intermittent glimpses of the river's curve, poplars and mill, the pinkish light of evening was fading, with a sliver of moon rising. I think that, by the time I had got down to the level of the river – it is always further than it looks from the hill above – and the water in the millstream was a continuous sound, the unreal light was going fast. It was as if the pinkish colour had been generated by the stone and was now seeping out of it minute by minute; the mill-house and its outbuildings at the end of the rough track were becoming one dark mass, the oak tree leaves overhead a black lace. A late bird was calling as if it were lost, and there were also disconcerting sounds from somewhere near at hand as if giants were trampling and breathing in the long grass: I was unused then to cows or to the country at all. With my knapsack on my back, and the mixture, usual to me then, of uncertainty and brash confidence, I strode down the track and then blundered around looking for the way into the house's central yard.

I got in, and was confronted by the high bulk of the mill and a low penthouse to one side with three doors. The shutters must have been drawn across the windows at that hour, leaving only chinks of yellow light. I fancy I could hear a radio playing softly, but, though I tried saying 'Hallo!' loudly several times, no one came. I chose a door at random and knocked, but still nothing happened.

I tried again, but although I thought I heard someone moving behind the door they did not open it. After a long moment, I put my hand to the door-latch. It gave way unexpectedly, and I almost fell down one step into a warm farmyard darkness and practically onto the horns of a small white goat. We staggered back from one another, both affronted, and were nervously appraising one another when a door further along opened and my host appeared.

'Good evening, good evening! You must be Monsieur Ferrier – I see you have already met Monsieur Seguin's goat. Come out, and let us shut the door quickly or she will

32

be off to her assignation with the wolf on the mountain. But I forget, you are English – perhaps you don't know the story?'

It was so typical of Jacquou kindly to ignore my unguest-like behaviour, but to set to work to instruct me at once in French folklore. I have always hoped, in later life, that I have as little regard for convention as he had. That, at any rate, is how people seem to think of me: no doubt I have worked to produce that impression. But I cannot help also noticing that I, too, tend to want to tell people about things. Jacquou himself used to say that teaching is in the blood, that if you are born that way it is best just to capitalize on it.

He took me into his lighted kitchen. A stocky man about the age of my own father – the age, I calculate with the customary twinge of disbelief, that I am now. A little shorter than myself: a good size for a Frenchman. Thick grey hair; a crumpled face with a protruding lower lip. His voice and manner were those of an educated man, his tattered clothes suggested a peasant farmer, which is a rarer combination in France than in England. I came to learn later that his tastes in literature, music and sport too were eclectic, in a slightly eccentric, un-French way. He spoke a fair English, when he cared to, and honoured the memory of several of the Englishmen he had met during his wartime activities. But I believe that that first evening he and his surroundings all struck me as deeply, exotically foreign, far stranger than anything I had so far encountered in Paris. I also had the dreamlike, exhilarated sensation, born partly of tiredness and a day of travel and expectation, that I myself was somehow transformed by being in this place with this person.

The kitchen seemed very high, crowded, old with the patina of other lives. Obsolete-looking farm implements and nets of root vegetables hung on hooks from a ceiling still blackened by smoke from long-extinct lamps. The slate slabs underfoot were as large and uneven as those in the courtyard, but the place was made comfortable, in a makeshift way, with rag rugs and battered cane chairs. There was a large, blanket-covered bed in the shadows cast

33

by the impromptu-looking dangling light bulbs, and stacks of books on shelves made of bricks and planks. More books and piles of papers covered the slab of wormy oak that was a table, except for one corner on which Jacquou had evidently been eating his supper: broken bread, pâté still in its tin, a wine-bottle and a purplish stained glass. A wood-burning stove wittered quietly to itself in the cavern of an open fireplace, the radio talked softly. Some intensity in the great room, in spite of its superficial disorder, suggested the hideout and clandestine power-centre that, ten years ago, I understood it to have been. But it also seemed like a place that had been lived in for generations without ever being completely cleared or renovated. Old earthenware bowls lay on a high shelf, worn lace-covered cushions were squashed back into chairs. There was a fearsome rat-trap standing rusty in one corner, and a shotgun on hooks above the door, but there were other objects that seemed to be there for decoration: a wooden angel with a broken wing perched high on the chimney shelf, a carved bird, whole and perfect, small dented clay figures such as children make. There were also pieces of furniture – chests, a child's chair – painted with birds, flowers and miniature country scenes, distinctive and elegiac.

'It's a very nice place,' I said at last.

'Wants a bit doing to it, like all old houses.' He divested me of my pack, poured me a glass of wine, and continued: 'Apart from the electricity, and that tap over there that draws off the well, nothing much has been done to the whole place since my grandfather's day. He was the last working miller here, before the steam-mills came in the big towns. And my parents didn't live here, except for holidays.'

'But you live here all the time?'

'I do now. I used to be at Poitiers and just come here for the summer, but after the war I decided to retire from the university and spend my last working years back in a local school. Part-time. That suits me, these days.'

'Professor Gombach said you had an important Chair at Poitiers?'

'Yes, but you can have enough of being important. After a certain time you should go back to where you began – like the retiring Abbé becoming the monastery doorkeeper. Gombach: yes of course, he sent you here. How is he, poor old Serge?'

As I have expressed his words, they sound patronizing, but in fact I believe that what Jacquou said was *mon pauvre vieux Serge*, with a rueful tenderness as if he and Gombach had indeed been close at one time. I attempted, hesitating for words that would not sound either trite or impertinent, to indicate how I had found Professor Gombach on our last meeting. Jacquou listened, nodding his head slowly, and finally said:

'We were together for a time in the war. He came to me because we had been friends years before as students. He was with my group for some time, till he was picked up in a random check and deported. They didn't realize he was a *maquisard*, of course, or they would simply . . .' He drew his hand across his throat. 'Poor Serge, the time he spent in Germany did his health no good . . . Does it surprise you to hear he could be quite brave? And dependable. He was here with me and several others in this house when we were running the network from here for a while in '43.' He paused, then said: 'I can see him now, over there by the window, very slowly peeling potatoes. He was the most incompetent cook ever, but determined to do his share . . . Excuse me, but what did Serge tell me your name was? Your first name, I mean?'

'Tom.' Still unused to the French reticence with first names, I expected him to call me that anyway.

'Yes, I thought that was it. As it happens, Tom was my own *maquisard* name, my pseudonym in the network, I mean.' His eyes, rather odd, light-grey eyes with ringed irises rested on me momentarily as if he attached some kind of significance to the coincidence. 'And I think, from your surname, you must be of Huguenot stock? So am I. We are Protestants in my family, originally from further south.'

Another happy coincidence, I thought. Or perhaps more than that? The out-groups – Protestants, unbelievers, Jews,

all the significant minorities of anti-clerical France –
naturally tended to figure more prominently in the
Resistance than did the mass of regular, Roman Catholic
Frenchmen. Yet when Serge Gombach had told me Jacques
Mongeux had been a Resistance leader, my first reaction
had been one of scepticism. In that extended period known
in France as *l'après-guerre*, a time of delayed shock and slow
reappraisal, the lives of individuals were dominated by the
enormous fact of the Occupation and how they themselves
had experienced it. By the early 1950s, the number of
people claiming to have been 'in' the Resistance passed all
probability and circumstantial evidence; even I, a relatively
innocent Englishman, was learning enough to be cynical
about such claims. But the detail Gombach had since told
me had convinced me that Jacques was a genuine example. I
was eager to ask him more about his involvement right
away: after all I was in his house for that purpose. But,
having just touched on the subject, he moved the conversation firmly back to Gombach, telling me what a tough time
he had had as a boy and how ambitious and hard-working
he had always been.

'I don't think he's very happy now,' I heard myself say.
Almost for the first time I was seeing a man much older than
myself just as an equal individual, and envisaging the boy
he had once been.

'No? People aren't always when they get what they think
they want. Like Monsieur Seguin's goat.'

'The one in the stable? You were going to tell me about
her. But who is Monsieur Seguin?'

'Ah yes, so I was. But you haven't quite understood.
Choufleur there is actually *my* goat. Monsieur Seguin's
goat, Blanquette, is the one in a story that all – yes, all –
French children read about at school. You know our
obsessionally centralized system of education? So now you
too shall hear about her – '

And he related to me, in perfect mock solemnity, that
story which I too was to come to know so well that the
classic schoolroom phrases have become part of me also,
and I too have within my own head the rhetorical cadences

36

of a nineteenth-century school teacher. Monsieur Seguin had a white goat, Blanquette, who was the apple of his eye and to whom he gave everything a goat could want etc., etc. And for a long time Blanquette was very happy. But one spring she took it into her head that she wanted to go up onto the mountain to graze on the new grass and the flowers. And Monsieur Seguin said, 'But Blanquette, you have everything here that a goat could want, plenty of grass, a long rope in the nicest part of the meadow, and here you are safe from the wolf of the mountain.' But Blanquette was not afraid of the wolf, or of anything else, and she kept insisting that she wanted to see the mountain until Monsieur Seguin, determined to keep her safe, put her into the stable and locked the door. However he had forgotten the window, and hardly was his back turned when Blanquette was out of the window and off. She trotted away to the mountain, where a friendly herd of deer received her like a small queen . . .

– And the story inexorably continues: Blanquette spent a delightful day on the mountain pastures, sampling the spring flowers and drinking from clear streams. She was enjoying herself too much to notice the coming of dark, and it took her by surprise. She was cold, and a little afraid, and was almost tempted to try to find her way back to the house in the valley she could no longer see. But then she remembered the hedge around the meadow, the rope, the closed stable, and knew that after her day of freedom she could never again live as Monsieur Seguin's goat, even though he blew his horn from the valley to try to call her home. Then, suddenly, she saw in the moonlight, among the rocks, a little distance off, two great eyes watching her. They came closer . . .

Poor Blanquette struggled all night to fight off the terrible wolf of the mountain with her small hooves and horns. But by dawn she could fight no longer. Her beautiful white coat was all stained with blood, and in the morning when Monsieur Seguin came to look for her on the mountain, Blanquette, ah, Blanquette – !

'When I was a very small boy,' Jacquou concluded, as,

later, I always heard him conclude it, so that it became part of the recitation: 'that story used to make me cry.'

'I'm not surprised. It practically makes me cry now. I'm sure the stories we tell children in England have happier endings. Perhaps we are softer.'

Jacquou inclined his head, as if he too had formed that impression but did not want to commit himself.

'What a moral tale, though,' I said.

'Of course. It's a warning to our children to stay at home and not to follow their instincts and go out into the world. As a bigger boy and a young man, naturally I despised it very much. But in later years, more recently . . . Well, I begin to have some craven sympathy with Monsieur Seguin's point of view . . .

'I told you I retired from the university after the war? Yes. Well it wasn't just that I wanted to cultivate my garden, as we say. My wife had died. I wanted to be at home more to look after my own little goat properly, so that she did not stray on the mountain.'

'The one in the stable?' I said, floundering. It seemed an unlikely preoccupation for such a man, and anyway where in the gentle Creuse were the mountains, where the danger?

'No, no! My other little goat, my own one – look, here's her picture.' He picked an inconspicuous snapshot off a shelf, and I found myself looking at a girl in her teens with long plaits looped up, Jacquou's obstinate lower lip and the dark eyes of another: Simone.

'That was taken a few years ago now,' he said, glancing at the back of it. 'Yes – just after the Liberation. She must have been fourteen. The next summer her mother died, and Simone and I set up house here on our own.'

'She looks more than fourteen.' I wanted to say something admiring, but could not find quite the right thing.

'Yes, she grew up early. She's twenty-one now, but she still looks much the same as in this photo. A couple of years ago she cut off her long hair, silly girl, but she's letting it grow again now, I'm glad to say. I'm old-fashioned about hair. If not about anything else.'

'Where is she just now?' I asked. Perhaps she was due to

38

appear at the kitchen door, dutifully home with the gathering dark.

'Away studying,' he said, and I felt a pang of disappointment. Maybe, apart from my own selfish young man's interest, I had picked up some unspoken yearning in Jacquou's own carefully casual tone.

'In Paris. I sent her there to do her degree. It was a great temptation to let her go somewhere near here where she would come home at weekends. Well, Poitiers was the obvious place. You know that is our usual system here in France, it is different from yours as I understand it. But – let us say I did not want to be Monsieur Seguin.'

'She's at the Sorbonne?' I persisted. Jacquou shot me a glance of amusement. 'Yes, yes. Don't worry, young man; if you like, you shall meet her. I'll arrange it.'

I set out to chronicle my meeting with Simone. But I see now that what I have done is to describe how I came to meet her father, and, in doing so, have said already almost as much as I am able about Simone herself. How can you 'describe' someone who is for ever part of you, the one who makes all the others seem like imitations?

I have tried, with an effort of concentrated memory, to isolate my first impression of my father-in-law and to recreate the mill-house kitchen as it was then, before Simone managed to banish a few of the ancient implements to the barn, before we persuaded Jacquou to have an extra window made in the south side and a proper sink put in beneath it – before, indeed, Choufleur's one-time stable became our own room for holiday visits. But I have no doubt made factual mistakes even so, endowing that first, so long distant evening not only with the accreted emotion of the years to come but with objects from the future also.

For instance, I know that the medieval angel with the broken wing must have already been in its place on the chimneypiece that first time, because it was Jacquou's own father, a local school teacher and sometime Mayor of the district, who had found it. One exceptionally dry nineteenth-century summer he came upon it in the exposed bed of the Creuse, buried in the peaty mud that had by a freak preserved it. Local antiquarian theory held that it had probably come from a nearby monastery chapel that had been looted at the Revolution. The family story, a mild anti-Catholic joke recounted to Jacquou as a small boy and passed on in turn to Simone and then to Marigold, was that the angel had flown rebelliously away from the chapel one beautiful summer morning, had been shot through the wing like a buzzard by an inept hunter and had plummeted into the river. Maybe on that very first evening I commented on the angel and was told this tale. But the other winged wooden carving, the swallow in flight formed from one perfect piece of chestnut wood, which I believe I remember noticing at the same time, was perhaps not there at all. Indeed on reflection I think the swallow only appeared in the house in the course of the following year, after its prototype had been admired in the local café and then taken from there.

Come to that, although I am sure the two painted chests were in the mill when I first went there – Jacquou kept his Resistance 'archives' in one of them, deceptively innocuous beneath a lid decorated with water birds and mallows – the little chair must have come much later, since we commissioned it ourselves, for Marigold. I have been thinking that it was, like most of Marigold's 'French home' possessions, once Simone's. But the man who embellished the deal boxes and chairs so gracefully, and carved the swallows also, only appeared in the district after the war when Simone was already in her teens. He was a Pole with a name full of s's and z's who was known locally as 'Monsieur Maryk'. A refugee, he had no family: he had nothing. He used to sit in the café in the evenings near the iron stove and draw sketches of animals and birds in charcoal on the backs of handbills. Jacquou befriended him, bought him some paints and other materials to replace those arbitrarily destroyed by Hitler, and the furniture and birds were the result. By the time I came on the scene Maryk had acquired a modest celebrity in the region and had a workshop in a barn some miles off.

★
40

There is a circularity in time, all the same. Even if the cycles do not renew themselves as we dream they might – our youth given back to us and the dead, like the seasons and the fruits, returning – there are patterns which seem to repeat themselves through families and lives. It is this, as much as the distortions of memory, which gives us the retrospective impression that in our past the then-future was already implicit, a pattern being intricately prepared in cipher, warp and weft. When I met Jacques Mongeux his wife was dead and the centre of his life was his daughter, Simone. Many years later, after Jacques himself lay in the Protestant cemetery in Limoges, I was to find that time had brought me round to the same situation. It was as if Jacques had been, all along, both my model and my dealer of fate, though he never knew it. Simone was dead, like her mother, at barely forty, and I in my turn was a widower in the summer mill-house, strong and active but alone, waiting for my own daughter to return – from a swim, or a bike ride, or a weekend with friends or, later, from the city. Or from another country. Or from some mountain I could not see.

Perhaps this sense of coming back, via the wide detours of living, to the same point, is why the way I met Simone now seems so critical to my life, to everything; pregnant at the start with all that was to come. But in between there were many, many happy, preoccupied years in which I would not have regarded the circumstances in which Simone and I had met as particularly significant. We married in 1954 when my thesis was done, and I brought her back to England with me. Because I was married I needed a job and so became a schoolmaster. Marigold was born in 1956. She was given that name because I, in my conceit, wanted an unusual one for her; and because Simone, convalescent after an unexpectedly difficult birth, was consoled by the idea of naming her after those flowers which, in French, are called *sans soucis* – 'without a care'. She turned out to be our only child: a disappointment to Simone, this, less so to me, since my limited imagination

41

could not encompass loving any further child so well. In any event we prospered. Simone taught too: French at a girls' school. My own career expanded.

If I had any sense, all those happy, busy, ignorant years, of life's circularity, it was located only in our regular return trips to central France, to the Creuse and the mill-house and Jacquou and his kitchen. How many times, under how many skies, was I to arrive, as I arrived on that first ever evening, and it was always a little different and always the same, the same. After the beginning, I usually came with Simone, and then after a few years with Simone and Marigold. Train and local bus gave way to a beat-up green Simca with several teeth missing in the gear-box: my first vehicle. Later Jacques used to lend us his pre-war Citroën Light-15, a low-slung black car like a symbol on a road-sign. By the time Marigold was there we had a Morris Traveller, whose wooden trims Jacquou's country neighbours, from their bouncing canvas Deux Chevaux, rather admired. Later came Triumphs, our first 'good' car; then, in 1970, the year of Simone's illness, a large, comfortable Peugeot which made us look back to the green Simca with patronizing amazement that we had ever been so content with it. Simone, who was a good driver, enjoyed the Peugeot: it was almost the last thing she was able to enjoy in that way.

But as we ourselves changed and progressed up the material scale, so did France, even the hidden Creuse. There, too, changes did take place, imperceptibly but cumulatively from year to year. I know that when I first walked beside Simone in the autumn fields of 1952, I was struck by the fact, already picturesque to British eyes, that all the ploughing was done with horse-teams, and the sowers went forth to sow from pouches like Biblical figures. I don't think there was then a tractor anywhere in that district. France, which had stagnated economically and socially ever since the blow of 1914, had been dealt a further blow in 1940 and the years of Occupation from which she still seemed barely convalescent, a wounded society huddled in her old ways. Rural France seemed to me, as a young man, full of old or simply ageless people in carefully darned clothes, perpetually fixing gates or carts with bits of wire, patching roofs with ends of wood, shepherding tiny flocks of goats, geese or chickens, hoarding obsolescent coins in worn pouches, relieving themselves on manure heaps, prodigal only with food and drink.

But I was wrong, all of us were, for great changes were coming, de Gaulle was coming, the *après-guerre* was after all passing and a hidden prosperity must even then have been on its slow but certain way. I cannot of course remember now which year the first tractors began to appear, or when the old push-bikes were gradually replaced by motorized ones and then by cars. Nor can I remember by what stages the smithy in the village up the hill turned itself into a two-stroke garage, nor when electric petrol pumps replaced the hand one, nor when – later, surely? – the first supermarkets grew monstrously from the earth beside the main highways. I cannot remember just when the village café, where Monsieur Maryk liked to sit, shed its round iron stove and acquired a jukebox and a pin-table, nor yet when the camp site was opened down by the reservoir and pedalos appeared for hire, and there began to be cars from elsewhere outside the restaurants on Sundays. Nor yet can I recall when we first began to hear that this or the other ancient farmhouse had been sold to 'Parisiens' (outsiders were always supposed to be from Paris) as a holiday home. But I believe that, throughout the 1960s, while Marigold was growing from a small child into a teenager and we were just busy being ourselves in cheerful unobservance, the great change was taking place. I think that it was more or less complete by 1970.

Coincidentally, at the extreme end of that year, in the blank, short days between Christmas and New Year, Simone ceased to live. It was more sudden, at the end, than even her doctors had expected.

There are blessings in life, all the same. Jacquou had died the previous year, not long before Simone's cancer was diagnosed. He was old; he had done most of the things he had wanted to do, indeed I think he had done those things by the time I met him. Certain things, which most men never have to confront however long they live, he had met in his prime and dealt with, for better or worse. Death held no terrors for him: he had seen his grand-daughter grow tall and beautiful, he never knew that his daughter was so soon to follow him. Happy Jacquou.

Under French law, the mill and all its contents came to Simone, and then, when she died soon after, to Marigold under my trusteeship. Which is how, by the early 1970s, Marigold and I found ourselves together in possession of the place, repeating the pattern established a generation before.

I wonder now if it can have been on my first visit to the mill that Jacquou told me the essence of his Resistance activities and showed me some of the papers lying so innocently under the painted lid of one of the Pole's chests? I remember it that way, but I suspect that the central conversation, so important to me that I have invested it with the intensity of my first visit, actually took place later. That first time, when I came alone and Jacquou received me kindly on Serge Gombach's recommendation, I believe I asked him a number of prosaic, exploratory questions about the size and composition of the underground network he had headed between 1942 and 1944. I was rewarded with an interesting general lecture on the difficulties of welding together in a common cause people whose motives – even declared motives – varied widely. I already knew, of course, that the Communist allegiance that was the backbone of much valid Resistance to the Nazis had created endemic problems for committed *maquisards* who were not Party members, nor even left-wing by upbringing or temperament. We must have spoken then of the charismatic figures of Frenay, the ex-military editor of *Combat*, and Jean Moulin who died under Gestapo torture, both of whom came from upper-class, essentially Pétainist worlds. 'For me, at least, there was no internal conflict,' Jacquou used to say: 'Our own family had a long tradition of non-conformity. Robin Hood was a favourite childhood hero.

44

And Jacquou le Croquant, of course. Clandestine resistance suited me.'

I think that on this first occasion he did also mention, and then brushed aside as if it were too obvious to discuss further, the 'rebellious adolescent' problem – the difficulties created, particularly in the final stages of the Occupation, by the number of rank-and-file *maquisards* who had joined not out of idealism and commitment but because they wanted to handle a weapon and to be in on the fun. 'Violent movements always attract congenital criminals as well as congenital idealists,' Jacquou used to say. 'The chance of history will mean a man gets recorded as a hero of the Resistance who, under other circumstances, would just have been a petty crook. Not that that necessarily invalidates his actions, you understand; it's a nice philosophical point . . . But it does complicate life when you're trying to organize and control such people.'

But I am almost sure that on that first occasion he did not let himself be drawn any further, into more personal reminiscences. Why should he? He owed me, an unknown foreign student, nothing. He was getting the measure of me. I was grateful enough – more than grateful, secretly thrilled – when, on the morning I left, he gave me, as well as food for the journey, a note of Simone's address in Paris.

Long after, he told me with wry amusement that seeing me off like that, making sure I had everything I needed including a contact, had reminded him of something. But not till after I had left, trudging purposefully up the hill with my knapsack on my back, did it come to him that in the war he had frequently seen off on missions young men very much like me. 'Some of them, it turned out, were going to their deaths,' he said. 'I felt most relieved that now my conscience was – more or less – quiet. You were only going to my daughter.'

My conscience was quiet. By the time he told me that we must have talked much more. Of course I sought Simone out as soon as I got back to Paris. I was lucky that Jacques' letter to her, recommending me, had already arrived: I had barely given it time to. But that was only the beginning of my luck, that summer, the first summer of my real life.

In August I went reluctantly on a camping holiday in the Lake District with Oxford friends. It had been arranged the previous autumn, in a spirit of let's-keep-in-touch, and I now regretted committing myself to it. By September I was back in France. Simone had been with relatives near Biarritz, cousins with whom she had spent part of her childhood during her parents' wartime activities. She and I met at the railway station in Clermont-Ferrand, I coming from the north and she from the south, and travelled on together by branch line and bus to the green depths of the Creuse. Jacquou was waiting for us at the last bus stop in his old black Citroën, together with the week's shopping.

Later that evening, while Simone was washing up after the substantial meal, Jacquou asked me to come and help him 'put the chickens to bed'. He always had several chickens, tame, affectionate creatures who pecked around the mill by day laying eggs in odd corners, and normally roosted for the night in a conveniently sagging mulberry tree. But he said that the present lot were too trusting for their own good; there was a fox about, and he'd taken to putting them in with Choufleur for the night.

Guessing that this might be a pretext to speak to me alone, I followed him self-consciously into the yard in the pink evening light. 'I wanted to ask you a couple of things,' he said, and I braced myself, but the first question suggested his mind was still running on the fox.

'The shooting season opens this Sunday,' he said. 'Are you interested? There's quite a lot of game up the hill and wood pigeons needing to be kept down as usual – they've been a pest this year. I've only the one shotgun, but I could borrow another for you if you like.'

Feeling English, urban and a little silly, I explained that I'd no experience of shooting. 'It's rather an upper-class activity in England, you know. Pétainist – in a manner of speaking.'

'Yes, one of the Englishmen I knew in the war told me that,' said Jacquou, looking vaguely sceptical all the same.

46

'I did rifle practice in the Army of course. But that was with bullets and a fixed mark.'

'A shotgun's much the same principle, except it doesn't have sights. But you'd better have a practice, I daresay, before joining a party. We'll take my gun out first on our own, perhaps?'

'Thanks. I'd like to.'

We succeeded in picking up the soft, silly chickens, and tossed them fluttering into Choufleur's acrid boudoir, where they settled fussily on the rafters. Then, partly wanting to defuse any further tension for my own sake, and partly feeling I owed this to him, I said:

'You wanted to ask me something else?'

'Yes I did, didn't I? . . . Just tell me, are you sleeping with my daughter?'

He was scratching Choufleur's head as he asked, not looking at me. It cost him something – in my youth and ignorance I could not measure how much – to ask. Was I sleeping with his daughter? No father, at the deepest level, wants to hear the answer to that. I had wanted to sleep with her the whole summer; she assured me passionately that she was not bothered by morality or prudence 'or any of that old stuff', yet she would not. She had told me a number of times that she did want us to be together and that we would be later, but that she could not – really *could* not – sleep with me for the time being, for a reason she did not think it right to explain. In my frustration and urgency I pretended at times to think she was playing 'the usual female game' with me; I even, to my lasting secret shame, jeered at her once, but I knew even as I did so that it was I who was trying emotional blackmail, not she. Her distress whenever I broached the subject was so apparent that after that occasion I did not have the face to press her further: I had resigned myself, like many young men of our generation, to a long wait. And then, the very evening before I was due to set off for England and my unwanted holiday, she appeared unexpectedly at the door of my garret and began weeping inconsolably, and we ended up in the bed and in each other's arms and in each other.

47

All those blank weeks with my Oxford friends, while she was so far away with unknown people near the Spanish border, I wondered – for she had given me no explanations – if this benison would be repeated. I nerved myself for the possibility that, when we met again, the mysterious problem would once again lie between us. But my fears turned out groundless: our encounter on Clermont-Ferrand station was followed by a joyful night in the railway hotel. And now her father asked me if we were sleeping together. God, were we not: I could think of little else. I felt myself beginning to blush, and was thankful the dark was gathering, as I tried to frame an answer that might be at the same time modest, enthusiastic, inoffensive and more or less true. Jacquou said brusquely:

'That must have sounded like an Inquisition question: I'm sorry, I didn't mean it to. How you and she arrange your private life is your own affair – she's twenty-one now. No, I simply meant, will Simone sleep in her old room and you on one of the camp beds in the room above the mill-chamber – or do you want to be offered beds together? – or will that make you shy? Would you rather matters remained private and I did not ask? I'm just seeking information.'

It is easy to forget, now, how few fathers in the early 1950s adopted such an attitude, whether it was real or assumed. It was hard for me then, with my mind and body full of his daughter, to convey my heartfelt gratitude to him. I hope he knew. I think he did.

Once, another time, he said to me:

'Am I a bad father? My sisters think I am. They think I should "control Simone more for her own good".'

'You must know that's ridiculous. You have your own standards. Anyway Simone isn't the sort of person one controls. She makes up her own mind. *I* can't tell her what to do either.'

'Yes. Quite . . . But I know what my sisters mean. There are a lot of things I don't care enough about any more.'

'Simone isn't one of them, however.'

'No . . . but they say I am "cold". And I know what they mean.'

Did he? Do I? For much of the last ten years I have believed myself to be cold. I'm sure that Ann, if she dared to be honest with herself, would say that of me. And yet look. See. To what has all this come –

On the Sunday morning, it must have been, Maryk the Pole called. I had heard about him but had not met him before. Simone had told me that, because her father had originally bought Maryk his materials and helped to set him up in his barn, Maryk seemed to feel a lasting indebtedness to Jacquou which the gift of the two painted chests had not assuaged. In consequence, a small but steady stream of offerings were brought to the mill: sketches, carvings, mushrooms, blackberries, once a baby owl whom Simone tried unsuccessfully to rear. That morning it was a bottle of home-made plum brandy. Simone made a face at me: 'That'll mean he'll be here half the morning talking and drinking the stuff himself "just to try it". Papa's so soft with people like that. I'm going to see old Madame Bernardet up at the cross. She used to mind me sometimes when I was little, and she's knitting me a jersey – or was last April. Papa! Can I take Madame Bernardet some eggs? We've got lots this week, for a change. I think Mistinguett's started laying again.'

'You're like Red Riding Hood,' I said, rather proud of knowing the French title of the story. She had tied on a spotted headscarf and put the eggs in a small round basket.

'Aren't I just? Dear me, I hope Madame Bernardet hasn't turned into a wolf.'

'Been eaten by one, you mean.'

'No, I mean turned. That's the original story, according to Papa. The nursery story's a watered down version. Really, it's a werewolf story. Grandma *is* the wolf.'

The French term, *loup-garou*, was unfamiliar to me. She explained it, adding, with one of those flights of fantasy which occasionally overtook her determinedly matter-of-fact view of life: 'Actually I think these stories are allegories, no I mean metaphors really I suppose, for the dark side of everybody. We each have a little bit of werewolf in us.'

I wasn't interested in that at that moment.

'Can I come with you?' I said hopefully.

'No, don't, we'll have the whole village talking if I take you to meet Madame Bernardet. Anyway – ' she lowered her voice – 'you stay and help Papa with Monsieur Maryk. Remind him loudly that you and he are going to go out with the gun. Then perhaps that old ruffian won't stay *all* the morning.'

In fact the old ruffian seemed rather gentler than I had expected. His French was barbaric, learnt very imperfectly by ear, but that was hardly his fault. His innocent eyes, in his ill-shaven, craggy face, were an astonishing dark blue. It was not hard to believe, in spite of his smelly clothes and bombastic manner, that he created beautiful things. Happy to find a new audience, he settled down to tell me something – at any rate one version – of his wartime experiences. It was not clear to me then, or ever, how he had eventually come to rest in the Creuse. In 1945 Europe was full of displaced, shattered people, fleeing or driven, but Maryk must have travelled farther and more effectively than many of them. 'I had no papers – no money – no one of my own left to me – nothing,' he declared. It was, I came to learn, one of his standard refrains. 'But when you have nothing and have to start your life over again everything is simple. You can do anything, on the far side of despair.'

This truth did not mean much to me, then. In any case I wanted to get out into the sunlit fields, newly bare in September, and try Jacquou's shotgun. With creaking tact I worked the conversation round to the subject.

'But you'll need a gun each,' Maryk exclaimed. 'You'd better borrow mine.'

'If you mean that old blunderbuss you bought off a tinker, I wouldn't care to put it in the boy's hands!' said Jacquou amiably.

'Old blunderbuss indeed!' Maryk sounded really hurt. 'It's a very good gun, I keep my pot filled by it. Anyway yours is hardly much if it's that antique object I see up there.'

'1860s. My grandfather's.' Jacquou lifted down the

50

double-barrelled twelve-bore. 'You wouldn't get that pretty silver chasing on a modern version and you might get a refinement like a choke in one barrel, but the basic design hasn't changed. Look – ' he broke it open: 'Breech-loading, double-pin action – safety catch – just what you'd have on a gun made today. Yours has to be front-loaded with a ram-rod, if I remember rightly.'

'Well what if it does? Cartridges are still cartridges wherever you shove 'em.' Maryk made a vaguely obscene gesture and, as if cheered by having done so, forgot his injury and grinned at us. 'Anyway, where are your cartridges? Don't you even keep the thing loaded?'

'No, of course I don't, Maryk. Dear God!'

By and by Maryk took himself off, assuring us with what seemed a mixture of generosity and aggression that he'd be back with his own gun to lend to us later that day or the next.

'I don't think he'll be back for several weeks,' said Jacquou meditatively. 'He has his own ways, does Maryk.'

'Do you think he really keeps his gun loaded?'

'I'm sure he does. And, at that, not up on hooks like this one but just standing in the corner where anyone might grab it. Silly bugger. And yet, for all that, you couldn't really find a sweeter-natured or more harmless man.'

I took up the gun, felt its weight and length. It was nicely balanced. Jacquou, watching me, said: 'A shotgun may seem harmless enough compared with a service rifle but, as you probably know, lead shot can be lethal to a human being at close range. Even without resorting to choking devices. We certainly made good use of shotguns like this in the Resistance.'

'Including this one?' I asked, admiring the silver round the breech. Jacquou paused a moment, then said:

'Yes. Including this one.' He took it from me, handled it a moment, then laid it on the table between us.

As if offering an explanation which was not really relevant to the question his last remark had put into my mind, he said after a minute: 'Shotguns are not ideal weapons of execution, of course. Revolvers were much

51

better and easier to conceal, but it was difficult for us to get our hands on enough of those. The whole time we were chronically short of weapons and ammunition. Shotguns and cartridges were ordinary objects in the countryside before 1940, as they are again now, so they were easier to get than anything else.'

I looked at the gun, thinking that it had taken the life of Germans. By and by I voiced this trite thought.

'Oh – Germans . . .' Jacquou was dismissive. 'Yes, the odd sentry. But they won't have left any – any moral traces, so to speak. Taking German life was simple, under the Occupation that posed no problem in itself. It was what tended to come after that cast its moral burden on us. I mean – ' (for I suppose I looked witlessly puzzled) 'that for every German the Resistance enthusiastically killed, dozens of hostages were apt to be taken and hanged. Just any people that were to hand, usually male – fathers, husbands, young sons . . . I must say, the taking and killing of hostages has always seemed to me a filthy crime. But perhaps I have an exaggerated concept of fairness – ' (he actually said '*le fair-play*', as Frenchmen do when they are both mocking and admiring the English). 'Some of my fellow conspirators used to say that I had.'

'Hostages. Yes I see. Of course, it's obvious now I come to think about it.'

'Yes. But one yearns for simple moral issues. Some people believed, when they were joining the Resistance, they had found just that. Huh! What a delusion. Of course the anti-German sentiment meshed with the old tradition of proletarian and peasant sentiment – that the poor, who sweated and suffered to feed the Wicked Lords, should rise against them. The French Revolution and all the subsequent risings – '30, '48, the Commune and so on – were being re-enacted once again under the Occupation, for people like Serge Gombach. The Wicked Lords were foreign this time, but that was no real change. Jacquou le Croquant with his firebrands walked the woods again. Huh! No, I am not sneering. I felt it too, at times. How could I not?'

Because he seemed to need some response from me, I

52

nodded, though I did not yet know who Jacquou's name-sake had been.

'You should understand,' he said, beginning to walk about the crowded kitchen; 'You should understand, if you are trying to write your dissertation on this period, that the real drama and tragedy of the Occupation lay not in the struggle between us and *les Boches* but in the struggle between one Frenchman and another. And not just between collaborator and Resister but between people within our own organization – amongst ourselves. Here in this house, even.'

'I didn't realize . . .' I felt young and ignorant, assailed by the unaccustomed force of Jacquou's emotion.

'Look,' he said, sticking his hands in his pockets and speaking now with deliberate flatness, 'there was this man. I lived closely with him at one time, before I was running the network myself. Shared beds and water flasks with him – that sort of thing. I rather liked him. Cheerful, heavy drinking kind of fellow. But – the time came when I and several others in the command decided that he must be disposed of. Why? Why, because we weren't sure of him, of course. That was the way it was.'

'You found out he was a double agent?'

'Yes, but not "found out": that would be putting it too strongly. We had a pretty strong suspicion. Various things, over a period of time, did not add up as they should. We had no means of verifying. We were fairly sure – even very sure. But that was as far as we could get. As far as we were going to get.'

'So – you killed him?'

'So *I* killed him. Yes.'

Into the silence, I said:

'Was it hard?'

'Yes. Oh, I knew all the utilitarian arguments – that to leave one man alive who *might* have it in his power to bring death to the whole company would be a worse evil than to kill one innocent man. But still . . . There was something about it which stuck in my gullet. The decision had not been mine alone of course, but the responsibility was

53

ultimately mine, you see, I was in command. I sat for ages down by the river – yes, here, not far from this house, with my gun – this gun – hidden under the lea of the bank, chewing it over in my mind. I had hours. I had asked the others to send him down to me when he appeared, and he was much later than I had expected. At last I managed – well, not exactly to still my conscience, but to quiet and comfort it with the notion of "rough justice" (*"justice en gros"*). It wasn't justice by the highest standards, I had to admit that to myself, but it was the best justice that could be managed in those desperate times. I knew my own life to be very cheap, and the lives of other people dear to me including Simone's mother. Many people inevitably knew of my activities, had penetrated my alias. I might be killed myself any time. So.'

'And so – he came in the end?'

'He came. The others at the mill-house had told him some cock-and-bull story we'd invented about why I wanted to see him alone: I forget what it was now. And he came down across the meadow, walking quite slowly towards me, with the sun setting at his back. But as soon as he was near and I stood up he seemed to smell a rat. Perhaps there was something in my posture, perhaps without meaning to I glanced towards my gun, hidden under the bank, and he guessed, knew . . . Anyway, he turned tail and began to run.'

'That looks like confirmation that you were right about him.'

'Yes! Yes, I thought that afterwards too. It consoled me. But at the time I didn't think at all, I was just bent on action. I believe it would have made no difference *what* he had done, even if he had gone down on his knees before me . . .'

'But he didn't?' I said at last.

'No. He didn't. He ran away from me across the meadow, away from the mill-house, towards that big elm at the far end, and I ran as fast as I could after him and when I was within three or four metres of him I shot him in the back. And that was all.'

There was indeed no more to be said. And when Jacquou

spoke again it was of something else. But later that same day or the next, when I had digested the story, I found an opportunity to ask him if he had ever felt 'guilty' about the business, later, after the Liberation. But I was uncomfortably aware, as I spoke, that there is no overall word for 'guilty' in French that does not carry either legal or religious overtones, which was not what I had intended. Jacquou was, rightly, rather irritated with me.

'Guilty – no, why? I told you, the decision was, on balance, justified. Oh, I regretted that it had to be so, of course – but that is not the same. If you are after guilt, my boy, in the Anglo-Saxon manner, I can offer you much more fruitful subjects for guilt than that. How, for instance' (belligerently) 'do you think the *maquisards* got their food?'

'Well – from friendly farmers . . .'

'Yes, but from less friendly ones, too. From peasants who were just bloody terrified that, if they didn't give the boys what they wanted, they'd be denounced to the other side as black marketeers. Between two fires, you see.'

'Yes, I see . . . But presumably some of them *were* black marketeers?'

'Some, yes. Others not, just understandably anxious to hang onto their own provisions. But the notion that they were illicit profiteers was a very convenient pretext for certain elements in the Resistance to mount raids. I told you, Resistance movements attract crooks as well as heroes. Didn't I?'

'Yes. Yes, you did.'

'Oh, I wasn't involved personally in any of this. But I knew it went on, at times. How could it not? We had to eat . . . People don't want to talk about this now – yet – probably won't for another generation, but it's all there and more, your material for guilt. Do you want to hear some more?'

'If you want to tell me.'

'Then look at this.' He crossed to the chest painted with Maryk's water birds and flipped up the lid. On top of a mass of papers and files lay a bulging folder which he took out and slapped on the table.

'Look. All this – and another stack of papers besides that are sitting in a lawyer's office in Poitiers – relates to an inquiry that has been trailing on for months now, ever since last year. The remains of a British SOE man were found in the forest to the south of here. He was identified by his watch. As you probably know, there was a showdown there in June '44 between our lot and the Germans, who were getting very rattled about events in Normandy.'

'The battle at l'Etang des Loups?' I felt glad to be able to supply the name.

'Just so. A number of people were killed on both sides – including my young cousin Philippe: there's a street named after him now in Boussac . . . Well: it had been assumed, as the SOE man had been parachuted into our area just before and had been with our boys, that he was one of the ones who fell. I believed that myself. The hidden camp had been burnt down, some of the dead were never properly identified. And there the matter rested for seven years. But when his body was discovered, it was not in the right place. And there was another thing – he'd died by strangulation. The cord was still round his neck.'

I felt that touch of sick disgust that the phrase 'cord round his neck' has always produced in me. Dead is dead, but some forms of killing seemed designed to degrade the victim as well as destroying him and thereby degrade the executioner.

'Could a German patrol have caught up with him as he was trying to escape after the battle, and hanged him?' I proffered diffidently, after some thought.

'Yes, quite, that makes you feel better doesn't it? And that, indeed, is what I have been suggesting to the enquiry. But *I* know it's nonsense, and so, I should think, do they. Because if the Germans had caught anyone, especially a Britisher, even at that late stage in the war, they wouldn't have made away with him quietly in the forest, they'd have strung him up in front of the Town Hall in Limoges for everyone to see. No, I'm afraid it points to one of our own men – one of my men – whose job it was to see this British contact safely out of our own zone.'

'Have you asked anyone about it?'

'I have. He was quite hard to find; he'd moved to the Nantes area. And then at first he lied to me that as far as he knew the Britisher had got away . . . By the way, Simone knows nothing of all this, and that's the way it's to be for the moment. If I think she needs to know in the end I'll tell her myself. But *you're not to*. Do you understand?'

'Yes.' Jacques Mongeux, in this mood, inspired dread.

'Where is she anyway? Still out cosseting that goat?'

'Yes. I think she may be back soon. So please tell me the rest quickly.'

'Right. Well this man, this ex-*maquisard* – let's call him Luc – spun me a tale at first, but then broke down when I threatened to put the inquiry-judge onto him. He told me that *he* had strangled the Britisher, but only because he had a bullet wound anyway and couldn't walk properly. They were a party of six, escaping, and in those circumstances one incapacitated man can bring death to all the rest. So, Luc says, he let the others go on ahead, pretended to lag behind himself to help the injured man, and strangled him quickly before he knew what was happening. For the general good. Better than leaving him to die in the forest on his own of starvation and septicaemia.'

'An extension of rough justice, I suppose,' I said at last. I found I wanted to comfort him.

'Quite – if you believe Luc's story.'

'And don't you?'

'I'm not sure. Oh, it's plausible in a way . . . But, though the skeleton was still wearing the rags of clothes, with the usual money-belt underneath the shirt, no money was found. You see? And I never entirely trusted Luc anyway. He was only on the fringe of the network – a paid agent, a local poacher who knew the forest well.'

I looked at the dossier lying on the table. This sort of material would have enhanced and extended my dissertation immeasurably. But I was young, still attached to my dreams, I suppose. I found I did not much want to study it.

'Shall you tell the inquiry about him?' I said at last.

'That's what I can't make up my mind about.'

I was surprised. I had innocently thought that Jacquou had made up his mind about everything.

'But if they believe his story . . . Mightn't it be better that way? For him to come out into the open and clear himself? Well – sort of clear himself.'

'Yes. Yes, that's what I have been inclined to think too. I've even told him so. Better, in any case, he should appear now than that he should just wait in fear for the hounds to catch up with him. And I think they will, one way or another . . . Ah, but you still don't see the crux of the problem. Rough justice is all very well in war, my boy, it's all we can aspire to – but it doesn't go down that well in a Court of Law in peacetime. And all sorts of rough justice was perpetrated, particularly in the days after the Liberation, some of it very rough indeed, some of it vindictive and questionable . . . For half a dozen years after the war ended everyone went quiet about this. France just licked her wounds in peace. But now the wounds are appearing again – opening – the questions are being asked. And, because the "justice" of that time was so summary, so hasty and brutal, now, in contrast, a fit of moral scruple is upon us. We have to be seen to be applying the standards of today, of calm reflection, not those of 1944. Everyone is keen to claim he was a "hero of the Resistance" but God knows how much will eventually be dragged out and questioned – well, look at this, for instance.'

He rooted around in the chest, glanced through several folders, and finally took something from one of them and held it out to me on the palm of his hand. I found myself looking at a photograph of what I realized after a moment was an execution. In the foreground, a group of men and one young woman, close together, watching. A few paces away another man, in the act of raising a revolver. It was pointed at a boy who stood tied to a fence, his hands behind his back. His thin profile was raised proudly to the sky, mouth clamped shut. He did not look at his killer. His dark eyes seemed fixed on another horizon.

I would have taken this for a German archive picture of a young Resister dying for his country, a village Jean Moulin

– except that his uniform jacket, that of the Nazi-organized local Militia, told another story. It was his executioner and others in the group who wore the berets and armbands of the FFI, the Resistance.

'A collaborator?' I said to Jacquou.

'Just so. One of the many who were dealt with like this at the Liberation.'

I said: 'He looks very young.'

'A boy of eighteen.'

'You knew him?' But of course. He had taken the photo.

'I knew the family. His mother still runs a tobacconist in Argenton. Poor kid. Poor bloody little fool.'

We heard Simone's rapid footsteps approaching the open yard door. Jacquou withdrew his hand and very quickly stuffed the photo back into its file, returning all the papers to the chest. But the boy's face remained with me. In the night, beside my sleeping love, I saw it again in my mind: young, rapt, fearless, ennobled to himself by dying for the cause in which he had chosen to believe.

Come to that, although I think Jacquou destroyed that photo later, along with much else – I did not find it in the chest after his death – that boy's face has remained with me all my life.

If you feel passionately that you are doing right, then your conscience is at rest, and 'guilt' can be dismissed contemptuously, as Jacquou dismissed it. Conversely, to act only within the Law can be to take the guilt-ridden coward's way out. This, I discovered for myself, long after.

I kept my word to Jacquou, I did not tell Simone either about the man Luc or about the boy-collaborator – and when, years later, I spoke to her of the double agent her father had shot in the river meadow, she already knew about that, had known all along. But in these days of our life together I could not stop myself talking to her, in a general way, about her father's war and whether she thought it had changed him.

'*He* thinks so,' she said.

'Do you?'

59

'Um – it's hard for me to say. I was ten when France fell, and getting on for twelve, I suppose, when Papa and Maman got so involved in the Resistance. I mean, that's just the sort of age at which your relationship with your father *does* change, doesn't it? He stops bouncing you around on his knee and so on. And presently I was sent south to the cousins to be kept safe out of the way. And when I came back again we only had about a year all together again before Maman died.'

'He thinks he's "cold" and doesn't care enough about things any more.'

'Yes, I know he does.' She sounded faintly distressed.

'But I think he's one of the warmest people I've ever met. And he seemed to care about – and for – a lot of people.'

'Yes. But perhaps more "people", you know, than anyone special.' Simone's voice had gone thin and toneless. After a long pause, she added: 'I think, perhaps, it's not just the war and having to kill people, or whatever it is he's told you. *I* think it's losing Maman really, just as much. But he never talks to me about that. He never lets on he really minds at all. And when people say "How sad – she was so young to die" he says things like "Well, she lived a lot longer and had a lot more in her life than many people" – he does, Tom, I've heard him. Of course he's quite right, I see that, but it sounds so odd somehow. And he doesn't even have her photo around. Yet I'd always thought, you know, seeing them together when I was a little girl, that he was very – *fond* of her . . .'

She was crying now, and so I comforted her and made much of her, and after that I did not refer to it again. I did, however, get her to explain to me who Jacquou le Croquant had been; and the following winter, back in Paris, I read for myself that inspiring, consoling, bourgeois folk-novel of an abandoned boy, orphaned by the acts of the Wicked Lord, who makes the forest his home, passes through lengthy trials and dangers, and at last avenges his family's misfortunes. Not only that, but he becomes a rural pillar of reformed, post-Revolutionary society and the father of numerous children.

I enjoyed the documentary, rustic detail of the book; I could see how it had inspired generations of left-wing Frenchmen, culminating (as Jacques Mongeux had said) in those who had made the dream reality again by taking to the forests themselves during the Occupation. But I suppose that the novel carried no particular emotional charge for me, and when I came to re-read it years later I found I had forgotten great tracts of it. That was in the early 1970s, when Marigold and I were having holidays in the mill-house on our own, and the area had developed not only camp sites and boats on the Creuse but summer entertainments of the *son et lumière* kind. 'Jacquou le Croquant' was being staged in a convenient nearby ruin; the head of the district high school, with a fine rolling delivery of his own, led and directed a large cast of people from the villages around, supplemented by horses, sheep, geese, superannuated carts and the firemen's band. I re-read the book in order to recount the story beforehand to Marigold and to another teenager staying with us, the nephew of friends. To my surprise, the part of the novel which now impressed and moved me the most was one I had overlooked in memory. It was the chapter where Jacquou's childhood love, believing him to be dead in the dungeons of the Wicked Lord, drowns herself in a deep limestone pit. He himself is rescued in the nick of time through the offices of the Good Squire, only to find that she is gone:

'*Maintenant, tout était fini; elle était au fond de l'abîme, couchée dans quelque recoin de ces grottes aux eaux souterraines, et ce corps charmant, perdant toute forme humaine, tombait en décomposition . . .*'

I passed some of that interminable summer evening on the wooden seats, in the scent of crushed grass and beer, blinded by tears. Luckily I don't think the children noticed. They were patient with the hours and hours of homespun French declamation and enthusiastic about the real live creatures galloped or herded about the scene. Marigold was also much taken with the Wicked Lord, a portly local garage proprietor in a frogged coat, though the boy Jeffrey, suddenly astute beyond his lumpy years,

61

pointed out that the only real evidence for this character's wickedness was that he never said anything at all, just 'Ho, ho, ho'.

So, year after year, Marigold and I continued to come to the mill-house that was now ours alone. Since she was still at school and I was still a headmaster our holidays coincided. Usually, in the spring, we came on our own, and Marigold would renew shy acquaintance with the French families she had known since babyhood. Her French was very good, and naturally, now Simone and Jacquou were gone, I nagged at her to maintain this advantage. In the summer, friends from England visited us, filling the house for the first time with English voices and jokes. I half wanted them there, for Marigold's sake, feeling that this was the right sort of holiday for her, and half did not: myself, I was most completely happy when we had the house to ourselves.

Of course we were 'alone' together in London, but so much else intervened: her school timetables, mine, and a jigsaw of other preoccupations. Marigold had grown up seeing her mother run work with one hand and the house with the other: now, from her early teens, she set herself to do the same. I, in love and gratitude for her efforts, made sure that she did not go short of school trips, theatres, concerts, music lessons and everything else appropriate for her age: between our two determined selves we led a life that may even have been – I came to think wretchedly in the great, echoing void of Afterwards – too full, too tiring for her. Yet how could I regret a day of it, when it turned out that was all, or almost all, there was ever to be?

She never acted the difficult teenager. She did not need to.

If those brief, packed years were to be documented now – as, say, Jacquou's war years were documented – it would be in the notes we scribbled to each other. At intervals they still crowd my mind, those notes, sometimes overwhelming it. 'Daddy, the rest of the stew is for you, I've had some. Please DON'T feed Woozcat again, she may pretend I haven't fed her but she is lying' . . . 'Lewis G. 'phoned. V. chatty.' . . . 'A Dr

62

Baines 'phoned.' . . . 'Humphrey 'phoned and Jeffrey may be coming to stay in France. Oh good.' Or, from me: 'I think I forgot to tell you this morning that your favourite, Humphrey, will be in London on Friday and is coming to supper. If you decide, Bosscat, what delicious meal you'd like to cook for us, I'll buy all the stuff tomorrow. And are we out of orange juice? I can't find any.' Or – she was, after all, not really grown up yet, for all her competent airs – 'Marigold! How many more times must I tell you DO NOT open the yard door and then just go out leaving it unlocked? It will be your things that get stolen, stupid, as well as mine.'

Innumerable messages, nearly all written on the kitchen memo board, and wiped as soon as they had been conveyed. They are nothing and nowhere now, like the joint life they embodied. But even had they been written on paper I doubt if I would have kept any. No one has ever accused me of sentimentality.

At the mill-house, those years, we both drew breath and rested. We did not need notes. Time ran differently there.

I think I can recall now, with yearning, transfiguring intensity, a few long walks we took, a memorable 'treat' meal or two in the best local restaurant (Marigold very much the lady being taken out, I in a tie doing my best to rise to the occasion with an odd self-consciousness I would feel with no one else), and a handful of conversations between us on love or child-bearing or death: such subjects as adolescents introduce readily, almost nonchalantly, in that precious, brief time before adult perceptions and reticences set in.

That time passed, as it had to. When Marigold had turned sixteen, she began going off on visits on her own, coming to join me at the mill-house once I was established there. Later again, in her university vacations, she several times stayed at the mill-house with friends from school or college, playing mistress of the house. I, in my turn, would be the traveller who eventually arrived, stained and hungry, in the light of the setting sun.

I did not really like her staying there quite alone. Some basic paternal emotion made me feel it was unsuitable, though the irrationality of this was apparent even to me. I would not have felt it had she been older, yet age has little to do with vulnerability. I knew Marigold to be, by now, well organized and sensible beyond her years. In any case she had always been a little shy of strangers. The idea of her making unsuitable acquaintances – for instance – in some camp-site bar, and letting them follow her back to the mill-house, was preposterous. Also, as she herself pointed out to me, I made no fuss about her being alone for a few nights in our London home, yet everyone knew the high figures for burglaries and crimes of violence in large cities. By comparison, the Creuse was almost devoid of incident, a great peaceful green womb. And, when it came to it, I, like Jacquou, did not want to be cast in the role of Monsieur Seguin. Choufleur-Blanquette had been dead for many a year, a little heap of bones beneath the roots of the mulberry tree, but her name and that of her owner had long passed into our family language as a cipher for an unnecessarily repressive or protective attitude.

I suppose that the accusation 'Don't be a Monsieur Seguin!' was such a useful one that we had lost sight of the fact that when Monsieur Seguin's goat did go free the result was tragic. Monsieur Seguin had been right all the time.

In 1977 Marigold would be twenty-one. That September, she and a friend from schooldays called Sophie were at the mill-house. I had to leave in the middle of the month although I had that term off, a sabbatical awarded to me by the local education authority on some amiable pretext. I was due to go into hospital in London for surgery, the removal of a knee cartilage I had injured playing rugby many years before and which was now causing me problems. The plan was that Marigold should leave central France just before I was due to come out of hospital, in order to be back in London to wait on me for a week or two before her own last year at university began. Sophie, I understood, would leave a little earlier: she had an arrangement to meet her boyfriend in Paris.

I would have preferred to think of the two girls travelling together, but to say so would have come so clearly under the

Monsieur Seguin heading that I kept my vague thought to myself and presently forgot it.

Neither of the girls could drive (Marigold had begun learning that summer), so when I left I took the car. I made sure they each had plenty of money for their respective journeys home. They waved me a cheerful goodbye from the corner of the track leading to the road, bright in their shorts and T-shirts. Marigold then had eleven more days to live.

My knee, in hospital, gave more trouble than had been anticipated. So I was still there, lying in bed, on 26 September, when the young police officer came into the ward and spoke to Sister, and they both looked anxiously in my direction and then came towards me, and my life was changed for ever.

A car crash, the previous day, they said. On the winding road down to Argenton. And however much I told them that she didn't drive, that she had been going to get the local taxi to take her to the bus, that she never accepted lifts from strangers, that Argenton was the wrong direction anyway – the fact still remained the same, the same.

A principal member of 'them' that terrible month was my old friend, the lawyer Lewis Greenfield. Because of the state of my leg, and no doubt for other reasons as well, it was he who travelled to the centre of France, who saw the local police and the equivalent of the coroner, who identified Marigold and had her quietly buried, at my distracted insistence, beside her grandfather in Limoges. (Simone, dying in London, had been cremated: there seemed no reason now to bring our daughter back for such a pointless ritual.) Lewis dealt with everything, asking me how much I wanted to hear and then, at my cry that I wished to hear nothing since nothing would bring her back, told me almost nothing and kept his own counsel.

He did just tell me that the car involved was a Paris-registered one, and that the driver had told the police he had given Marigold, who was hitchhiking, a lift. He apparently lost control going round a bend. The car hit a bollard, went off the road, and the door burst open. Marigold, flung down a rocky slope above the river, had been dead when she was picked up, among the ferns and heather.

'The police did consider prosecuting him for dangerous driving,' Lewis told me some weeks later. 'But I heard yesterday that they've decided to take no action.'

'No action? . . . I see.' Dear God.

He murmured something apologetic about there having been no witnesses to the accident . . . driver injured himself . . . no other car involved . . . a dangerous road . . . such a bloody lot of accidents on French roads anyway.

'It doesn't matter,' I said at last, for his sake, because he sounded so miserable. 'Forget it, Lewis. It wouldn't make any difference anyway.'

'No. It wouldn't. I'm glad you see it like that, Tom.'

'. . . Just one thing, though. You said the driver was injured himself. Badly?' I hoped so, yes, I hoped so. In a couple of seconds I envisioned paraplegia – no, tetraplegia – life never ever the same again for him either.

'Mm – no. Just slight injuries. Or so I gather. But you said you didn't want to hear any details, Tom.'

'No. I don't. You're right. Forget it. It's happened. That's all.'

He took my hand.

And so, for several years, I carried in my mind the stereotyped image of a bad French driver, some arrogant fool of a Parisian, passing casually through the Creuse in his over-powered car, an almost incidental agent of destruction. Of course I hated him, bitterly, eternally. But it is safe to hate the unknown enemy, the cardboard cut-out: Wicked Lord, German Gauleiter, rotten driver.

The Mayor of the district wrote me a flowery letter of condolence, assuring me in passing, as if I cared any more, that he had personally checked on the mill-house and that everything appeared to be locked and shuttered and in good order. Evidently Marigold's final car ride was to have been the first lap of her journey home. How, why, she was in that car at that moment, was not something I could understand.

I did not even want to. As Lewis said, no knowledge now would make any difference.

That autumn, I would simply have left the mill-house and everything in it to the spiders and the field mice and the encroaching damp of the river, locked and shuttered for ever. But my two oldest friends in France, Hermione the American and Paul, whom she had married, came to London in December, when Sophie and her parents and other friends organized an informal memorial ceremony for Marigold. Paul and Hermione had several times stayed with us at the mill-house. They did not try to convince me of anything, but told me that the house – Marigold's house, Simone's house, Jacquou's house – must not be left to rot, and that they would like to take charge of it 'for the time being'. So I gave them the keys, and after that, every few months, they sent me unasked-for rent and a report on taps repaired, roof tiles replaced and grazing rights re-let to a local farmer.

For the first years, I was not at all grateful for these attentions. It was only later, after I had married again, and it was borne in on me that I would never want to take Ann to the mill-house nor she to be taken there, that I began to be relieved that Paul and Hermione were looking after the place, all the same.

PART II

I realize that, all this time, I have said nothing more of Evan Brown and his girl Joyce.

In fact it was through Simone that I met them, or rather met him. He seemed to me just one of the usual loose-knit band of students that, for want of more select company, then formed Simone's Parisian circle. It is like that, when you are young and consciously making a life for yourself: discrimination and cynicism are only gradually acquired. It took me some time to realize that Evan was not in fact following any courses at the Sorbonne. He was one of the shadowy army of *étudiants fantômes* who had once signed on for a minimal course in order to acquire a student card for the university canteens. When I discovered, by chance, from his own laughing reference, that he regularly updated his card 'with a bit of art work' I was inclined to be Britishly disapproving. I was a little disconcerted when Simone, normally scrupulous herself, defended him.

'After all, he has to live. It's his painting he cares about, nothing else. Perhaps, you know Tom, he's right?'

She sounded hopeful but troubled. I did not think much of this hackneyed Vie de Bohème argument, which I accounted unworthy of her, but I did not say so: I would rather think she might be right.

I'd noticed that Simone seemed to like Evan, and indeed when he was on form no one was better company. I saw him charming his way into a nightclub for free and then amusing even the jaded, naked hostesses with his impersonation of an American tourist. He sang well too, in an effortless Welsh tenor, and played the guitar. Wary of being caught out myself in a dislike born of envy, I agreed with everyone that Evan was great fun, talented, *un numéro*, would go far. Actually I rather wished he would go away. But when he did, temporarily, on missions to sell pictures or other

68

unspecified 'business', I had to admit that the evening gatherings in the café were less amusing, and that by comparison the French students seemed rather an uninventive lot, 'unconventional' only in a noisy, conventional French way.

At first, that summer, Joyce was not there. I heard her name mentioned, but it seemed that she had gone back to England to see her sick grandmother. She was an orphan, Evan explained, and 'Nan' had brought her up.

'I'm not sure she's coming back,' said Simone to me.

'Really? He seems quite sure that she is.'

'Oh yes. He's very loyal to her – in his way. But I'm not sure she will.'

She did not elaborate. I had not then noticed, though I did soon afterwards, that Evan was discreetly promiscuous, and had clearly slept with more than one other girl in the group. I did not, however, mention this to Simone, partly out of some vague sense of masculine solidarity and discretion, and partly because of the tension that had at that time begun to surround the subject of sex between herself and me.

But Joyce did come back. Her Nan had died; she had no one else to keep her in England. Simone, I thought, must have been mistaken about her. Pink-cheeked, smiling but rarely talkative, she adored Evan with a desperate single-mindedness. She seemed to like me, probably because her own French was very poor and I was therefore the only other person besides Evan with whom she could talk freely. (Simone's English, eventually to become so good, was then rather sparse. That first year, and for several years afterwards, she and I normally used French, so that it became my true second language and, in the circumstances, the language of my deepest emotions and experiences. I had been happy enough as a child. But now I had found a different country of the mind.)

Joyce's homely Midlands accent, so at variance with her cosmopolitan urban-gipsy appearance, was akin to the one that had been ironed out of me by education. I could imagine so well – though I did not tell her so – the little brick

69

house in Northampton from which she had come, and she probably knew I could imagine it. She was quite intelligent, but poorly educated; Evan was not just her man, charismatic and handsome, but a whole world to her. With that too, I could empathize.

Once, trudging by the Seine with me, carrying the portfolio of Evan's drawings that she offered tenaciously round café terraces, she asked me if I could recommend some 'literature' to her. She had, she said, never read anything: she felt that if she read a few 'proper books' she would be a better companion for Evan. She sounded wistful. What about Sartre, was he translated into English? And wasn't there a writer called Madame Bovary?

I had no doubts as to whether Sartre and Flaubert would really give her much in common with Evan. Though he flourished the names of famous writers, I suspected that he had never read them. It was hard to imagine Evan just sitting and reading for long, even in public on a café terrace. He always seemed to have something more pressing to do. I told Joyce that I thought Sartre over-rated (an arrogant if truthful line of mine which seemed to shock her slightly) but that she could read Camus. I lent her an English translation of *L'Etranger*, telling her it was an important study of an abnormal personality, superficially like anyone else but deficient in deeper feelings. I lent it just because I appreciated Camus myself and because it was, for a 'great work', manageably short: I do not think I reflected at the time on whether, as reading matter for Joyce, it had any particular appropriateness.

I'm not sure I ever heard what she thought about it. I don't suppose she gave it back to me. The next image that comes to me is of her giggly-drunk in one of those packed cellars where we used to dance to traditional jazz in a haze of cigarette smoke. Evan, probably drunker but betraying it less, was showing off about how he and Joyce had managed covertly to move themselves, their clothes and all his painting gear from one Left Bank hotel to another without settling their account.

This time, talking to Simone afterwards, I had fewer

scruples about appearing priggish. Such hotels, in those days, charged trifling amounts, and the broken-down old Parisians who ran them often seemed poorer than their obstreperous, careless clients.

'I know.' Simone looked troubled. 'I know Evan shouldn't behave like that. It's different about the canteens, but one shouldn't exploit actual people . . . As a matter of fact, I'm rather sick of Evan and a lot of the crowd and I'd really rather not spend so many evenings with them.'

'Suits me.' I glowed to hear her say it. 'We often have a nicer time on our own, don't we?'

She squeezed my hand gratifyingly, but went on looking preoccupied:

'Only – you see, Evan particularly asked me if I'd be a friend to Joyce and look after her, you know . . . So I don't like to let him – her – down.'

'Oh?' I said jealously. 'When did he ask you that?'

'When Joyce was coming back again from England. He and I went for a long walk and he asked me then.'

It was the first I'd heard of this long walk. It was Simone's business of course, not mine, and she had known Evan before I came on the scene, but I had not realized she was such a particular friend. As for Joyce, Simone's attitude to her had vaguely puzzled me. She seemed solicitous, like an elder sister, but faintly censorious, and had continued to hint at intervals to me that Joyce might not be going to stay in Paris.

'Joyce had an abortion while she was in England,' Simone said suddenly. 'She told me just the other day.' Her voice sounded flat, strained.

'Good heavens,' I said, 'I thought they were much easier to get here. I mean, people seem to *have* them here so much more.'

'Well, but she was in England . . . She told me about it. Some woman in her home town with a syringe. She said it hurt dreadfully. It sounded *horrible*.' Simone shuddered compassionately. 'And she said she minded too about the idea of the baby, killing it you know . . . So you see, Tom, why I feel I must go on being her friend. She doesn't really have anybody. Except Evan himself, of course.'

71

'Yes, I see. Does Evan know about this, by the way?'

'She said he didn't, she hadn't wanted to bother him, and I said he ought to know. That was right, wasn't it?'

'Of course it was! I'm surprised she managed it on her own anyway. What did she use for money? It's very expensive in England – so I'm told,' I added hastily.

'Her grandmother had just died, at last . . . She said there was a clock and one or two other things her grandmother had left her, so she sold those. Poor girl.'

'Poor girl – yes.'

I suppose my tone was faintly ominous. Simone looked anxious again, but a mixture of emotions prevented me from saying anything more then, or even knowing what I wanted to say. I had difficulty with Evan, to whom everyone, even my thoughtful, finely-reared Simone, gave such ready admiration and forgiveness. Once she came to meet me, happy and talkative, clutching a large bunch of flowers – white daisies – which she said that Evan had presented to her when she ran into him near the flower market on the quay.

'That was nice of him,' I said. Concealed jealousy ignited in me. Girls liked me all right too, but I had never yet, I thought furiously, bought any girl flowers. Why had I never thought of it? From whence Evan's natural grace?

Simone must have sensed my tension. She said quickly: 'Oh, it was just one of his pretty impulses, you know what he's like! But it *was* nice of him – they're country flowers, you see, and he knows how much I miss the country here in Paris, now that it's got so hot. I think he misses it too.'

'I see.'

It must have been not very long after that we were both due to go on our separate holidays, and I found Simone weeping in the dark passage by my door, and she became mine.

That autumn, after our successful visit to the Creuse, Simone's life and mine took on a more regular pattern. Till then, she had been living in a university hostel in the south of Paris. Now she found a room even smaller than mine but

72

nearby, vertiginously overlooking the tracks of the Petite Ceinture railway, and we went back and forth between the two eyries. Instinctively nest-building already, we spent much less time sitting in cafés or wandering the streets, and more buying bargain vegetables in Les Halles and concocting stews with them on an oil stove. My thesis – now known as the Great Work on the Left – thrived in the tranquillity of this new bourgeois idyll, and so did Simone's studies: she was due to take her own degree the following summer. After that, she was hoping for a part-time teacher's job like mine in the Paris region. 'I'll have to sign up for some research project as well,' she said, 'to justify being in Paris. Otherwise the Ministry might send me absolutely anywhere.'

'Could they?' Lapped in my British independence, I was still unused to the centrally regulated nature of life in France.

'Oh yes. It's the way they work. Otherwise, I suppose, they'd never get high school teachers in remote places. But actually people say they do it to be contrary also. When Sartre and de Beauvoir were both teaching, he was sent to Caen in Normandy, I think it was, and she was sent to Marseilles!'

'Poor them.'

'Yes. They used to meet in Paris for the weekends – which must have come quite expensive, for her especially. She took a room in Marseilles by the station, and used to have breakfast every morning in the station buffet, pretending to herself she wasn't really living there at all. I do feel for her . . . All the same,' she added after a moment, with some spirit, 'if it had been me, I think I'd have tried to enjoy Marseilles for its own sake, while I was there . . . Oh *dear* Tom! One shouldn't think one can't live without a particular person, should one? It's too dangerous. I do see that really.' We smiled weakly at each other, trying to store up principles for the unknowable years to come.

(But can we really have had the conversation on quite those lines then, or have I displaced it from another time? Surely it was not till the late fifties or sixties that Simone's

73

namesake began publishing every detail of her life? But my Simone had long been interested in the other one, having been given the earliest novels to read by her father when she was in her teens. Indeed on reflection my own less-than-respectful view of Sartre had been strengthened by Jacquou, who held that Sartre, because of his coldness and conceit, had been a bad influence on most of his associates. Jacquou had told me that the most interesting figure of that group was Camus, who had worked through the bleak fields of existentialist theory to the idea of the necessity of commitment and solidarity 'notwithstanding'. Thinking about this afterwards, I saw something of the same pattern in Jacquou's own life.)

That long, happy autumn, Simone and I saw less of our old group – though more of Paul and Hermione – and seldom saw Evan and Joyce at all. I was relieved. Perversely, though, I found I sometimes missed Evan's jokes (which occasionally he and I had shared at the expense of all the French-speaking others), and his skill in telling his tall stories – his gift for turning his own life into an amusing if self-aggrandizing saga.

Then, near Christmas, I received word from Evan that he wanted to see me on 'business'. Would I come alone to a certain café to meet him? Knowing that he meant 'without Simone', I complied with rather ill grace. I was surprised to find Joyce was with him, though, as usual, he did all the talking.

Joyce was pregnant, he said. He spoke without rancour; he was at his best, lucid, warm, 'more than ready' (he said) to admit his own part in the matter. When I took a second look at her, sitting docilely at his side, I could see she was pregnant, in spite of her usual voluminous, dark clothes. It was clearly far too late to 'do' anything this time, and none of us mentioned the previous occasion. Perhaps Evan really did not know about it, and I was not supposed to know either.

They had decided, he said fluently, to have the baby adopted. It was clearly just not on, was it, for them to keep it? They had looked at it 'from all angles' and had decided

74

that, in the circumstances, adoption was the best thing for everyone – particularly for the baby. He continued for a while in this vein, and my eyes kept sliding to Joyce's face beside his, round, pink-cheeked, impassive yet anxious all the same. I wanted to ask her what she really thought about it. Or rather, I did not exactly want to but felt that I should. But it was not easy, with Evan so voluble and so ready with answers to every query; when I tried, Joyce said simply:

'I never knew my father and my Mum and I had a rotten time, tatting round different jobs in other people's houses and institutions and things. It killed her, really. I'd like our baby to have a better chance in life than that.'

Well, it was an impeccable viewpoint, as far as it went. Inexperienced, and a prig still in spite of everything, I let it go at that. How, I asked on cue (as I was meant to) could I help them?

Ah, that was the point. Evan hoped very much that I could. As they were both British it would surely be simpler to get the baby adopted in England than in France, and, as I was British too, they were counting on me to tell them how to go about it. With my education – so much better than theirs – and my contacts and general know-how . . .

Flattered, as I was meant to be, it did not take me very long to produce the name of Shirley Gilchrist as a likely source of advice, if not actual practical help. (I reflected in passing that poor old Shirley would probably like to hear from me again, whatever the reason, and then felt rather ashamed of this thought.)

In no time Evan had extracted from me a promise to write to Shirley and 'set something up'. The baby was due in less than three months. Would it be simplest if they both went to England for its birth? Like good children (Evan seemed now to be tacitly emphasizing their youth, perhaps to underline the idea that they could hardly be expected to take on the responsibility of a *baby*, for God's sake) – they were prepared to do just what they were told.

Cast in the attractive role of responsible adult, I promised to do my best. I was going back to England myself for a Christmas visit to my parents. Probably I would be able actually to see Shirley Gilchrist. I also found myself promising not to tell anyone else of the plan – 'not even Simone, for the moment, if you don't mind very much, Tom.'

'But,' I said, floundering, 'Joyce's pregnancy can hardly be a secret now. I mean – look at you, love. Lots of people must have noticed already.'

No, that wasn't what Evan meant. Of course everyone would see there was a baby coming. But they would rather that, for the moment, the other plan – the adoption – remained a secret between the three of us. OK?

'OK,' I said uncertainly. 'I promise. I can see you might not want to discuss it a lot. But you'll have to tell people in the end, won't you? I mean, when you come back to France without a baby.'

'Oh,' said Evan casually, 'we thought it might be simplest just to tell people it'd died. Didn't we, Joyce?'

She nodded, and looked away.

'But we can talk about that later,' he said.

Just why adoption was such a sensible, reasonable idea but at the same time must be treated as a dark secret, was not explored between us.

I saw Shirley Gilchrist in London. She said she knew more than one family who might be interested. She said she would make the hospital booking for Joyce, who would then be able to leave the baby there for collection. Only from a momentary glint of excitement and suspicion in her eye, did I see that she was wondering if it might be my child I was attempting to dispose of thus, and I quickly set to work to dispel such a fantasy with circumstantial detail about Evan. I found myself emphasizing the scrappiness and uncertainty of Evan's daily life, his inability to support himself and Joyce adequately, let alone a child . . . No doubt it was myself I was convincing as much as Shirley.

I minded, rather, not telling my parents about this domestic drama during our cosy, dull family Christmas. I was as fond of them as ever, but I shared so little with them these days; my mother particularly would have been interested, concerned, full of irrelevant practical suggestions. They had not been young at my birth, and now they were getting old. I kept my word to Evan.

I found it harder not to tell Simone. She was intrigued by the idea of the coming baby, planning to buy for it, when it arrived, a special French quilted garment known as an 'angel's nest'. But in the end she learnt abruptly what the plans were. For the carefully arranged birth in a London hospital in February never took place. In January, Joyce went into labour unexpectedly ('She fell down the stairs, silly cow,' said Evan angrily) and was taken to a large Parisian infirmary. There, three days after the birth, Simone and I visited her. On our way on the Metro, I had hastily told Simone of Evan and Joyce's intentions, realizing that I could conceal this no longer or Simone would say all the wrong enthusiastic things. Simone looked stunned, but at first said little.

It took a while to locate Joyce in the long ward full of the clatter of metal pans and the weak cries of the new-born. We sought her among rows of women, some of whom seemed to my eyes almost old; she lay propped up, looking pale but over-voluptuous in a skimpy hospital gown. Simone kissed her warmly so I followed suit, rather embarrassed. Joyce's transparent sexuality, I had long thought, must be a major part of her appeal to Evan, and it appealed vaguely to me also.

The baby was a little girl. I gazed obediently into a canvas box at the end of the bed at a small red face, two fists flung up in a posture of drowning. I felt dejectedly that I could see why Evan didn't want it.

'Evan and I agreed I shouldn't feed her myself,' said Joyce. 'He told the doctor so. But the nurses say I've lots of milk and should. It's a nuisance for them to have to prepare bottles, I think. The chief nurse is so nasty . . . And my milk *hurts*.' She burst into tears.

Simone said that the baby was lovely. She said it looked wonderfully healthy for one born suddenly and prematurely. She asked – and this seemed the height of tactlessness to me at that moment – if Joyce had a name for her? But

Joyce seemed to like being asked this: 'Well, not a proper one. I suppose you know we're going to give her away? – probably . . .' Her eyes filled with tears again. 'But I do have a little name for her myself. I call her Penguin. Because she flaps her little hands like a penguin's flippers when I pick her up.'

I could hardly bear the 'probably'. Everything seemed suddenly awful, with Joyce's distress and her swollen breasts and the baby real after all – not just something one took a moral position about. It got worse when Simone enquired diffidently about the birth and Joyce said, with a dreadful stoicism, that the whole thing had been worse than she had expected – the pain simply awful – and that she didn't really think she could go through it again, ever. At that point I got up, took my leave, and went to wait for Simone in the shabby hospital entry hall.

When Simone joined me she was still untypically silent. But she did say she thought Joyce and Evan might, after all, keep the baby. I did not contradict her.

The following day Evan appeared before me in a canteen near the Sorbonne where he knew I often lunched.

'What the bloody hell have you been saying to Joyce?'

'Nothing. Why? Sit down Evan, for God's sake and speak more quietly. Everyone will look at you.'

He sat down, but continued in his tone of fury: 'You and Simone between you have been going behind my back, haven't you, changing Joyce's mind for her? Huh. Fine friend *you* are, Mr Worldly-Wise.'

I suddenly felt extremely sick of both Evan and Joyce and the whole venture. Outside it was bitterly cold, Paris a uniform grey under a low sky. It was warm in the canteen, but my own room was barely heated, nor was the hotel garret Evan and Joyce shared. Could you take a new baby out into such cold? Mightn't it die anyway? Nebulous apprehensions assailed me.

'Look, Evan. *I* haven't said a thing to Joyce. I don't care what you do. It's your business, not mine. Simone may have said something – I don't know, they were cooing over

78

the baby, you know how girls are – but surely that was only to be expected?'

'Oh was it?' he said nastily. 'Well, so long as you and Simone realize you may have buggered up everything.'

'Look, Evan.' I struggled for a position of reason in the tempest of emotion in which he now seemed to be surrounding me. 'Did you really expect to keep Joyce away from anybody else's opinion for ever?' (But, of course, I suddenly saw, he had.) 'Even if the birth hadn't happened here, in Paris, where we could see her, there would still have been doctors, nurses, social workers or whatever. And now Joyce's going to have to bring the baby out of hospital with her when she leaves, isn't she, simply in order to get it to England?'

'Oh bloody hell,' he said, putting his head in his hands. Evidently that had not occurred to him, till now.

'So,' I went on, emboldened, 'is it really so vital that poor old Joyce makes up her mind to give the baby away now at this moment? The poor kid's had a hard time, Simone told me . . . Have a heart, Evan! You and I can't appreciate what it's like for them. Can't you at least wait till she's on her feet again?'

'Oh yes?' he said, 'And by that time she'll be all for keeping it, won't she? Particularly with *Simone* getting at her – '

He had a point, I knew, but I became angry myself now at the tone of voice in which he said 'Simone' and told him so.

He put his head in his hands again, and said after a minute in a different, almost childish voice: 'Don't you see, I *can't* let her bring the baby out of hospital. I've been telling everyone it was stillborn – the old bag in our hotel, the crowd who go to the Deux Magots, Jean-Paul and Sylvie and everyone. Of course they all believe me, with Joyce having had that fall and being taken there by ambulance. They're all so sorry for us . . . How can we turn up now with a live baby? I'd look such a *fool*.'

Suddenly I almost wanted to laugh. The idea of the baby being adopted in spite of Joyce's feelings, in spite of everything, simply in order to save Evan's face, was so ludicrous that I wondered that Evan, ordinarily no fool, did not see it himself. But of course it wasn't really funny, not at all. I did not know what to say.

'Tom, you've got to help us.'

'Dammit, I have. And you don't seem entirely grateful.'

'I'm sorry, I know, I'm just so upset about it all. I'm sorry I was rude, Tom, I really am.' He sounded so pathetic now that, in spite of myself, I believed him. *He's angry with himself really*, I thought – instant psychologist coming to the rescue, the soothing fantasy of others' 'guilt feelings'.

'Oh, I'll help you,' I said. 'But I do think you may have trouble with Joyce' – I found myself hoping that he would – 'And you're not to blame Simone for anything. Whoever's fault it is if things go wrong, it's not hers.'

'I won't, I promise I won't. Simone's a great girl – a real friend. I've always thought so.'

So we helped them. In spite of Simone's own voiced forebodings and my own silent, less formed ones, we were evidently both too committed to the idea of ourselves behaving well in one particular way. A week later we went with Evan to collect Joyce and the much swaddled Penguin from the hospital by taxi, and deposited them straight at the Gare du Nord. Fortunately the weather was milder by then, a greasy, dreary day. Worried that the winter Channel would be rough, Simone urged Joyce to take Penguin below directly they were on board the ferry and lie down with her. Joyce said she would: she still looked pale, and said her stitches hurt. I walked away at this point, and bought everyone over-priced croissants from a station barrow. I did not want to hear about stitches. But Joyce seemed quiescent: after all, she was no 'trouble'. At one moment in the business of organizing their untidy belongings out of the taxi, she had even handed Penguin to me to hold. In the miniature revelation of the baby's warmth and compact weight, I had felt a human stirring for which I had been quite unprepared and for which I did not even have a name, a foretaste of the instincts which one day my own infant child would rouse in me. It disconcerted me very much, and, making some joke about male ineptitude, I handed the baby on to Simone as soon as possible.

Naturally I had paid for the taxi, and had 'lent' Evan some of the cross-Channel fare. I believe Simone had provided the clothes the baby wore.

Evan himself was cheerful, but in a subdued way so as not to seem insensitive, and was full of eloquent thanks to us. Of course he was.

As we left the station – a forbidding name it had always seemed to me, the Gare du Nord – I noticed that Simone was crying unobtrusively. She said it was because it all seemed so awful, but did not elaborate, and I did not ask her to. I felt bad enough as it was, though I did not then, or for many years, give my sad, uneasy feelings the name of guilt.

That morning, I just thought I should be quite glad if I never saw Evan or Joyce again. And yet, as the days went by, I found I missed them. In absence, they seemed faintly glamorous.

In the spring, they were back. Both seemed almost exuberant at being in Paris once more. There had, Evan conveyed, been some unspecified 'trouble' in London with people out to do him down: the English really were a putrid race, he said, sounding more Welsh than ever. Joyce had recovered her figure and her pink-cheeked smiles. I felt almost annoyed with her, yet at some deeper level much relieved. Perhaps, I thought, Evan had been right after all: women were emotional and unreliable just after childbirth and one should not take their desires then too seriously.

Joyce confided that Evan was now doing some marvellous new pictures which she was sure the French would appreciate much more than the stupid Londoners. She only looked sad when she spoke to us of the baby, and that was just once, to tell us that its 'new family' (whom she had not met) had called it Amanda: 'Shirley Gilchrist says that means "deserving of love", Tom. I do think that's a good sign, don't you?'

'Yes. Oh yes I'm sure it is. Of course.'

'She's awfully nice, Shirley, isn't she? So kind and sort of efficient. I wish I knew more people like her.'

Being Joyce, I don't think she meant to convey anything particular to me. She was simply speaking out of her limpid self. But of course Simone and I both, silently, took the remark as a challenge. In any case Simone still seemed bent on helping Evan and Joyce. I wasn't quite sure why.

'They seem fine now to me,' I said. 'People like that bob up again like corks.' I had just come to realize that myself.

But a few weeks later it was apparently important that they leave Paris again. Evan had been let down by someone on whom he had counted: a promised sale had fallen through, there were dark references to people being 'double-faced' and 'crooks': now there were bills mounting up . . . I hoped cravenly not to hear too much about that. But Joyce had a heart-to-heart with Simone, whose own English was improving under my influence and who seemed, since the baby, to have replaced me in Joyce's affections; Joyce expressed to her the idea that if only she and Evan could 'get away somewhere into the country', live quietly for a bit, amass pictures, spend little, they could 'get back on their feet again'. Evan, she explained, spent too much in Paris, as in London, on buying other people drinks: 'He's too generous.'

It was true that Evan could be expansively generous when he felt flush for some reason. But I mistrusted the idea of a restorative country idyll. In spite of the daisies he had given Simone and all those landscapes with sheep, I thought that Evan was essentially an urban creature.

Simone recounted this to me but, for better or worse, she was always inclined to take her own decisions, an only-child trait I have noticed in myself. (And in Marigold too, come to that.) She listened to Joyce, and to Evan, wrote to her father, and then came up with a proposal: the owner of a small château in the Creuse – more prosaically a forlorn nineteenth-century mansion with a couple of turrets – was going to spend the summer in Canada with his married daughter, and was looking for a couple to caretake mean-while and look after his two wolfhounds. They would live rent-free, and he would pay them a retainer. Didn't that sound, said Simone, just the thing for Evan and Joyce?

Apparently they thought so too, and were at once enthusiastic about the idea. I, however, was extremely taken aback. I was also hurt. I had felt that the Creuse was a magic land into which Simone had introduced me as a mark of special favour and intimacy, and now here she was opening the gate to Evan and Joyce. In particular, I resented the idea of Evan and his ready charm, his pastiche French with its Parisian *argot*, insinuating his way into Jacquou's favour – Jacquou, whom I already valued so much. I could not say any of this, I would have felt ridiculously possessive. On the face of it, what could be more natural than some of Simone's other Paris friends spending the summer in her home territory? But I was greatly relieved when I heard that the château in question was some thirty kilometres from the mill-house, on the far side of Argenton. I had imagined it in the next village. Without a car, they would be decently distant there.

I had recently acquired a car myself – the toothless green Simca, a model from the 1930s, which had somehow survived the war years. Till then, I had been looking forward very much to driving Simone down to the Creuse in July when her exams were over. Now I felt this idyll impinged on by other presences. I confined myself to grumbling at Simone that I hoped Evan and Joyce wouldn't be wanting lifts all over the place. I knew already (but did not say) that they would never pay for the petrol.

Simone remarked coolly, and reasonably on the face of it, that I didn't have to offer and, if it came to that, I could always refuse.

But later that evening she relented and said:

'I know you don't really want them in the Creuse. I'm sorry.'

'Good heavens, it's not for me to dictate.' (It was my turn to be on the high horse.) 'If *you* want them there, it's entirely up to you.'

'I don't,' she said quietly. 'Not really. It's just that . . . Oh Tom, it's just that I feel so *sorry* for them. It really hasn't been much, to do this for them. And they're both so pleased about it.'

Sorry for them? At length I said, 'Well I can see you might feel pretty sorry for Joyce. After all – '

'No, no, you don't see; it's more general than that. It's just that I've had so much given to me. Such a good childhood, such layers and layers of security, a proper education. Proper love . . . Neither of them has had any of those things, you can see it. Evan even less than Joyce, I think.'

'Well her childhood seems to have been bleak enough.'

'Yes, but I think his was actually worse, in its way. Not as poor, perhaps, his father worked at a racecourse – betting, you know. But I think he was a bit *louche*, and Evan's mother . . . Well, by the time Evan was in his teens it was American soldiers and so on.'

'I didn't know there were many of those stationed in Wales,' I said annoyingly. But in general terms I could believe in the truth of what she said.

'He told you all this?' Again that hidden pang of resentment. Where, when, had Simone and Evan had these confiding talks? Before I met her? Or more recently?

'So that,' she said helplessly after a bit, 'is why I feel I want to do what I can for them. Sort of redressing the balance. What Papa jokes about as *le fair-play*. But I'm sorry if it sounds silly, or makes you cross . . .'

After that, I couldn't decently be cross, could I?

At the last minute before they left, I had to do some giving myself, of a more prosaic sort. Joyce appeared at the door of my room early one morning. Simone, as it happened, had spent the night at her own place. Perhaps it had been Simone Joyce was hoping to find – or had been sent to find: she seemed very embarrassed at having to make her request to me, biting her red lips. They were all ready to set off but there was this little trouble at the hotel. She was afraid Evan might lose his temper; the stupid concierge wouldn't let them go without settling the bill, even though they were leaving a suitcase there and Evan had explained it all to her . . . She was so very sorry to bother me again.

I remember now with niggling clarity that the outstanding bill amounted to roughly what I was paid for a month's part-time teaching. It must have been mounting up for weeks. Dourly I enquired about the train fare to the Creuse.

Oh, they were going to hitchhike down there. Joyce looked quite shocked at the luxurious idea of the train. But she admitted she was worried; it might take several days to get there, and even though they would sleep in the open they must have a little money for food . . .

I now know, as perhaps I had not then yet realized, that there are two sorts of people in the world, those who always manage to have some money put by and those who don't, and that this has almost nothing to do with the scale of income. Without any choice in the matter, I belong in the first category. Unenthusiastically, I took Joyce with me to the post office and drew money for her out of my account. It was supposed to be my car-repair fund.

We drove down to the Creuse ourselves after a joyful Quatorze Juillet in Paris. As usual, in Evan and Joyce's absence, my heart had grown fonder of them. I was even quite looking forward to seeing them again, and I know that Simone was. She had received a couple of stilted little notes in Joyce's childish hand, telling her how beautiful the countryside was and how enormous and greedy the wolfhounds. Evan had appended funny messages to these with little drawings – of him and Joyce being walked by the dogs, swimming naked in the lake and being surprised by a gamekeeper. Joyce trying to ride a cow . . .

On the way down in the car – a minor hiccup with the oilflow in the southern suburbs of Paris, a puncture at Tours – we vaguely discussed possible picnics and excursions for the four of us with pleasurable anticipation. But when, two days after settling in with Jacques, we drove over to the chateau, damply sequestered among pine trees, I picked up from his defensive greeting that Evan had become my enemy, and perhaps Simone's as well.

Sometimes you sense something in this way which

rationality and optimism then reject. It is weeks before mounting unease forces you to realize that your instant impression was the true one. So it was that summer.

Isolated pictures of the four of us come back to memory, but most are blurry, overlaid by others from numerous later, better summers. Pursuing the desperate charade that we were all the best of friends, I'm sure that we took Evan and Joyce to some of our regular favourite places – deep pools under the cliffs of the Creuse downstream where it entered the limestone ravines, standing stones hidden in the forests that the local guidebook misleadingly referred to as 'Druid altars'. Since Jacquou himself knew the countryside minutely for fifty kilometres around he had taught much of it to Simone, and she in turn had shared it with me the year before. No doubt, in wanting to show that this was *our* territory, mine and Simone's, I sometimes seemed arrogant. No doubt, too, the difference between the sort of education Simone and I had received and Evan and Joyce's historical and cultural ignorance, yawned more obviously when the four of us were thrown together alone than it had in Paris; we should have been more on our guard against this and more tactful. But the fact remains that, however we had behaved, Evan, at some deeper level, wished to discomfit us, and more particularly me, and succeeded all too well.

He seemed continually on edge, restless, whistling through his teeth, exaggeratedly uninterested in any ancient monument by which we passed, except as a possible source for cigarettes or 'a nice cold beer'. It was as if he'd deliberately shed his Parisian veneer for the time being and was acting the part of the down-to-earth Real Man, bored stiff by fancy cultural pretensions. He was indeed, I suspect, profoundly bored in his country retreat, missing the daily audience that elsewhere reassured him of his existence. He teased the girls relentlessly, inanely – hiding their clothes when they went swimming, constantly telling Joyce she was too fat and Simone she was too skinny, revealing a line in fatuously coarse jokes (at which Joyce laughed shrilly while Simone pretended not to hear). He

86

tried to enlist me as an ally in this dirty schoolboy sport, and then, when he did not succeed, changed his pattern and became delightful to the girls while excluding me.

He murmured to them in corners, joking and sniggering, and more openly in cafés when I went to pay for our drinks at the bar. Standing self-consciously there, I tried to calculate whether I was really paying, overall, much more than my share, as it seemed to me, and at the same time felt petty. I guessed that an image of myself as a stuffy odd-man-out was being skilfully promoted behind my back. In contrast with Evan's persuasive charm, his relentless, aggressive gaiety, I must indeed, I thought dourly, seem dull, a spoilsport. My spirits were sinking with every expedition. I was beginning to harbour a deep, suppressed anger – not just with Evan, but with soft, corruptible Joyce, and, far more painfully, with Simone for not defending me. Once or twice I caught her looking stricken at some puerile, sadistic sally of Evan's, and took grim comfort from the knowledge that she wasn't really enjoying herself any more than I was, but felt still more cross with her that she said nothing. We were both failing to stand up to Evan, but that fact in itself was no comfort.

Had I ever been bullied at school, or in the Army, I should no doubt have got some practice in dealing with it. Later, as a teacher, I had little difficulty putting down the class trouble-maker from my position of strength. But I was unused to being cast in the role of victim: I had no devious skills and was as defenceless and stupid as a bear being baited.

One evening, in the village café nearest to the mill-house, Evan drank a good deal. At first he was charming, singing to his guitar, getting the bemused but enthusiastic peasant farmers to join in the refrains. He complimented the café-owner on the beautiful little bird, carved from one piece of chestnut wood, that hung over the bar, delicate but strong among the advertisements for Ricard and Brrh. The owner took it down for Evan to examine with an air of expertise ('I'm an artist myself, you see, and I'm thinking of moving into sculpture') and it continued to lie on the table while the man explained that it was the work of a refugee Pole who had settled in the area. 'Monsieur Maryk, we call him. What a gift! Lots of people have admired that bird, but I'm not parting with it, not for any money. He paints too: that's one of his pictures up there. He's a good customer. He's not in here tonight, but he often is. You ought to meet him, M'sieur, you both being in the same line – '

'I most certainly would like to,' said Evan fluently, and, with a sinking heart, I heard plans being mooted for Friday evening. But they seemed to be forgotten later in the general clamour, the click of dominoes and smoke of the advancing hour. I took comfort in the thought that next week, thank God, Evan and Joyce were supposed to be going back to Paris. I had rashly promised to drive them to Châteauroux in the adjacent Department where the express trains stopped. Evan had apparently got some more money from somewhere.

At last I managed to get us all out of the café. Evan stood swaying a little in the sudden cool of the night air. I thought I could hear the river rushing far below us; I felt a longing to go down there now, on my own, without even Simone, rather than driving my ungrateful car-load nearly thirty kilometres in the dark and then returning the same distance.

'Into the car,' I said, surly.

''Scuse me, Sir, can't I have a pee first, Sir?'

'Oh go on then,' I said, turning my back on him. I could tell, from Joyce's subsequent giggles, that he was having it in an exhibitionist way.

When we were all in the car Simone suddenly said, in a strained voice:

'Tom – sorry: could you let me out again? I think I won't come over there with you to drop Evan and Joyce off. I think I'll just walk down now to the mill-house. I'm tired, and Papa might be wondering where we've got to. You don't mind, do you?'

'Of course not,' I said, relieved on several counts. 'But you needn't walk down in the dark. We'll drop you off.'

'Isn't it in the other direction?' said Evan loudly, lolling in the front seat.

'Only a couple of kilometres,' I said firmly. And added under my breath '*You sod.*'

I did not know if he had heard or not, and did not care. At the corner by the mill-house he made a great performance of getting out of the car to let Simone out of the back. Later, on what seemed to me an interminable journey round dark tree-hung bends, far longer than usual, like a drive in a bad dream, he wanted to get out for another pee. When he settled back in with a great sigh and a graphic comment on his bladder, I thought I heard something crunch under his feet, but felt too depleted to enquire what he was doing to my car. One of his frequent lines was that I drove too slowly on the winding roads, 'like a nervous old lady', and that if I'd any sense I'd let him take over sometimes because he'd driven trucks in the Army. With a kind of weary incredulity, I heard him embark on this topic again.

'You haven't got a licence,' I said as usual. And just managed not to add: 'And you're drunk as well.'

'How do you know I haven't got a licence? In your superior, goody-goody way you just assume it, don't you. As a matter of fact I have. I'll prove it to you tomorrow.'

'He has, actually, Tom,' added silly Joyce from the back of the car.

Not trusting myself to speak (or not having anything to say) I drove tensely on, and presently realized that he had fallen asleep.

In the end we reached the château, which I had begun to think of as an accursed place, dank among its dark, balding pine-woods. I could hear the neglected wolfhounds baying inside at the sound of the car. Evan was snoring faintly. I got out, releasing Joyce, walked round, opened the front passenger door and stood with elaborately feigned patience waiting for him to come to his senses. He did so abruptly, with a snort, and bundled out.

'You dropped something, I think,' I said bleakly. By the moon, I could see something pale glimmer on the floor of the car. I had no idea what it was.

'Not me, mate – unless it's me trousers.'

I stooped and picked it up. It was the carved bird,

cracked across its neck and one wing where Evan's heedless feet had earlier trodden on it. Like a real dead bird it flopped across my hand, neck broken.

The scene that followed was brief. I was numbed myself by a kind of disbelief, the weakness of the ordinary person in the face of evil. Had I not been handicapped by this, I think I would have hit Evan. Afterwards, I wished I had, and replayed the scene in my imagination with myself in a more heroic role. I was bigger than he was, and almost certainly stronger: I might have managed to inflict some satisfactory damage on him. But not necessarily. The comfortable idea that all bullies are cowards is, unfortunately, not true, and Evan was a tough boy; he would surely have been a dirty fighter. Perhaps it was as well I kept my hands off him.

He blustered at first that the café-owner had given him the bird; that I just hadn't been around at that moment. But I had heard the man say that he would not part with it.

' – And anyway, Evan, bloody hell, you've broken it. Not content with stealing it, you just trod on it, didn't you? You didn't even want it enough to look after it.'

'I'm sure Evan didn't mean . . . Perhaps we could mend it?' Joyce hovered, her face a pale oval, decapitated above her clothes that merged with the dark. I took some minimal comfort from the fact that she, at least, looked suitably upset.

'I trod on it because I didn't know it was there, you fool,' said Evan, getting his second wind. 'I'd forgotten all about it. Like Joyce says, I didn't mean to take it. I was a bit tight, that's all.'

'Oh yes?' I said, consciously nasty. 'And are you tight each time you go pinching odds and ends in the village shops? Don't think I haven't noticed – yes, *and* Joyce hiding them inside her blouse for you.'

I hadn't really meant to come out with it. I had not been quite sure of what I had seen: on both occasions it had happened so quickly, and anyway I had not wanted to believe the evidence of my own eyes: perhaps the sleight of hand had just been one of Evan's 'jokes', a trick to goad me into further displays of 'stuffiness': But I could see by the expression on his face, hastily erased, that I had hit home.

No one said anything else. The hounds still barked forlornly inside the house. 'Oh, shut up, you fuckers,' muttered Evan. I got back into the car and turned it round, its weak headlights swinging across the old, dreary mansion. It must have been a fine house, once. Just as I was moving off Joyce's face appeared agitated at the window.

'Oh Tom! What about next Tuesday?'

'Well, what about it?' I said, savouring the moment.

'I mean – what arrangements for collecting us to take us to Châteauroux?'

'If you think,' I said, 'I am taking you two anywhere, on Tuesday or any other day, you've got another think coming.'

'But – Châteauroux? How'll we get there? How'll we get away from *here*?' She sounded frantic.

'You got yourselves here. Get yourselves away again. And don't come back.'

I accelerated away, so that she had to jump aside. I half expected a volley of stones to pursue me, but nothing happened. Soon the peaceful, cricket-haunted night surrounded me once more, though it seemed to me to be blowing up for rain and I drove faster as if to escape from that as well. Perhaps I was a little drunk too.

Simone was asleep in our room above the mill-chamber, with the light on and the sheet rucked around her. There were dark smudges under her eyes. I thought she had been crying. She looked drowned. Dead girl. Dead bird, broken thing . . . In a sudden, irrational panic I woke her. I wanted, selfishly, to tell her what had happened.

' – And,' I concluded, 'I mean it. I'm not having him in the car again. I'm not having him anywhere near me.'

Simone was quiet for a bit. Then she said miserably: 'Of course you're right, I see that. He – he's awful, isn't he?'

'Yes. Awful.'

'But he can be so – nice.'

'Quite.'

We said nothing else for a while. She rolled onto her face, and presently I realized she was crying again.

91

'For heaven's sake, Simone,' I said. 'He just isn't worth it.' I felt deathly tired now. A thin spatter of rain had come as I parked the car: now I heard it crepitating on the bare tiles above our heads. There was something in all this that was beyond me, and always had been.

'I know it sounds silly,' she said through her tears, 'but I did try so hard to go on being friends with him and to be a good friend to Joyce. It – it seemed important. You see . . . Oh, I don't want to talk about it, and probably I shouldn't anyway. But he and I were quite close, once, just for a little while.'

I stood still, arrested in the act of unbuttoning my shirt. 'I didn't know that,' I said at last.

'It was a sort of secret. He wanted it that way – said it was better for me. It was before – you understand . . . Over a year ago now. Quite over.'

And that was all she ever said on the matter. I never asked her any questions. But in those few, bleak minutes while I mechanically went to wash and returned, stripped off my clothes and got onto the mattress beside her, I realized that she was telling me he had been her lover. (I knew there had been Someone before me.) She must have allowed herself to be seduced by him while Joyce was in England, during the period that she and I had first met. She had (of course, I realized now) gone on letting him come to her up to the time that Joyce returned, and perhaps even after that . . . Hence her problem about me, and its sudden, tearful resolution.

What a fool I had been, I thought with conscious bitterness, not to see it before. I tried lying on my back, ostentatiously not touching her, thinking of Evan and hating him in an intimate, corporeal way. But by and by I began to feel rather silly. Simone had not wronged me, she had not been unfaithful to me. No other person's life, when one walks into it, is a blank sheet, if the life is worth walking into. If she had wronged anybody it was Joyce, but no doubt Evan had pitched her some devious line about that – 'wanted it secret' did he? I could well imagine he did, the creep. What I could not now imagine, and it was like a black hole in my perception, a small acid burn on cloth, was why, with Evan she had ever – ever wanted . . . desired . . . fallen in love . . .

Everyone has some dark side to them, I thought in pain. Even my Simone. Perhaps especially Simone. Because so much else was radiance.

I lay there trying to think of my own darker side. Shirley Gilchrist and various other girls hardly seemed to qualify for such a dramatic category. Perhaps I didn't even have a dark side – too ordinary a chap. Stuffy. I hadn't even hit Evan.

I drifted unhappily off to sleep.

And then woke later, in ravening anger, and replayed the whole programme over again: accusing bitterness, then conscious philosophizing, finally blank tormenting incomprehension. How *could* she. . . ? Why the hell did *he*. . . ? In that interminable and near-sleepless night this cycle was repeated. And repeated. Each time that I believed I had overcome black emotion with common sense, and drifted into insensibility, the emotion reasserted itself and I woke, in twitching horror, graphic images of *her* lithe body entwined with his, *his* hands and mouth at the vulnerable heart of her, searing my shut eyelids.

Yet it was not really, even so, the idea of her sleeping with him that I could not bear. It was the sick, unvoiced knowledge that she had loved him. Whatever love means.

As I say, I never asked her any questions, neither then nor later. It is not my way. I would have despised myself had I done that. You might say that, in the very long run, it would have been better had I exposed my distress to her, made a scene . . . But that is not my way.

Of course I got over it all right. I do get over things. Or believed I did, then and for very many years. It was very many years later, decades I should say – indeed, only quite recently – that it occurred to me that something permanent may have been laid down in me in the course of that night. Something implanted, that lay dormant but would one day grow. Something dark, after all.

★

In the morning Simone still looked exhausted. Her eyes were faintly swollen. She said:

'Please don't tell Papa about any of this. I feel so ashamed that I brought Evan and Joyce to this part.'

For a wild moment I thought she meant 'Don't tell him about Evan and me'; I was about to say disgustedly that I would not dream of doing so, when I realized that what she meant was about the shop-lifting and the bird stolen from the café.

I promised, but felt that something ought to be done about the bird, and I did not know what. I was still worrying about this the day after, when I was sitting in the kitchen concocting a cheerful letter to my parents and Joyce suddenly appeared at the open door.

'Hallo Tom! Am I bothering you?' A tremulous pink-and-white smile.

I felt that the proper answer would be 'Yes. Go away', but I hesitated weakly about making it. After all – poor Joyce. None of it was really her fault. (Indeed I never did decide to what extent Joyce, already a ghost-designate in Evan's variegated, busy life, was simply his dupe, or something more culpable.)

With a frigid air, to show I was being kind, I made her a cup of coffee instead. She had, she told me, hitched over on a series of farm carts. 'It took *hours*,' she said gaily, without rancour, tucking into some bread and cheese I had also produced for her.

'You shouldn't have bothered,' I said, with a heavy irony that was evidently lost on her. Two minutes later, busy munching, she said:

'Tom – about Châteauroux – '

Exasperated, and contemptuous now of her for her lack of pride, I said: 'Joyce, I am not taking you to Châteauroux. Not you, not Evan – no one.'

'Oh please – '

'*No.*'

'You're too critical, Tom, like Evan says – '

'Right. I'm too critical. I'm not such a nice person as you thought at all. Let's leave it at that.'

94

She drooped.

'Evan will be simply furious with me when I tell him I haven't persuaded you,' she said fearfully. Poor little cow, he probably would be, I thought.

I was not going to be pushed. But, as a useless sop to her, I said I would drive her back now to the outer gate of the château, or near to it. She need not spend the rest of the day in farmers' carts.

We emerged into the mill-yard looking, no doubt, reasonably amicable with one another. So, at any rate, Evan must have thought, for he suddenly appeared from round the side of the wood store.

'All fixed up, are we?' he said chirpily. 'Thanks, Tom – I really mean it. You're a good friend. And about the other night – I really am sorry. Shouldn't drink so much. I get carried away. No harm meant. Let's forget it, shall we?'

I felt almost angrier than I ever have before or since. So angry that I heard myself stammering, something I never ordinarily do. But I believe I managed to convey to him nevertheless that, far from forgetting the other night, I was thinking of going to the police about it – yes, *and* about his shop-lifting. That he and Joyce had better take themselves off that very minute and that if Evan ever showed his face at the mill-house again it would be the worse for him.

Somewhere over the last two days my conflict about him had evidently disappeared. Bourgeois upholder of right was firmly in the ascendant. Embryo magistrate was already alive within me.

Not till afterwards did it occur to me that my fit of moral rectitude might be fuelled by something much stronger and less admirable, but by then I didn't care.

In fact, had I taken my tale to the local Gendarmerie, I doubt if they would have been impressed. It might have sounded to them like a holiday quarrel between a couple of tiresome foreigners, and therefore not their business. But this did not seem to occur to Evan. The word 'police' had a startling effect on him. His cockiness all disappeared. He looked ill. His mouth literally sagged, so that I suddenly saw an ugly pattern of creases that would be there when he was fifty. When he pulled himself together, he still looked extremely nasty.

'You bastard,' he said slowly. 'I'll get even with you. You wait.'

Even to my emotion-wracked ear this sounded like a line from a B-film. Yet something beyond bravado was working in him, even as it was in me.

Suiting my stance to his, I waited, hands on hips.

'Come on, Joyce,' he said at last. 'Let's go. We don't want anything more to do with these shitty people.' And they went.

I was still standing there, breathing hard, when Jacquou emerged from Choufleur's stable.

'I heard all that,' he said equably.

I groaned, and abandoned my pose. 'Oh Jacquou – Oh God, I'm sorry about it . . . Did you understand it?'

'Most of it, I think.'

'I owe you an explanation.' I embarked heavily on the saga of the broken bird. He cut me short:

'Don't bother. I already know about that. These things get around a village in no time, you know.'

'Yes of course, I should have realized . . . I thought of going to apologize to the café-owner myself. Should I?' I couldn't bear the idea of being associated for ever in his mind with Evan, without distinction.

'No, it's not necessary. I've seen him myself. And I'll speak to Maryk about a replacement. No, one thing you can do, is – don't let my daughter invite anyone else like that down here. If you have any influence with her.'

I said it had been my fault as much as Simone's – that I'd been fooled by Evan too. I apologized further. He cut me short again.

'Don't get in such a state about it, my boy. These things happen. You've been disgusted by – what's his name? Evans? Heavens? – and think he's exceptionally bad, but I've met lots of Heavens in my time.'

'In the Resistance?' I thought of our previous conversations.

'And elsewhere, but particularly there. They make good

soldiers, often, but bad citizens. You've met some too, I'm sure; it's just that you haven't recognized them because you haven't been so involved with them.'

I thought of National Service, and agreed that he was probably right. I felt young and stupid.

'He is evil, though,' I said, with a sudden conviction. I understood for the first time that an apparently trivial crime and a serious one may have the same ugly roots.

'Yes. A lot of people are – or can readily become so. In stories, evil is presented as something exceptional, isn't it? The Wicked Lord . . . The Bad Fairy . . . Ghengis Khan . . . People regard it as a perversion of normality. They even like to say now, "Of course Hitler was mad." But he wasn't mad, he was merely a bad man with unusual opportunities. So were the SS troops who burnt the people of Oradour alive in their church. So were the torturers of Jean Moulin. So were some of the best saboteurs . . . Evil can be commonplace, Tom. That is one of the terrible things about it.'

I listened submissively. I had been instrumental in embarrassing Jacquou in the village and putting him to trouble and expense. I felt I deserved his homily even though I was not entirely convinced by his view, which was then more unusual than it would be today.

Early the following Tuesday, Evan stole the Simca. The ability to start a car without the ignition key was evidently one of his many skills.

I had no time to speculate on its disappearance, because I did not notice it had gone till a police van drove down the track to the mill-house and three Gendarmes tumbled out. Having established that I was the owner – they had found a book with Jacquou's name on the back seat, and they were local men – they told me that the Simca was now in a ditch some miles away. A young Englishwoman had been found near it, in a state of distress, with various minor injuries. She had been taken to the hospital in a neighbouring small town, and said she did not know where the driver of the car was.

'Well I certainly don't,' I said furiously.

'Did you give him permission to take it?'

'I did not.'

Then did I want to deposit a complaint? (In my disorientated state that's what it sounded like.)

Oh God. Simone had now joined me. She looked extremely apprehensive. I hesitated. I remembered the effect the very word 'police' had had on Evan.

'No,' I said wearily at last. 'He is – or was – a friend. I don't want to bring proceedings against him.' It would have seemed tempting fate to do so. I would rather settle for this as the simple result of his melodramatic, cheap threat 'You wait, you bastard'.

'What about the car?' said Simone. 'Can it be repaired?'

The gendarmes looked dubious but wouldn't say. It wasn't their place to, they indicated. A garage had been called out to tow the vehicle away.

Just so long, I said to Simone, as I never had to see him again as long as I lived. B-film had clearly taken me over also.

Joyce, however, we did have to see. As Simone said, we could hardly leave her injured, friendless and nearly French-less, unvisited in a country hospital. On the Thursday, we nerved ourselves to go over there. Jacquou lent us his Citroën.

The place was a shock to me. It made me realize after all how deep my Englishness went. The word 'hospital' had suggested to me some more or less efficient institution, bleak perhaps but clean, with bossy staff. Even the nineteenth-century maternity ward in which we had last visited Joyce had fallen within this category. But this small rural institution was a throwback to a much older use of the word, the *hôpital* of medieval Europe where the lame, the halt and the blind, lepers and the destitute, were gathered into a minimal shelter by religious orders. The buildings, charmingly set by the river, were several centuries old. The standards of organization and hygiene seemed hardly more modern. Joyce was lying in dirty sheets, wearing her petticoat which was still stained with blood. Her other clothes were piled on the bed-end. Various grubby bandages decorated parts of her. Her hair had not been washed or brushed. Around her, between the stone pillars of the ward, the other female patients, many of them extremely aged, lay, sat, wandered, ate things, gibbered, moaned, squatted in corners, wet themselves and otherwise pursued their own individual devices. At the sight of us, Joyce burst into tears.

'It's all my fault,' she said after a while, when she could speak. 'I know it's all my fault.'

I thought she was talking nonsense, but seeing her so pathetically alone shifted her again in my perception. In the past weeks she had become for me Evan's faintly repellent accomplice, an example of evil-through-mere-weakness, like (I thought) the women who had a good time with Nazi officers during the Occupation. Now, as at the time of the baby's birth, I saw her again as a victim, a sufferer.

Simone stroked and patted her, while I wandered around the ward scowling at senile old ladies and at a girl with an abnormally small head who sat masturbating on a commode. When I came back, Joyce was saying to Simone:

'I tried – I did try to be what he wanted me to be. And to do what he wanted – '

'I know you did.'

'But he's so changeable, gets in such moods. I suppose that's his creative temperament? He says it is . . . Sometimes I think I shouldn't have given in to him so much. It seems to make him worse. He can't bear to be grateful to anyone. You know: the more people do what he wants, the naughtier he gets. It's as if he's testing you out all the time.'

Simone just nodded and went on patting her hand. I lolled at the bedhead, interested that Joyce seemed to have perceived something fundamental about Evan that I had not. She must be quite bright after all.

'Tested to destruction,' I remarked conversationally. Joyce stared at me, then burst into tears again. Simone gave me a reproachful look.

'Oh where is he now?' wept Joyce. 'When I came round after the accident he simply wasn't there. On his own, with so little money and maybe concussed as well . . . Maybe he's lost his memory? Oh Evan – '

'I expect he's hitchhiked back to Paris by now,' I said promptly, and Simone, meaning the same thing, said: 'Oh, I'm sure Evan's OK. You'll probably hear from him soon.'

'But he doesn't know I'm here – '

None of us heard from Evan, not to my surprise. The following week an ill-shaven hospital 'doctor', smelling of wine and garlic, pronounced Joyce fit to leave. We saw her onto the train – she finally achieved her desire to be taken to Châteauroux. Jacquou gave her some money. She was bent on going to Paris to look for Evan: she rejected suggestions, reluctantly made by all three of us, that she should stay at the mill-house for a few days to convalesce. We were all relieved.

'I've seen too many girls like that in my time,' said Jacquou sombrely, as the train diminished in the distance towards the plains of the Loire. Then he burst out laughing, and apologized for being 'old and cynical'.

I felt I wanted to be old and cynical too. I had had enough of being young, I thought, if that meant sitting in cafés drinking too much, listening to rubbish about creativity, and being beholden to proper adults to bail me out of trouble. I was in my mid-twenties and was within a few months of finishing my dissertation, if I worked hard. Simone would soon be twenty-three. I thought it was nearly time we got married.

I was not to see Evan again for very many years.

I ran into Joyce once, on the Metro, the following winter. She looked fairly well, if rather fat. We greeted one another with mutual embarrassment, and conversed for a few minutes without mentioning Evan's name. She said that she had a job looking after some children out at Vincennes, which is where she was going. I got off at Bastille, as Simone and I were now living in two rooms above a bakery in the Marais, among interesting whiffs of new bread and drains.

I believe it was at the end of that same summer but perhaps it was one soon after – at any rate it was long, long ago – that

100

Simone and I, driving north, stopped at a small town on the Loire. I have always thought it was Richelieu, but I have never been back. I do not remember if we sought out a particular church, or if we were simply wandering, buying a picnic lunch and taking a stroll – it must have been that, for no one had told us what we would find in the church. Unusually, it had an upper room to one side of the main building, a light, stone-vaulted chamber like a setting for some Renaissance painting of the Last Supper. It was arranged as a chapel, with an ornate nineteenth-century altar at one end and the usual unresponsive-looking statue of the Virgin. Almost all the wall-space was covered with a patchwork of stone and marble plaques, their inscriptions variations on the eternal, wishful theme of 'Grateful thanks, Mother of God, for favours received'.

'It must be some specific cult,' Simone and I said to each other. 'They've probably got a grubby little relic here.'

'I wonder what this Virgin does,' said Simone. 'I mean, what she cures.'

'Must it be one particular thing?'

'Yes, I think so. I think that's what they – ' (she meant the Catholics, the traditional Other of Huguenot France) – 'believe. Such-and-such a Virgin is good for infertility and that other for tuberculosis or – or liver complaints or something.'

'How prosaic.'

'But convenient. Like knowing which shop to go to.' She wandered round the chapel, reading the variations of abject gratitude and conviction, personal letters to Dear Mary in stone. She seemed to like them, but I found them cumulatively claustrophobic.

'Well whatever it is it must be quite a common complaint,' I said, 'and one that you can kid yourself is improved by praying . . . Shall we go?'

'Do you think perhaps it's cancer?' she said.

That had occurred to me too, as the most likely disease for such obsessive attention, but I had not liked to say so because of Simone's own mother.

'Very probably,' I said. 'Let's go.'

Down the stone stairs, in the main body of the church, we found some pamphlets. It wasn't cancer, after all, that this Virgin was reputed to protect one from: it was fear.

'Dead clever!' I said. 'Wonder who dreamed that up? The one thing no one could ever prove prayer wasn't efficacious against. A bit of a cheat, I'd say.'

'I don't think it's a cheat,' she said slowly. 'It's actually more honest than most of the cults. If people believe they are conquering fear by prayer, then they *are*. Anyway it's what I always wanted when I was a child . . . I wish I'd known then that this Virgin was here.'

'Well I shouldn't think your father would have been keen on you traipsing off to petition her.' I was surprised. I was inclined to think of Simone as braver than myself, and – in most things – clear-sighted. I found the thought of her, at ten or eleven, praying to a sentimental Victorian image, vaguely offensive. 'What were you afraid of anyway?'

'Oh – lots of things . . . Yes I was, you don't realize. Lots and lots. I used to talk to – to either of my parents about the things I was afraid of, and at first whichever one it was used to try to talk me out of that particular fear.'

'But what *sort* of fears?' I couldn't remember being afraid of much as a child myself. Crassly secure, no doubt, I thought.

'Oh – the dark and accidents and the river rising suddenly in the night and savage dogs and a boy in the village with a huge head and Maman or Papa dying,' she said rapidly, and added at once: 'But *what* is beside the point. Because when I was reasoned out of one fear I used to think up another one, so reasoning was no use. Eventually Papa noticed that. He said to me once when I'd been carrying on at him – oh, about some silly, unlikely thing, I can't remember what – he said: "I think you are frightened just because you are frightened, and the only thing you really have to fear is fear itself." '

'That was probably true. But did it help?'

'Yes, eventually it did. We made a sort of joke of it after that. Any particular thing I was afraid of – the Germans coming, or whatever – Papa and Maman used to be

102

absolutely dismissive about, but they used to accept that I *was frightened*, and be fairly sympathetic about my fear, as if it were a tiresome pain in the leg or something. That's why I think that chapel full of "thank you" plaques is right. Often it is fear itself that is the incapacitating disease to be overcome.'

'I am familiar with the theory,' I said stiffly, as we left the church, 'but there seems to me a fallacy in it.'

'What?'

'Well – you said that one of your fears as a child was of either of your parents dying. But your mother did.'

'Yes. But by that time I had become braver. That's the point.' There was an edge of childish 'so there' in her voice but I, from within my carapace of reason, confusedly perceived the point she was making. Did she still pray for courage, translating her father's secular advice into something more mystical? I had a hunch that she did.

Throughout our life together I tended to scoff at any signs of mysticism or superstition that she betrayed – taking upon myself, I suppose, her father's rôle, copying what I took to be his steadfast rejection of illusion. But after she herself had died (unafraid, her eyes open towards a dark that seemingly held no terrors for her), I wanted to bring Marigold to this Loire town and show her the chapel in the upper room and tell her what her mother had said.

I never did. I was going to, but on one journey together we were late or I thought I must have misremembered the town, recognizing nothing, and the next year Marigold was older and travelled out on her own to join me. I think . . . Anyway, I never did. One conversation she and I did not have.

I never let Simone herself speak to me properly of these things either. I mean, of the balancing act of living with the dark void and not living with it, minding but not minding. I regret that we did not speak of it. Now, I find myself longing obscurely for Simone's concealed fount of belief rather than the anodyne goodwill of the person I live with now.

Ann believes that she has no religion. Yet she operates

103

under a great, bland load of assumption about charity, progress, and humankind being essentially good. She does not recognize this value-pack for what it is: the squashy, standard baggage of a post-Christian era that wishes to retain the comforts of religion without its dark heart. She vaguely imagines herself to be emancipated 'from all that'. Instead, she has made a restrained 'good Socialism' her faith; she is one of those who vote Left from conviction rather than self-interest and innocently imagine others do as well. Similarly, she cannot grasp why the entire world is not in favour of nuclear disarmament, and indeed pacificism. She seems to suppose that war is an aberration, that blood sports are a perversion, even that vegetarianism may be more natural to humans than meat-eating . . . She is intelligent, by general standards, sensitive and civilized. We have the same mother-tongue.

Yet this time it is like living with someone from a foreign country. She knows nothing. Is this why I married her? Is this the best that, weighted by grief, I could manage? God. God.

PART III

When did the search begin in earnest?

Certainly, in the early stages, I did not know what I was seeking, and the first moves may seem in the telling, and seemed to me at the time, random. I twitched, shifted, like a drowned man, moved by currents undersea: I knew nothing myself. Or almost nothing.

It is only now, looking back from the end, that I can see that the cycle of blind exploration began earlier than I thought at the time, perhaps even as early as that afternoon when the irrelevant girl who was another Amanda stood in front of me in Court. And I drove home afterwards in the rain and told Ann, in a desultory way, about Evan and Joyce. Joyce and Evan. That was when the sea began to cast forth its dead. Not the literal dead (Marigold had been dead five years then, but was never, for one day, absent from my mind), but those who, for thirty years, had been dead to me.

Of course I did not at first realize that anything was beginning. Having dredged these bodies up, coated in the slime of my own outdated emotion – resentment, a sense of inadequacy and something other and deeper without a name – I would have been glad to cast them back again. But, once exposed, they kept returning unbidden to my thoughts. I had no idea why.

I had not (it seems to me now) much idea about anything at that time. It was indeed I who was the drowned man. I had left my job as a headmaster after Marigold was killed: or, more exactly, since I was starting my sabbatical term off then, I never returned to it. Already, in any case, there had been tentative soundings about a job change: the successful Grammar School I ran was due to go Comprehensive, and my own lack of total enthusiasm for the project was well known; I had recently published a book on the history of

105

state education. Now, when I was asked if I would like to become an Inspector – a rôle in which the pursuit of excellence was considered less of a handicap – I accepted, not thinking very much about anything, intent only on putting one foot before the other; this was a state in which I remained for some time.

So I had been an HMI for about five years, and was married to Ann, when my search got underway. But at first the moves were so inconsequential and (it seemed) dependent on chance, that I did not recognize them for what they were.

It must have been some time after that day in Court, later in the winter, that I called on Lewis Greenfield to discuss my Russian prisoner.

Lewis it was who 'looked after everything' when Marigold was killed, but that was sheer kindness on his part, for these days Lewis is no family solicitor but a specialist in international legal wrangles. We have known each other since we were both at Oxford. I have a photograph still of our year, taken in the quad, and it makes me smile. I suppose I must have changed a bit, though I never feel I have changed at all in myself, and even the mirror tells me that I am merely thicker and greyer. But who would recognize in the heavy, bald, formidable, expensively-suited Lewis of today the thin, dark boy with a nervous smile and an East End accent that I remember? In the photo he stands a little apart at the end of a row of stolid, tweed-jacketed young men, as if not quite certain he ought to be there. He wears a blue suit that I remember and a row of pens in his breast pocket; his cowlick hair is greased into a quiff. 'It *was* my first week of my first term,' Lewis protested when I showed him the picture the other year, almost indignant that I still had it. 'And you're not to show it to Myra! I mean that.'

Actually I think Myra would find that photo as touching as I do, even though she is rather a snob these days. She is a frankly fat but still pretty woman, who manages to conceal emotionalism under a façade of serene matronhood. They have four well-brought-up children and live in a neo-Georgian house in one of those wooded suburbs where you have to take the car out to buy an evening paper or a loaf of bread: fortunately they have several cars. Their daughter, a portly little girl with Lewis's covert sweetness of nature but without his aggression, was a pupil of Simone's at one time; afterwards, the Greenfields used to invite Marigold and me regularly to supper or to Sunday lunch. Later again, when I came out of hospital with my barely-mended knee and no Marigold, not at home, not anywhere, ever again, I more or less lived in the Greenfields' house for several weeks. Was it then, on a particularly bad day, that Lewis told me the Treblinka story? I think it must have been. It was, he said almost dismissively, a well-known story: I must stop him if I realized I had heard it already . . .

There was a group of Hassidic scholars in Treblinka Concentration Camp. They wished to mark Yom Kippur, the Day of Atonement, and the only means available to them was to hold an informal debate, a kind of vigil. So they discussed for many hours, with scholarly references and precedents, the likely existence or otherwise of God. And, through these time-honoured means, some arguments won over others and a group-consensus emerged: it was at last regretfully agreed that the balance of probability was that God did not exist – that what they had seen and what was happening around them made the existence of a powerful, caring God *ipso facto* unlikely. There followed a silence, while the implications of this decision were digested. Then at last the eldest scholar got shakily to his feet and said:

'My friends, it is time to say the evening prayer.'

Of course, I could see that Lewis meant the story to be for me, in the state I was in, but I didn't want to talk about myself. Unlike the eldest Hassid I had not quite made up my mind whether to go on living. So, for something to say, I asked:

'Do you have a God, Lewis?' I was fairly sure he did not.

'Well I wouldn't say I have Him personally, so to speak. But the older I get the more I appreciate the idea of keeping faith with my ancestors. And it's like an old uncle of mine used to say: I believe in standing up of my own accord to be counted before someone drags me out and counts me.'

'No one will do that to you today, in England.'

'Very possibly not, but I don't believe in being too sure of anything. One can get caught out nastily by counting too much on something.'

I wasn't entirely convinced by him. Oh, I believed in the objective truth of what he said – how could I, of all people, not know now that one should never count upon anything – but I was sceptical that Lewis kept this daunting fact much in mind these days. From the depths of my grief I had been sourly envying him his secure, unbroken life. There were moments when I turned from the big, warm, expensively-furnished house, scented with Myra's baking, a child playing a musical instrument somewhere in an upstairs room, another studying for his own Law finals by a log fire, all mess removed by the Filipino couple, plus Daddy himself arriving on cue from Zurich, Strasbourg or Hong Kong after another successful professional foray . . . Moments when it all seemed to me just too like, shall I say, a transatlantic commercial for some discreetly ethnic but by-adoption all-American product: Israeli claret, perhaps.

But possibly Lewis, for all his ostentatious enjoyment of what he had made of his life, really thought something like this too. For when at last I murmured my bitter feeling that he and Myra were living in a happy country from which chance events had now excluded me for ever, he said promptly: 'Oh – me. Well, yes, of course *all this* is all right in its way. But a lot of the time I live As If . . .'

'As what?'

'*As If* there were some purpose to it all. I mean – what other feasible option is there?' He glanced at me with a shrewd, half-amused, half-cynical expression, perhaps waiting to be asked to elaborate. He might, I thought afterwards, have had an impulse to unburden himself to me. His loss of faith in other things, besides religion . . . But, if so, I had been too self-absorbed to invite him to. Maybe it was just as well. Sometimes, no doubt, it is better just to say the evening prayer instead. Or to observe whatever secular rituals and obligations have, for people like us, replaced prayer.

Another time, it must have been later, I forget the immediate context, he said – 'Oh we all have a bit of free-floating agony around, don't we? It's a mistake to think it's necessarily *because* of anything. You can torture yourself that way . . .' But then, before I could agree or disagree with him, he put a hand on my arm and said: 'I'm sorry, Tom. That was a bloody stupid thing to say to you.'

I was recalling this conversation, and the Treblinka story, on the day several years later that I went to talk to Lewis about 'my' Russian prisoner. He was a Ukrainian in fact, a history teacher imprisoned by Soviet Russia for his supposed Ukrainian nationalist sympathies, his tendency to teach history according to facts rather than according to accepted Party concepts, or for some other specifically Russian misdemeanour. I had heard of him through an international historical association to which I belong and which interests itself in such cases. Long ago, when I joined this association, its most eminent members specialized in the Marxist approach to history: I was then busy with my Great Work on the Left. Time, and such events as the demoting of Stalin and the Hungarian Revolution on the one hand, and the rediscovery and popularization of Marxist theory on the other, subsequently undermined many of the assumptions on which the association was originally founded. Today, its ethos is slavophile but anti-Soviet, and it has developed a sideline in campaigning in favour of imprisoned or persecuted academics.

I had never met Piotr Mihailovitch Malenko, but a photo of him looking bespectacled and cheerful, with his dog, in happier days, stood on my study mantelpiece. I used to greet him out loud when I was alone, for we were twins; on the day in 1927 that I saw the light of Birmingham he too cried for the first time in a village on the Dnieper. It was for this reason, together with less childish ones, that I had asked the Prisoners' Committee secretary to let me have Piotr Mihailovitch as 'my' prisoner. As for the rest of his details, the very ordinary pleasantness of his face, the normality of his domestic record (a wife and two daughters, currently living bereft 'somewhere in the country') and the modest decency of his achievements (deputy-head, until his arrest, of a high school in Kiev) made me warm to him all the more. I did not want to believe him to be an exceptional person – except in so far as any man may be called exceptional who does what he believes to be right knowing that he may suffer for it. I saw him, rather, as an ordinary chap like myself, but one forced by circumstances to find within himself exceptional resources. I used to look at his picture and hope that he was finding them. The news of him, via the association and contacts in Eastern Europe, was that he had become seriously malnourished on the prison diet, that he had kidney problems and that his eyes were troubling him. I used to stand in front of him and try quite hard to imagine myself in his place. I have never had much time for the idea that contemplating another's misfortunes makes you feel better about your own, but, for whatever reason, it did seem to help in some way to have Piotr Mihailovitch's photo there with me.

I knew too that he was of Jewish origin but was a believing Christian: neither of these facts can have endeared him to the Soviet authorities. So I was thinking about the Treblinka story as I drove to the Greenfields that day, and while I was there I said to Lewis, 'I wonder if Piotr Mihailovitch is living "As If" in Perm camp.'

Lewis took off his new half-moon glasses and put them on again while he worked out what on earth I meant. Having apparently located my reference and understood it, he just said:

'Must be, I should think, wouldn't you? Hope so, poor sod.'

Lewis was helping me draft a letter to a delegation in Vienna who were supposed to be looking into a number of Human Rights cases including that of Piotr Mihailovitch Malenko. I had some time ago enlisted Lewis's support as legal adviser to the Prisoners' Committee.

'If we want to make this letter usable in itself by the delegation we have to work within Soviet Law as it stands,' he said. 'Like I said before, it's no good banging on about it being scandalous that Malenko is in prison anyway, that would just be counter-productive. He's sentenced to ten years and there it is. What I suggest we stress is his rights within that context – make the buggers feel that, at the end of the sentence, they've got to produce him to the world in reasonable nick. How much longer has he got to serve, by the way?'

'Nearly six years still. What I'm afraid is that, as things are, he won't live that long.'

'Exactly, and that's what we have to harp on. Ask specific questions about diet and medical treatment. Nag to know more about the kidney ailment. Embarrass the bastards.'

We worked on the letter some more. I said: 'Health is a matter of morale too, isn't it? I just wish we could think of some way of letting *him* know people are fussing on his behalf.'

'His wife knows?'

'We hope she does. We're never sure what letters get through to her.'

'Any chance of her getting a message to him?'

'We think the current situation is that she's not allowed to visit. Or send presents. That's part of the bleakness, isn't it? I mean that there isn't any hard news, nothing to take hold of. As if the powers that be were making him fade out of existence even before they've actually killed him off . . . You know, Lewis, yesterday for the first time when I looked at his photograph I had the sinking feeling that perhaps he isn't alive any more – that campaigning for him is just an empty act of faith. No real point to it. Not good.'

'Not good at all,' said Lewis promptly, 'since that's probably just what the Soviets are hoping we'll think. No news, nothing to go on . . . Emptiness. *Nacht und Nebel.* No, however non-existent the evidence, you must hang on to the idea that he is alive, can be helped.'

'The "As If" situation again, in fact. Not believing specifically in God, I mean, but just believing it's all worth it.'

'Quite so.'

111

I thought for a bit. Till then, I had had some cloudy feeling, to which I would not have owned in words, that by having Piotr Mihailovitch on my mantelpiece, talking to him when we were on our own, I was somehow doing what I could to keep him going. But perhaps it was rather he who was keeping me going? When I woke in the night and could not sleep again, which I had begun to do with depressing frequency the last few months, the thought of him, my shadow-twin, my *semblable*, surviving privations immeasurable by me, was an obscure source of strength to me. I had formed the habit of reaching for him mentally in the dark, for consolation and company, as a child will reach for its teddy or a man for a woman, real or fantasized. But if in reality *he* had given up, had abandoned his own more specific faith and was already dead, or dying . . .

After a while I attempted to convey this to Lewis. He gave me a penetrating look – or rather, a parody of one. I could see he was wondering if I was 'all right', which irritated me quite a lot. Of course I was 'all right' fundamentally, I always am. Except just in those first few weeks after Marigold went, it never occurred to me I might give up on life, and even if it had I don't think I would have known how to. Some people seem to be able to stage spectacular crack-ups, incontrovertible statements that they refuse to cope any longer, but that option never seemed to present itself to me. Some seemed to think this was stoicism on my part. However I had a suspicion it was a form of cowardice in me.

Lewis said: 'When I wake in the night – and I often do these days, it's middle age I think, I don't seem to need as much sleep as I used to – I read for a couple of hours. I recommend that. Doesn't matter what – Updike, Henry James, Law Reports, detective stories, whatever. Print is sweet, in the night. I enjoy it, then, much more than I ever do now at times when I'm supposed to be awake.'

'Doesn't Myra mind? About having the light on, I mean.' I'd tried that, but Ann had woken at once. No, she hadn't complained, but she'd been enormously, invasively concerned about me, so I hadn't tried it again.

'Myra complained like mad at first,' said Lewis promptly. 'So I said in that case I'd move into the spare room, and she didn't like the sound of that so she shut up quick. We bought one of those small tunnel spots which means I can direct a beam just down onto my own pillow, and Myra bought about six yards of tulle in different colours to bandage her eyes. Now, most nights, she does her head up in it last thing – I'm telling you, it's like sleeping with a corpse! I warn her I'm getting a taste for necrophilia, but of course she says it's my fault, well most things are – '

He was trying, among other things, to make me laugh, and he did, but I was not to be deflected from what else I wanted to say. I had realized only just now, as I was trying to tell him how Piotr Mihailovitch was present to me in the night, that someone else seemed to be there also.

Someone far more shadowy, without a face or a name, but deadeningly, pointlessly fettered to my life for ever. Several times recently when I had woken in the dark, the fact of his continuing existence, his unknown life going on and on when other lives were over, had presented itself to me like the weight of some unpleasant dream. But he was not a dream, and it was to stop my imagination dwelling specifically on him as much as anything that I had taken to summoning up Malenko. Better set one good, innocent man up as an ikon of purpose and contemplate him than brood upon his opposite, the one I can only hate: the French driver who killed Marigold.

By and by I told Lewis this. I did not think he would be surprised, and he wasn't. But something was bothering him. Presently he said, sounding accusing:

'You said at the time that you didn't want to know anything about the man.'

'I know I did. I thought, that way, I wouldn't think about him much. But it isn't so. Tell me what you know, Lewis. It might help me, to know – something.'

'Tom . . . It won't do any good. We said that at the time.'

'It won't do any harm either. Tell me, Lewis.'

'I don't know anything about him.'

'Then why are you acting as if you're hiding something?'
There's nothing like a wretched obsession for sharpening
one's perceptions.

Lewis got up from his vast desk and began wandering
round his study fiddling with the exhibition of exotic junk
he keeps there: bits of semi-polished rock from the Negev
desert, dark saints from Latin America, Buddhas from
South-East Asia. I waited. He turned round and said
heavily:

'All right then, I will put you right on one thing. You
have assumed the driver of that car was French. So did I,
initially.'

'It was a French car. Wasn't it?' I felt as if some small,
hard object had shifted slightly inside my head.

'Yes. But since you want to know – and I warn you, I
don't think it will be any help – I ought to tell you that the
driver appears to have been British. When I was shown the
police report that was stated. And his name was British too.'

'What was it?'

There is power in knowing a name. That, I suppose, is
why I wanted it. But there is also dread. In the several
seconds before he answered, I suffered the fear that the
name would be one already known to me. So, perhaps, does
a husband dread that the name of his wife's lover will turn
out to be that of his friend. And looking into Lewis's
crumpled face, as he stared into mine through the space
between his bushy eyebrows and his absurdly truncated
glasses, I saw in the instant that he shared the same fear.

'It was a David Hughes,' he said at last.

I found I had been holding my breath. I let it go.

'No one she knew?' he said very quickly.

I shook my head. The name meant nothing to me. It was,
after all, just a name, and a commonplace one at that. I felt a
shaken sense of anti-climax.

'I didn't think so either,' Lewis said. 'The police asked
me. I said I thought not, had never heard the name
mentioned . . . It didn't make any difference anyway.'

It didn't make any difference. Whether Marigold had
died due to the idiotic folly of an unknown Frenchman or of

an Englishman with a name, it made no difference. She was still just as dead, and would have remained so however many enquiries had been pursued. All the same, I indulged my bitterness by saying:

'The police hardly exerted themselves much, did they? But of course, if there wasn't even a French citizen involved, just two foreigners . . . And they weren't our local police but the Argenton lot. No wonder they didn't bother to bring any charges.'

I saw from his face that he was inclined to agree with this interpretation, but then he turned away. Perhaps he was afraid I was blaming him for not pressing the police harder himself. But if I did eventually come to feel that, I do not believe I was aware of it that afternoon. The information that the driver was British was enough for me to digest for the time being. So I really was only speculating when I said flatly:

'He was on holiday, I suppose, this David Hughes? But why the French car? Oh – hired, I imagine . . .'

'No, it was his own car, or so I understood. Paris-registered. I suppose he lived there. I seem to remember his statement to the police said he'd been staying somewhere in that part of France – that he often did. That was the reason the police asked me if he and Marigold knew each other before – though he'd already told them not, I believe.'

He looked at my face, and added quickly: 'Oh, they were just checking up in a routine way. It didn't amount to anything. So many accidents on French roads – I told you that at the time.'

'So he lived in Paris,' I said.

I really did not, at that moment, mean anything by the remark. I was just processing, with painful inefficiency, what Lewis had imparted to me. But he must have thought I was trying to find out more with some purpose in mind, and he became evasive and finally stubborn.

So, though I still accepted the idea that no good would come of vain questioning, I went home obscurely angry with him. And presently angry at myself too. For during the night that followed, the now-named man tormented me

115

more, closer to me now that I knew him to be a compatriot but still more shadowy. Or rather, he now took many chimeric forms in relentless succession. What sort of Englishman lives in Paris? A young man? A man near my own age? (Lewis might have told me his age, but I hadn't thought to ask.) An international businessman? A writer? A teacher of English? Someone maybe with a life's pattern not unlike my own – perhaps even a man with a French wife and a daughter. *Mon semblable, mon frère.*

I tried to think that he might have suffered from the accident himself, might have felt guilty, have grieved . . . He might even have wanted to write to me, to say, however inadequately, 'Sorry. Oh God – sorry', and been warned off any such compromising act by his own lawyer. For a time I played with this fantasy. But then suddenly it did not seem likely any more. The sort of conceited fool who picks up a pretty girl by the roadside and then, showing off his driving (or worse?), crashes the car and kills her – why should he know what grief meant?

I lay awake for what seemed much of the night, and for once my twin far away in Russia was no help to me, nor I, I am sure, to him.

It must have been shortly after that, and it was no doubt a sign of how on edge I was, that Ann and I quarrelled about Melvyn Baines.

For some years I had been successfully avoiding Melvyn. I liked to think that, following one or two occasions when I had been, professionally, less than polite about his Child Guidance Centre, he had got the message and had been keeping out of my way also. Of course he, for his part, must have regarded me as misguided – 'unenlightened' was probably his term – but he was profoundly pleased with himself, as those who aspire to the rôle of guru tend to be, and I have noticed that such people will go to ingenious lengths to avoid encountering those who do not admire them. In that respect Melvyn was no fool. Indeed, as I had always been annoyingly ready to concede to Ann when she tried to defend him, he was a cultured, intelligent fellow

116

with considerable charm and a number of talents – 'Yes, Ann, he's good at getting people to slave for him and I know he paints, and sings in a choir – yes, *and* reads Proust – but these aren't, in themselves, reasons for me to like him. Sorry, but they just aren't.'

'You don't like him because you think he's homosexual,' Ann said once. She can be quite sharp in that sort of way.

'Yes, as a matter of fact I *do* think that – and so, presumably, do you, or it wouldn't have occurred to you that I might – but *that isn't why* I don't like him, Ann; surely you know me better than that? But you could say, I suppose, that I'd like him better if he were open about it.'

'Oh well – poor him,' said Ann. 'In his position – I do see . . .'

However, we may both have been wrong, for Melvyn belatedly married: a sly, pink-complexioned Swede many years younger than himself. They had two children in quick succession, and I gathered that Proust and painting had been displaced by highly participant fatherhood. At Christmas we, and very many others, received a printed notice announcing that Birgit and Melvyn were not sending cards this year but were donating the money to a charity concerned with Natural Childbirth. The rear window of his car had for years publicized his moral commitment to CND, saving the whale and racial equality, but now it also bore a large notice proclaiming 'Pull back – Give my Child a Chance'.

'As if he thought everyone else goes around driving into the backs of cars for the hell of it,' I grumbled neurotically to Ann. 'Hasn't he noticed that having children is the common lot and so is caring about them? Giving yourself special sensitive airs because you are a father really is terminally conceited.'

'Oh, have it your own way.' Ann gets tense when I talk like this. 'But basically Melvyn has his heart in the right place, I promise you.'

I let it go at that, I even told myself she was probably right. But then Melvyn's concerns took a new turn. I suppose I would have heard about it sooner or later anyway, but in fact it came to my attention directly not through the education circuit but because I am a magistrate. Magistrates are sometimes sought out at home by the police to sign search warrants or arrest warrants after Court hours; our local force knew me, and quite often came to me. Now and again, though much less often, I was asked by them on behalf of the Social Services to sign a Place of Safety order for a child to be removed from its home. I think I had only signed three of them in about ten years, and I did not much like dealing with them because neither I nor the policemen who brought them to me could really know anything about the cases: the police were only going on what social workers told them, and I was just acting as a legal rubber stamp. So, when three more cases were brought to me within the space of two months, I became uneasy – though not in any focused way, since this was several years before a national scandal on these lines erupted in the north of England. The third time, I asked to see either the reports in full or, preferably, the social worker in charge of the case in person.

The police went away with the long-suffering air of those merely doing their duty, and returned an hour later still unaccompanied but with a sheaf of papers. The principal report turned out, as I expected, to be by the same social worker who had been quoted to me on the two previous occasions and, as before, the family were said to have been 'drawn to the attention of the Social Services' by Dr Melvyn Baines.

I asked the police to wait and took the papers in to Ann, who was making a dress on the kitchen table.

'Something's going on,' I said. 'Take a look at this lot.'

Ann removed many pins from her mouth – funny, and touching, how all women dress-make with the same gestures – and read through the papers with close attention.

'Goodness,' she said seriously when she had finished. 'How awful . . . Lucky that Melvyn found this out.'

'Unless,' I said, 'the whole thing's a figment of his over-active imagination.'

'Oh Tom.' She looked completely taken aback. 'You don't mean that?'

'Yes I do. I've read this carefully, twice. I agree it's a dramatic situation, if true – but do you notice there isn't a shred of hard evidence for it, not in these reports anyway? There's all this circumstantial stuff about the whole family having been "in therapy", and "counselling sessions" and "tension" and so forth, but the social worker and Melvyn seem to be basing their entire case on the fact that no one in the family will actually admit anything. It's the well-known Freudian trap: if you admit it then it's true, and if you don't then that in itself proves you're "repressing" it. Great.'

'It does say here that the girl seems upset and preoccupied with the subject, and . . . Where is it? Yes, here – "precociously aware of sexuality".'

' "Precociously aware" – yes, I bet she is, with Baines showing her dolls and working her up and encouraging her to make up dirty stories! It's a great mistake to think that when a kid is upset what you hear is the truth: on the contrary, it may be a lurid pack of lies. Surely I don't need to tell *you* that?'

'No. But – '

'And if you read these reports again you'll see there's no real evidence at all for the idea that the father's been interfering with her *or* the elder sister – just this brief note from a GP saying, in effect, that he can't be sure, that there are no gross physical signs and no evidence of rape as such.'

'It does say the bigger girl isn't a virgin.'

'So? She's fourteen, and from a crummy background. Nothing unusual there. Certainly nothing to implicate the father. Could be anybody . . .' Suddenly the realization of how profoundly I had distrusted Melvyn all these years came over me in a wave that was almost an exhilaration.

'I'm not going to lend myself to his power-grabbing fantasies,' I said. 'I'm not going to sign these papers.'

'But Tom, suppose it *is* true? Surely you can't take that risk? Surely, to be on the safe side – ?'

'What safe side? What's *safe* about removing a child from her home and branding her father as a danger to society and her mother as a pervert and inadequate? You're talking like a fool Ann – ' I know I should never speak to her like that, I do know, it is cruel and pointless, but I was now launched, and swept on:

'That's just the sort of herd-reaction that Melvyn Baines counts on provoking. Him and his empire-building and his harem of admiring unmarried female social workers! Shall I tell you what that man's particular talent is for? Not, for God's sake, for understanding the complexity of people's lives but for picking up just a bit quicker than anyone else what the next fashionable subject is going to be: Marriage Guidance – Non-Accidental Injury – God, he tried to conduct an absolute witch-hunt on that in a primary school a few years ago, I've just remembered . . . Counselling – Family Therapy – now Child Sexual Abuse – what's the next flavour-of-the-month eh? Watch Baines and you'll find out. Well, I'm not one of his fan club, and I'm not going to join this particular bandwagon. I won't play "Dr Baines is so perceptive". I won't sign a Place of Safety order for these girls.'

Ann's mouth was set in a thin, miserable line. Her small chin trembled.

'I think you may be making a terrible mistake,' she said.

'So be it. I'll carry the guilt then, won't I? I'd sooner be wrong by my own judgement than wrong by following the judgement of someone I don't trust.'

'What will you say to the police?'

'I'll tell them I haven't been given adequate evidence. And I'll spell out to them what I mean.'

Ann said, bravely for her: 'Well I just hope they find another magistrate to sign their order.'

This made me deeply angry, but I just said coldly: 'I expect they will.'

And I expect they did.

The next day, Sunday, I wrote Melvyn a long letter, expressing in temperate, impersonal terms the doubts I had conveyed to Ann with such wildness. I laboured over it all the morning, feeling increasingly paranoid about Melvyn but also increasingly unhappy with myself. Ann went about the house with a wretched, drawn look and hardly spoke. Clearly, I had gone much too far.

120

To my letter, I received an acknowledgement, but not at that point anything more. It seemed that Melvyn was in no hurry to enter into debate with me. Probably that was wise of him.

Neither Ann nor I had recovered fully from my outburst when I went to Edinburgh. I was going to visit my only surviving relation, my mother's sister, and also an old friend and his new wife. Neither my own dark mood nor Ann's hurt, withdrawn one made this a propitious time for me to travel, but the visits had long been arranged: anyway, I went.

I have known Humphrey for almost as long as I have known Lewis. In fact Humphrey was one of the Oxford friends with whom I had spent an inopportune holiday in the Lake District in the middle of my first summer with Simone. I remember eventually confiding in him, in oblique terms, why I was so restive and absent-minded. 'I feel I've had to leave her just at the wrong time,' I said glumly. Humphrey listened, full of sympathy and interest, asked tactful questions – and yet, in spite of the relief of speaking of Simone, saying her name, I began to feel more tense and frustrated rather than less, for it was borne in on me that Humphrey did not entirely understand what I was saying. He enquired at one point ('with apologies, Tom, for even raising such a personal thing') whether I had asked Simone to marry me. When I must have gaped at him, and insisted that our relationship was nowhere near that point, he went on to suggest, with great delicacy, that perhaps I should make the offer without delay. ' – To reassure her, Tom. Don't you think it might be what she very much needs, after – after what you have told me? It seems to me she must desperately want to trust you. And since you had to leave her like that yourself right after . . . You should have brought her here, Tom, we would all have understood. Laura would have understood, I would have had a quiet word with her . . . But perhaps you felt the relationship is too private to expose in that way?'

'Yes,' I said after a pause. 'Yes, I expect I did think that.'

I did not know what else to say, for Humphrey's apparent mental image of Simone now pining away in France, fearing herself seduced and abandoned, seemed so far from the reality of her and me that I could not think how to disabuse him of it. I even wondered wildly if he could possibly be right and if I, certainly less thoughtful and sensitive to others than he was, had failed, in the traditional male way, to understand Simone? But even in my present over-anxious state I knew that Simone had other strengths, other preoccupations, than those Humphrey ascribed to her: that, indeed, was one of the things that was worrying me – that very likely her mind was not now on me at all, but on things at which I could not guess.

'Anyway,' I said flatly, 'she was going off herself. To relatives in the south-west.'

'Poor love, I *see*,' said Humphrey.

'Humphrey, you know . . .' I felt ungrateful, unworthy of his sensibility. Had he been a different sort of person, one who would have greeted my confidence with conspiratorial male levity, I should no doubt have been annoyed. But, as it was, I felt indignant on Simone's behalf to see her cast in the rôle of the insipid and lachrymose Nice Girl of the period, British model. I had met enough of those at Oxford; the memory of several of them now made me feel uncomfort-able and vaguely sad – partly because I almost never did remember them. 'Simone isn't like that. She isn't – well, like Laura,' I ended tactlessly.

Laura was Humphrey's fiancée, whom he had met in his first year at Oxford: soon they were due to marry. In fact Laura was not insipid, being rather beautiful, very musical and formidably hard-working; but she came from much the same slightly grand background that Humphrey did. Though I liked her I could not quite imagine singling her out, as Humphrey had done, as the person with whom I wished to spend the rest of my life.

To my surprise, I realized that Humphrey was blushing. 'Well of course Laura *is* different,' he said firmly. 'I mean she and I don't . . .'

'You don't – ? Oh. Oh, I see.' It was my turn to be

concerned and taken aback. Our spartan holiday in Youth Hostels accompanied by several others had allowed little opportunity for private relations, but I had assumed that in more convenient times and places . . . In short, it had simply not occurred to me that Humphrey and Laura were not already lovers.

'Actually, Tom – I don't see why I shouldn't be frank with you, I'm not ashamed of it, God knows – I haven't ever, personally . . . I mean, Laura has been my first serious relationship, as I have hers. And we've decided to wait till we're married. We both prefer it that way.'

All that, of course, was a lifetime ago. Strange as it may seem, Humphrey and I were genuinely close friends: he was far too diplomatic and uncensorious a person to allow any hint of disapproval to escape him regarding Simone and myself, and I was careful not to let him see that I did not, in fact, find his and Laura's self-controlled idealism admirable.

Through the years we kept track of each other's diverging careers, exchanged holiday visits. When Marigold was born Laura endeared herself to Simone (who had been wary of her for some reason) by sending us a tiny dress that she had hand-smocked herself. Other carefully chosen gifts followed at birthdays and Christmases and I believe it was Laura, on reflection, who was the first person to notice that Marigold had perfect pitch. She encouraged her to sing and, later, to learn the guitar. Humphrey himself was delightful with children, his face lighting up over a game, a puzzle, a bedtime story, and was enthusiastically beloved by Marigold in return. We had imagined him and Laura conscientiously planning and then producing a family of talented, well-behaved children of their own, but as the years succeeded one another it was Lewis Greenfield who settled down after all and fathered these while Humphrey and Laura's life seemed to remain in tasteful, studiously occupied suspension. (Laura, on marriage, had given up her job at a music-publishers, to take on the busy non-occupation of Public School master's wife and presently house-master's.)

123

Eventually, trying in my elephantine way to emulate Humphrey's own real concern for his friends, I 'wondered' tactlessly to Humphrey, while we were on one of our long walks, whether he and Laura were 'seeing anyone' about their childlessness? It was then I learnt, in Humphrey's unspectacular, almost diffident phrases, what he and Laura had known for some time: Laura had multiple sclerosis. That was why she had made excuses not to come on any walks recently, that was the real reason she had abandoned the violin which she had played in a string quartet – and that was why she and Humphrey would never, now, have a child. 'Of course, as soon as her MS was diagnosed,' said Humphrey, 'we decided a child was just not on. It's terribly sad – Laura minds awfully, though she doesn't show it; she's terribly brave about the whole thing. But it just wouldn't be fair on the child.'

I nodded, I think, adopting his own restrained manner, but privately I disagreed with him. Perhaps (although I had at that time quite forgotten Evan and Joyce) I had been alerted to something too facile in not-fair-on-the-child arguments. I thought it rather a pity, in the circumstances, that Humphrey and Laura hadn't had a child already before her disease had declared itself. I said this to Simone, who agreed vehemently with me.

'There's worse things than a sick mother – many worse. It isn't as if Humphrey and Laura haven't got plenty of money for nannies. And living in a boarding school like that, they're surrounded by people who would lend a hand . . . Anyway, Laura may go on still for years and years, mayn't she? Why, by the time she dies the child might be as big as I was when Maman died. And it wouldn't have been "fairer" on me not to have me. There's such a thing as being too good and careful.'

Laura did live on for many years, though she had to take to a wheelchair and then to many other devices, as her strength and capabilities declined. For some time she and Humphrey continued to come on motoring holidays in France (Humphrey's old-fashioned phrase), spending time with us at the mill; but in her last few years the primitive bathroom arrangements at the mill, and then the difficulties of travel for her anyway, made these visits a thing of the past. Instead, she would go determinedly to a health farm, sending Humphrey to us in France on what she insisted now was a necessary holiday for him from her. She also encouraged him to take with him her nephew, Jeffrey, son of a less monied home, a less idyllic marriage, a clever, awkward boy, unhappy at boarding school, in whom she and Humphrey took a concerned interest. Jeffrey, it was felt, would be company for his uncle on the journey and company for Marigold, who was more or less the same age, when at the mill. In fact this well-intentioned plan worked out better than such plans often do: Jeffrey and Marigold, after initial mutual suspicion, found sufficient interests in common and, as they progressed through their teens even seemed to become quite fond of each other.

By this time Simone herself was dead, going, like her mother, from health to death in barely a year, suddenly contesting and outstripping Laura whose own eventual demise had been in laborious rehearsal for so long. Laura lived on another two years – if 'living' it was, immobile, incontinent, deprived in the end even of speech. It goes without saying that through her whole illness Humphrey looked after her with the utmost devotion, and mourned her desperately when at last death released her. I am tempted to put quotation marks round this last sentence, so much does it sound as if it were lifted from an obituary notice, but it is merely a statement of truth: this was the sort of man Humphrey was. Many people would have said he had long been a widower already, in most respects, but Humphrey did not see it like that. Two widowers together, and a little self-conscious in this joint identity, we roamed the cliff above the downstream gorges of the Creuse one hot afternoon, while the idle teenagers lay sprawled on sunlit rocks far below us, and Humphrey said to me suddenly at the end of a conversation about something quite other:

'You know, Tom, there isn't *one hour* when I don't think of her. Not one. People don't realize that . . . But of course you do, I know. I expect it's the same for you?'

It wasn't quite, but I didn't have the heart to tell him so. I used to think then that, much as I grieved for Simone and would have given a great deal for her life to go on – for her sake as much as my own – I probably was not as capable of such intense and exclusive love as Humphrey was. Later, when other things had happened, I became less sure of this. But that was what I thought, at the time.

Humphrey had inherited a flat in Edinburgh; he and Laura had used to let it to university people, and stayed in it themselves during the Festival until Laura became too handicapped for that. Later, I think, the boy Jeffrey lived in it while he was a student there: his edgy intelligence had developed into a taste for computer studies. Now he had moved on to a research post elsewhere, and his Uncle Humphrey had temporarily repossessed the flat.

There had been a temporary feeling about a number of Humphrey's arrangements in the years since Laura had died: he had left one school for another, then returned to the former but no longer as a house-master. When I had remarried myself I had not, for a combination of reasons I expect, liked to make my invitation to him to come and stay with Ann and myself in London too pressing; at any rate he did not come. But he had recently married again himself: someone who had come to his school as an assistant matron, he told me. He had also changed posts again, and was now teaching for the first time at an independent day-school – in Edinburgh. His letter to me, suggesting a meeting, was affectionate and eager. I thought it was time I went to see him.

I had, in any case, another reason for visiting Edinburgh. My mother's sister had married a Scot she had met in the war. He had died, but Auntie Madge (as I still found myself calling her, in an absurd throwback to my schooldays) lived on, old and fat and cheerful, in a house in Morningside.

On the way up in the train I tried to console myself for everything with the thought of how pleased both Auntie and Humphrey would be to see me. I was, I suppose, in the reduced state of needing consciously to count my blessings;

126

at such a time old friendships, old alliances, can seem the only refuge. Even as I reflected on this, I recalled the fatuous way Auntie, more consciously Scottish for years than the genuine article, loved to go on about the 'Auld Alliance' between Scotland and France and used to ask Simone daftly unanswerable questions about this supposed relationship. But there are worse things – ah, many worse – than being bored by an elderly relative, and in my present mood I felt grateful towards Auntie Madge for still existing, and looked forward to her welcome.

She seemed delighted to see me, and was merely a little reproachful that I had not 'after all' brought Ann with me, though there had at no stage been any question that I should.

'It's term-time, Auntie! Ann sends her – her very best to you, of course.' (I have never managed to get my tongue round the word 'love' in patently inappropriate circumstances, and sometimes have difficulty in appropriate ones too.) ' – But she couldn't possibly have got away. Even at half-term she was up to her eyes in paperwork. She takes on so much. She's a deputy-head now, you know.'

I always find it vaguely comforting talking *about* Ann: she sounds so suitable.

'So clever . . .' said my aunt with radiant vagueness. 'I always feel quite silly beside people like that,' she added comfortably.

'But Auntie, you know Ann isn't a bit intimidating. You met her – ' But my aunt wasn't listening. She was of course, at one level, quite right: she *did* seem silly beside people whose energies were more focused, and indeed had always been regarded as 'a silly woman' (almost, as it were, an official sample of the type) by my own consciously more austere and well-organized parents. But it was, I think, her chosen rôle. In fact she had the liveliness, adaptability and taste for new experience that rarely goes with real stupidity, but she dated from an era when a semblance of muddle-headedness was supposed to be 'more feminine'. Unlike her elder sister, my mother, she had turned her back on all education at fourteen. In my youth she worked in a hat shop, the pre-war epitome of the determinedly frivolous, and then, in the war, was said by my father to have 'gadded about' in one of the women's services. Even when she subsequently retired into the respectability of a belated marriage, and took to Edinburgh and being Scottish, a vague aura of luxury and levity still surrounded her name in my parents' household. They were fond enough of her, but thought she ought to have 'something proper to do', albeit of a charitable and voluntary nature. The fact that, in her improper idleness, she always seemed busy, even breathlessly so, did not please them either. It was rather remarkable how Aunt Madge, though clad in the matronly Caledonian uniform of quilting, fur and tweed, and given to orgies of baking what she now called 'pastries', managed nevertheless to live with a hint of un-British flamboyance within Edinburgh's damp, sooty confines. She somehow managed to treat that deeply provincial city as if it were an oriental bazaar: from the mildest foray to Princes Street – and her forays were frequent – she would return, flushed and elated, bearing with her some 'bargain', some long-sought knick-knack, some newly discovered heartfelt want now cunningly supplied. A top-dressing of Scots 'canniness' thinly veiled a ravening consumerism; no January or July sales time could pass without Auntie 'replenishing' her already bursting wardrobes, her full linen cupboards, her more-than-fully-fitted kitchen.

'It's lucky she's got a rich husband and nothing else to spend it on,' my father would say, with a disapproval that the years rendered ritualized.

'But Bertie, I think that's why she does it,' my mother had regularly responded in an equally traditional tone of conscious concern.

As a young man, I accepted this standard view, that 'poor Madge', childless as she was and married to that boring (if well-to-do) Scot, was sublimating unhappiness in the obsessional provision of embroidered napkins for tea parties. But even I, with my inherited work-ethic and my acquired intellectual arrogance, couldn't help noticing that Auntie Madge seemed perfectly happy. She had many friends, and a boundless and rather attractive enthusiasm for trivial excursions and treats which she indulged all the more fully once her husband had retired and was available as a full-time, if dourly unresponsive, chauffeur. I don't think she ever learnt to drive herself: perhaps it would have seemed to her unfeminine.

When her husband finally died, I wondered if this airy, concocted life of hers would collapse onto its empty centre, but the next time I visited her she seemed as busy as ever and quite happy, having joined innumerable clubs. She was learning highland dancing ('Yes, at my age, Tommy!'). She was singing folksongs with a choral society and she had 'taken up dressmaking again'; the dining room in the high, narrow Morningside house was covered in a rich profusion of silk and wool and tweed, and the excuses for 'running up to Princes Street', to match a cotton reel or choose some buttons, were now almost continuous. I felt then that, in her own way, my aunt had discovered some secret of life that many more intro-spective people never find, and that I need not worry about her: Madge would be all right.

I was therefore unprepared, on this visit, to find a new development. But perhaps, after all, she *had* been rather lonely in her great, soft, draped bed without her husband beside her, or perhaps some more recent deaths of contemporaries had dented her self-confidence and made her wish to replenish her life with people. At all events, Auntie Madge had discovered Spiritualism.

She did not call it that, but then I believe its present-day adherents often avoid the name, wishing to distance themselves from connotations of table-rapping and ecto-plasm. The weekly session at the home of a 'sensitive', which Aunt Madge now attended, was not called by the debased word 'seance' but was a 'Communication evening'. The assembled company did not receive 'messages from the dear departed' but were 'put into natural touch with those on the Other Side'. However, the banal and sentimental content of some of these communications, as retailed to me by my aunt with many pauses for effect, seemed to indicate that the cult was in essence the traditional death-denying bromide.

All my life I had felt a mild contempt for cults of this kind; that attitude is, I suppose, the usual one among people like me. But now, superimposed on this, was a sharper and more personal sense of offence, of territory that was rightly mine being violated by cant. Could my aunt really fail to realize this? She was babbling on about her friend Moira who had messages from her cousin about bills and the new curtains – 'things he couldn't possibly have known about unless there was Something In It' – and about a Mrs Cullen who had had such interesting experiences with her plants growing before her eyes . . . I felt anger, dark red, beginning to swell obscurely in me.

'Don't – ' I said suddenly, interrupting her in full spate of language and also with a buttered tea-cake in arrested motion half way to her lips. 'Don't you say anything to me about people close to me, Aunt Madge, I warn you. My wife – my dead wife, that is – and my daughter are mine, not yours. I won't have your group laying a hand on them, or – or using their names.' (I had been about to employ the old, biblical formulation 'taking their names in vain', but at the last moment I shied away from it.) 'Just you lay off them,' I finished, rudely but lamely.

My aunt had set down her tea-cake and put her head placatingly on one side. I saw that she was not entirely unprepared for some such reaction from me; my horrid suspicion that she had been leading up to a 'tactful' mention of my own loved ones had been justified.

'Oh *dear* Tommy,' she said – in obvious sincerity, damn her – 'It distresses me to see you so bitter, so closed up to Communication. We won't talk about it any more just now if you don't want to, but I do wish you'd have a little think some time about what I've been telling you – the proofs I've been giving you . . . I can't tell you what a *comfort* it is, as well as so exciting, when you are able to accept that it really is all true. They're alive, Tom! Alive and continuing just as we are.'

'Aunt Madge, I *don't want* a belief as a sort of hot-water

bottle. That's exactly what I've got against Spiritualism – '

I wanted to go on to intimate that I also found preposterous the idea that the dead, if sentient at all, should have nothing better to do than fuss over the bills, curtains and house-plants of those still on earth. But I was afraid that I could not embark on this without invoking the two names I had just loudly banned.

'Anyway, Auntie, what makes *you* so keen on bothering the dead? Uncle Andrew was all very well in his way, but you never had that much in common with him, don't kid me you did. He wasn't particularly interested in new bedroom curtains in his life, or in anything much in his last ten years come to that, so he's hardly going to join in cosy chats with you over astral air-waves, is he? In fact I should think he'd disapprove of any such attempt – a low churchman like him. Or is part of the idea that the dead stop being themselves and lose all their bad temper or stupidity or prejudice or whatever other distinguishing traits they had, and turn into uniform ideal old pussycats?'

I knew I was behaving 'badly', in a way the many bright adolescents I have taught might be allowed to behave, but not a man well into middle age and not to an old woman. But if I expected, or even unkindly hoped, that Madge's rouged cheeks would be drawn in, that she would purse her lips in distress so that the lipstick disappeared into the small lines of age surrounding the once-full mouth, I was disappointed. Madge was more resilient than that, and her adventurous life long ago, before she settled down into the respectability of Uncle Andrew's carefully invested fortune, must have taught her a degree of resourcefulness. Mustering some dignity, and even a slightly patronizing manner, she informed me that Uncle Andrew was 'at rest' after all his hard work and his last illness, and that she had no intention of disturbing him. Her interest, she said, was not with those who had 'moved to the Other Side' after a long, fulfilled life, but those who had been snatched from life prematurely and suddenly. Did I imagine, she enquired, warming to her theme, that they were immediately happy with what had happened to them. Did it not occur to me they might need comfort and support for a while, just as the living did? What, for example, could poor, darling little Marigold have felt, when she first woke after the accident and realized that she was on the Other Side?

There was more of the same kind, but somewhere in the middle of her impassioned and obviously predetermined lecture I got up, abandoning tea-cake, pastries, Earl Grey tea and the rest of the afternoon, and announced that I was going out. I would be back later, no, *much* later, that evening – and when I did return could we please regard this subject as closed for good and all?

Then, of course, having made my demonstration, I had no alternative but to go, out into the raw, misty, darkening avenues of surburban Edinburgh, with nothing to do and nowhere to go till I was due at Humphrey's flat towards eight o'clock.

> *. . . She's gone forever.*
> *I know when one is dead and when one lives;*
> *She's dead as earth.*

Another father, another daughter. Lear and Cordelia. Marigold had *King Lear* as an O-level text; I took her and a school friend to a performance at Stratford. I had barely known the play till then, read it for the occasion, watched it, stunned but wary. And read it again, with passionate concentration, several years after. After, after.

> *. . . Do you see this? Look on her, look, her lips,*
> *Look there! Look there!*

With a dead person, the best-loved photo (I have it in my study) becomes an ikon. You get used to that particular version of the individual and to the idea that that one is dead. This is, however, no protection against the repetitive stab to the heart when other versions of that unique person abruptly present themselves to memory. Marigold as a small child, solemnly fingering Aunt Madge's fur coat and asking if it had been a bear . . . Marigold at about twelve, induced to play the guitar and shyly sing *The Four Maries*, to her aunt's effusive Scottish acclaim.

. . . *'Oh little did my mother think, the day she cradled me,*
What lands I was to travel through, what death I was to
dee . . .'.

Marigold at fifteen, chattering passionately to me across a restaurant table in the Creuse about the differences between the various world religions, shovelling in *confit de oie* the while.

Gone. Nowhere. Over, finished, wiped out.

Simone, though just as surely vanished, had had a whole life before she died – too short a life, but one full of joys, fulfilment, things done and seen. Like Jacquou before me, speaking of his own wife, I feel the need to affirm this. And Simone had achieved Marigold, and seen her grow big and left her to me as a legacy. But Marigold, in whose death I had also lost Simone more completely, had hardly had time to live at all. Not what we call living. She was all promise. But the people she would, as an adult, have loved, the things she would have experienced, the children she might have borne – these were lost with her. I would never be called Granpa. And never again Daddy. It was not for weeks after her death that these flat, chill facts suddenly came to me, like another death in miniature: a death of some key part of myself.

When my aunt was gone there would be no one left who called me 'Tommy'. As a younger man I had been embarrassed by this childhood version of my name on her lips. Now I found myself mourning in anticipation its passing: Aunt Madge had always been fond of me and I, in a vague way, of her. But as I strode along, shoulders hunched (my anorak had been left with my suitcase in her spare room), I was filled with an angry misery that this, this indecent old woman, with her cowardice and gullibility in the face of the human lot, was my only surviving relation.

As I went on under dripping trees, I passed one of those

Scottish churchyards full of heavy wet stones like dwarf billiard tables: such an inappropriate image to be evoked by a religious cult not noted for its tolerance of earthly pleasures. Or its tolerance of many other enterprises. When I had said to Aunt Madge that surely Uncle Andrew would not approve of bothering the dead, I had been summoning up almost random jibes. But now I realized that among the general repugnance I felt for my aunt's attempt to appropriate the dead, *my* dead, was a sense of atavistic fear and disapproval. For what, essentially, were she and her accomplices doing but trying to raise the dead, a practice frowned on by most Christian churches, high and low? I felt my decent low-church ancestors (hers too, come to that) stir within me in revolt at this spirit-raising. A few minutes ago I had been condemning Spiritualism as naïve, but now, as I walked on fast and unseeing, muttering to myself inside my head and perhaps audibly as well, it took on a more sinister aspect. I now saw my aunt as playing with fire, or at any rate dabbling her fat fingers near it. It was a fire I had skirted with dread, turning aside my eyes.

That dream I had, five months after Marigold's death . . . I had longed, and dreaded, to dream of her. By which I mean that I had flinched from the possibility of dreaming that she was there, that life was ordinary and whole, and then waking again to sickening disappointment. But my dream, when it came, was not like that. In it, time had passed as in waking life, everything had happened as it had happened. But Marigold still existed. She did not understand what had taken place, and was distressed because she thought that it was everyone else who was dead. She was alone and I longed to comfort her, but could not reach her.

I knew, too well, how Aunt Madge would interpret this dream. The idea made the hair prickle on the back of my neck. Not because I thought she might be right, but because I recognized the temptation the dream represented.

I had longed so much for my daughter – longed for her now even more, though differently, than I had done immediately after her death – that I felt weak with the effort of maintaining my own creed, which is to say my own lack of belief. In my darkest moments I became afraid that integrity and intelligence (the very qualities I had prized and encouraged in Marigold herself) would become casualties also of that murdering driver; that I would be reduced to a pathetic old man whoring after a debased cult, pampering my imagination with spurious 'messages' and empty convictions. We betray the dead in any case simply by continuing to live, and thus willy-nilly driving a great wedge of alien days, months and finally years between them and ourselves: I felt this keenly. But how much worse a betrayal it would be to attempt to negate this process by self-deception?

And yet I longed and longed for another dream – all right, all right, what a believer would have termed another *sign* – to keep a tiny spark of agnostic hope for reunion alive in me through whatever long years still lay ahead.

Strung out between shamed longing and disgust, growing colder and damper as I walked and as the rain came on more definitely, I finally reached the edges of the eighteenth-century New Town where Humphrey's flat lay. It was long before the hour for which I had been invited, and I did not like to appear early given that I had not yet met his wife; in any case I was in no state for company. Instead I took refuge in a pub which, in spite of its genteel location, turned out to be the usual Scottish drinking house, shabby and male, with a raucous juke box. Here I drank several whiskies, and read and re-read uncomprehendingly sections of the barman's local newspaper. '*Weir site in dispute*' . . . '*Mackie 7–4*' . . . '*Girl in heather, man sought*' . . . Scots wha' hae' wi' Wallace bled . . . Oh bugger Scotland. I'd never liked the place anyway. I yearned briefly for France, with its superficial similarities to Scotland, its profound differences. But what remained for me now in France, after thirty years of passionate identification with the country? Only the space where others no longer were.

By a quarter-to-eight my mood had not greatly improved, but I was a little calmer. I was also very slightly drunk.

And in the end I turned up rather late and breathless, having forgotten the exact route to Humphrey's address and mistaken one ponderous neo-classical crescent for another. On the doorstep as I panted up was a figure already stooped towards the answerphone. It straightened up and greeted me by name with a mixture of warmth and embarrassment, but even so it took me a moment to recognize who it was: Jeffrey, unseen for several years, and now seeming taller than ever; Marigold's contemporary and one-time admirer.

'Admirer': I use the old-fashioned, non-committing word deliberately. When Jeffrey, as a schoolboy, had got over his shyness and natural defensiveness with Marigold, produced as she was to be a 'nice companion' for him, he had become loquacious towards her, even proprietorial. On holidays at the mill Humphrey and I used to listen with paternal amusement to him lecturing her on his latest interest: geology, or buzzards, or traditional jazz or economic theory. Sometimes, in London, bulky letters for her would arrive from his boarding school, later from Edinburgh. Marigold never said much about him, but I knew she had been flattered by his continuing interest and was eager to talk to him when, at long intervals, he telephoned her.

Marigold was pretty, and matured early: by the time she was in her mid-teens many young men came to our house, and some of them were much better looking and more obviously engaging than Jeffrey, but she seemed to go on valuing Jeffrey, which pleased me. Perhaps it was because, as she maintained, he was 'just a good friend', but I felt that, on his side anyway and potentially on hers, there was something more. Unlike many girls she seemed in no hurry to acquire an official boyfriend: I vaguely perceived, without quite wanting to look harder at the matter, that with me still as the centre of her life, she did not really need a boyfriend.

When she was killed Jeffrey wrote me a long, agonized letter in his chaotic handwriting, raging at fate, full of reminiscences of their times in France together – of swims

136

and picnics and bicycle rides and 'Jacquou le Croquant' with the local garage proprietor as the Wicked Lord: real memories abruptly revalued as the archetypal, idyllic childhood. 'Some of the happiest times,' he wrote, 'that I ever had as a kid.' Of course, I thought, if they *had* clasped each other on hot afternoons beneath the prickly, concealing bracken, he would hardly tell me that. But I wanted now very much to believe they had and, yes, more – that my lovely, desirable Marigold had at least known that . . . It was in fact just as likely or unlikely that some young man at college who was only a name to me had shared all that with her. She had spoken quite often of a Peter, a Daniel used to telephone in the holidays . . . But Jeffrey was the one who was real to me.

It was a great temptation to build on this insubstantial link, to cast Jeffrey in permanence as the lover of my girl. I told myself I must not behave like that. The boy had his own life to live; I must not impose on him; the young (as the French say) cannot live with the dead. And similar stifling truisms.

So, in an uncertainty and distress which was, I think, mutual, we had, after Marigold's memorial service, drifted apart again. I had been quite unprepared to find him at Humphrey's that night. But it only occurred to me afterwards that the well-intentioned obtuseness on Humphrey's part which this indicated had set the tone for the evening.

Some three hours later Jeffrey and I set off together again from the same doorstep. Humphrey and Carmen (such was her name) stood entwined, a tableau of marital happiness, in the lighted doorway, waving us off with glad cries of 'See you again very soon!' I was returning to my aunt, reluctantly – though less reluctantly than I would now have accepted a bed for the night from Humphrey and Carmen. Jeffrey, too, had refused pressing offers of a bed, claiming a friend elsewhere in the city.

We trudged for a while in silence. Was the boy as depressed as I thought he was, or was I attributing to him the sickening heaviness of my own heart? I slid a glance at him. In response he said with cutting enunciation:

137

'Women like that make me feel I want to go and have a bath.'

'Oh come on.' Feebly, half indulgent uncle, half brisk head master: 'She's not as bad as that.'

'Oh yes she is,' he said, with a bitter passion I had not quite expected from him, 'She's *just* as bad as that, and you know it, Tom, so don't pretend . . . Her queening it there among Laura's furniture, surrounded by muckage . . . Christ, my own Ma and her gin bottles is bad enough, but at least she doesn't have china doggies everywhere and open packets of biscuits and soft-porn historical novels. Carmen's like some great dirty bird sitting on a nest of regurgitated fish-pellets.'

'If you mean those fish-cakes and chips she eventually produced for supper – ' I was momentarily entertained, in spite of myself, by the cruel aptness of Jeffrey's description.

'I partly mean that – I loathe people who can't be bothered to cook and who pride themselves on it – but I mean, oh for Christ's sake, the whole squalid set-up. And Humphrey sitting in the middle of it with his paws up, wagging his tail – "Go on, admire us, aren't we spontaneous and lovely?" – *Yuck*.'

'I know.' I was really too depleted to argue. After a long silence, I said:

'But I think you attribute too much affectation to Carmen, you know. She didn't strike me as particularly conceited. Just a simple, self-centred soul who's thrilled to have landed Humphrey as a husband and is letting the world know.'

'You'll be telling me any minute that she *means well*.'

'So she does. But of course I do entirely agree with you really. I loathed the evening too.' Naïvety should not come across as a vice. And yet it does. I thought of my Aunt Madge too, but did not have the heart to mention her now.

'All that about her brother who's *quite mad* and *such a hoot* – ' (vicious impersonation) – 'and whom we must meet.'

'I know. And that long, coy story about a dog peeing on her shoes . . .'

We walked on further. At last, with the biting humour now gone from his voice, Jeffrey said heavily:

'The trouble is, the worse we think of her the worse we have to think of old Humphrey for marrying her.'

'I was thinking that myself.' I was also thinking this was probably still harder for the boy than it was for me. Humphrey was merely – merely? – one of my oldest friends, whereas to Jeffrey he had been a father figure, a substitute for Jeffrey's own absent and undutiful parent.

'I can't understand it myself,' I said. 'He used to be so – fastidious.' As I uttered the word I felt it was not quite right; I ploughed on: 'I mean discriminating. Not intellectual, quite, but almost the archetypal decent cultured man of his background. He has changed. It's daunting, baffling really. . . Did you hear that conversation about music?'

'I did.'

Humphrey had never been musical as Laura was and, though educated by her, his taste had remained unambitious. Nevertheless the four of us in the old days had enjoyed Mozart or Brahms together and the occasional opera. I had hardly been able to believe my ears when I had, this evening, heard Humphrey joining in enthusiastically as Carmen extolled as 'marvellous' the numbingly mediocre score of a musical currently running in London.

'That vulgar bilge,' said Jeffrey, implacable in contempt.

'Oh come on, Jeff.' (It was awful, I confusedly felt, to be talking like this.) 'I didn't quite mean that. Lots of reasonable people do enjoy musicals. I find the change odd, but I don't think we can indict the poor chap just for that, just for – well, widening his tastes.'

'I didn't get the impression he knows whether or not he likes that sort of musical hogwash at all,' pursued Jeffrey keenly. 'He wasn't using any judgement, just suspending it. It's that nauseating "darling, they're playing our tune" attitude to music. Oh, it's common enough, I know. But I just didn't expect it from him.'

We walked again in silence. I reviewed the look of fatuous adoration Humphrey's crumpled face had worn as Carmen had regaled us with her merry trivia, his overeagerness to praise the slovenly meal she had eventually dished up, his ready collusion with her image of herself as a vital, fascinating person. Carmen, though not particularly young, was considerably younger than he was – even, as I reminded myself firmly, as Ann is considerably younger than I am. Vital, Carmen might be considered, I supposed, in a dark, curly way. She was rather too large all over for my taste – too tall, too bosomy, with too many teeth and too bright a trailing scarf round her thick healthy neck. But I could see how another man than myself might be attracted to her, yes particularly a man who, for many years, had been cut off from association with a whole body, with plumpness and sleekness and energy and, yes, sheer animal health . . . And because Humphrey had incontinently married Carmen, this passion must be given the name of 'love' and cherished by him as such.

But perhaps it was indeed love, by all identifiable measures, just as much as his feeling toward the infinitely finer Laura for all those years had been? The objects might be utterly different, but there was no reason to suppose that the quality of the emotion was. I did not want to reason like this: it devalued retrospectively his dedication to Laura. But Jeffrey's scathing remarks about Humphrey's musical tastes, or rather his lack of taste, had set up a reverberation in my mind. 'Darling, they're playing our tune' indeed. Perhaps he had always been like that, really; it was simply that in the past the tune called by the woman was different.

'When I think how he used to be,' said Jeffrey after another long silence. 'I mean, he never set the Thames on fire, but he used to be – oh, interested and concerned about things. Good causes and so forth. Environmentalism. Preserving Venice. *You* know. And look at him now with that female sow – "Another drink, darling? . . . Gosh, aren't these bickies good . . . Gosh, did we tell you what happened on our honeymoon? . . . Are you warm enough, darling – Oh *yes*, darling, lovely and warm, just the two of us, aren't we wonderful . . . And bugger the rest of the globe." No moral agenda to life at all.'

'Sows are always female.' However much I agreed with

him, I objected to the raw priggishness of his tone. I felt exhausted, too much so to order my thoughts properly; I said hesitantly:

'Marriage to a different person must always change one a bit, I suppose. Or just marriage in itself, to anyone. Different bits come to the fore, others go into abeyance . . . You marry a world, not only a person. We aren't lone stars.' I was talking almost at random, in the murk of my own preoccupations. 'You'll see what I mean yourself, one day,' I finished lamely.

'I shall never marry,' he said, as if it were a foregone conclusion.

Well, we won't go into that, I thought. Marigold's name had remained unspoken all evening, but I must not assume it was relevant anyway. Jeffrey would in any case, I thought, have a long and complex road in life to travel. The knowledge that he had barely started out on it, with all his restless energy, and his human deprivation which this evening had only deepened, exhausted me further.

'I know you were fond of Laura,' I said helplessly. 'So was I.'

But Jeffrey, now his mind was working on Humphrey, was not to be lulled by this acceptable thought.

'Oh – fond,' he said dismissively. 'Yes, she was OK. I mean, she tried to be a "good aunt" to me and I always respected her. But I didn't *like* her as much as Humphrey.'

'No?'

'Well she was a bit of an old prune, wasn't she?' he said casually. 'Even before her MS got so bad. And awfully sort of pleased with herself for behaving so bravely. That was it, you see – Humphrey thought she was so marvellous and went round telling everyone so, so we were all suckered into thinking it must be true. At least, I was when I was a kid, and I rather think you and Simone were . . . Marigold never liked her much.'

'Didn't she? I didn't realize. Oh.' And all those presents . . . I longed to hear more, now Marigold's name had been spoken, but would I enjoy hearing it with Jeffrey in such a bitter mood?

'Nope. She didn't. I remember her telling me that one day at the mill-house when we were about sixteen. She thought Laura was very dominating. Funny, I've only just remembered that. I ought to have thought of it before. It all fits, doesn't it?'

'I'm afraid it does. Oh dear. Yes. Laura did rather run Humphrey, even from her wheelchair. She made him what he was, I suppose. I never knew him before he met her. And now we're complaining that Carmen has made him into something different.'

'He always was a bit of a wanker,' said Jeffrey. 'We should have expected it, after all.'

His tone suggested that was his last word on the subject, his verdict on my lifelong friend. I was unwilling to let him get away with that.

'I will offer you another explanation,' I said after a bit.

'Well – please offer it,' he said when I still remained silent. In the end I said:

'Humphrey looked after Laura devotedly for years. Yes, I know devotion and besottedness are two sides of the same coin, but she needed him to and he did. You saw him do it. And I've come to suspect that, contrary to popular belief, an experience like that doesn't necessarily do a chap any good.'

'You mean that it doesn't necessarily make him into a more deeply wonderful human being himself,' said Jeffrey nastily.

'That's just what I mean. It – it deforms life, all that sort of thing. I'm wondering if Humphrey was somehow strained beyond his proper capacity by all those years of devotion and restraint and *being good*, and has now, when it's all over, just – collapsed.'

'You don't mean physical collapse. Or even emotional.' Jeffrey's ability to apply himself carefully to any suggested idea had always been one of his better features. 'You can't mean that, because he's full of beans. You mean a sort of collapse of integrity?'

'Yes. Yes, I suppose so. Something like that. Overstrain in the moral fibres, let's say.'

'System overload.'

'Is that what you'd call it with computers? Yes.'

'Well that's just a general term. There might be a closer analogy . . .' Jeffrey pondered, his own system fully engaged. 'There's something called Deadly Embrace,' he said.

'That meant to refer to Carmen?' I could feel my own system collapsing into a feeble levity.

'Ha, ha. Or Laura, come to that? *Both* of them, and that might be the point . . . No, actually, Deadly Embrace – well, it's a bit complicated to explain, but its effect is that opposing demands within the system make it impossible for a bit of information to be accessed by either side. No advance can be made, no further development; the program just blocks itself.'

'It might fit,' I said uncertainly. I tried to visualize, in general terms, what was being blocked, the things we cannot afford to let ourselves know. If I had those, by definition I could not perceive them . . . Jeffrey too seemed daunted by the prospect of translating his recondite metaphor back into the terms of the human mind. He sighed.

'Well. As you say, poor old Humphrey.' He suddenly stopped and turned to face me in the dark.

'I think we must have walked past your turning,' I said.

'I don't know. I'm not fussed. Tom, can I ask you something?'

'Ask away,' I said easily, but my heartbeat increased and I found myself illogically thinking: Marigold. Something about Marigold.

'Do you feel that – that everything you've been through may have affected you like that?' he said.

After a long interval – so long, I suppose, that even Jeffrey lost his nerve and began to peer at me in the dark to see what had happened to me, I said:

'Do *you* think I have been – blocked. Or weakened?'

'No. Not at all. You seem to me just the same. It was just – the way you spoke about it.'

'Well I'm not the same,' I said, after another long silence.

'No?'

'No.'

He did not ask any more, but after a few yards I said:

'I thought – up to a few months ago, I thought – that the rest of my life would just be a sort of – retreat. In your electronic terms, a different, smaller program. Or a different circuit. A leftover life to make the best of and maybe harvest something from after all. But now – I'm not sure.'

After another long pause, I added obscurely:

'I think something else may be surfacing.'

'I'm not quite sure what you are saying,' said Jeffrey, humbly, for him, and suddenly sounding young and almost scared.

'No, nor am I, that's the trouble.' What the hell *was* I saying?

After a while I tried again. 'You used the phrase "collapse of integrity". Before we got sidetracked onto computers.'

'Did I? Oh yes – about Humphrey. Don't you agree with me, Tom?'

'Well yes, as a matter of fact I do, in Humphrey's case. But what I wanted to say is . . . One doesn't always know for oneself where integrity lies. You get used to the idea that it lies in a particular direction, in a particular set of values. But then one day you wake up to the possibility that actually there's something quite other you ought to be doing. Something special to be undertaken. That perhaps there is – you're not quite sure.' *Was* that what I really wanted to say? If so, I had only just formulated it.

'I'm still not entirely with you,' Jeffrey persisted, eager as ever for intellectual debate. But I had had enough. We were passing the corner pub where I had sat and drunk whisky hours earlier. It was shutting, an ejected customer was being sick by a railed garden. I smelt vomit and stale beer and soot and wet old leaves; such smells might have recalled nostalgically the Birmingham of my childhood, but that Birmingham had gone, vanished under motorways years ago, and the amalgam in the night air merely seemed like the suffocating deposit lying on my heart.

Whatever I had hoped in the train coming north, there

was to be no uncritical retreat into the past for me, no refuge there. I wanted and expected nothing now from friend or relative. Marigold had been gone more than five years, I would soon be an old man. Jeffrey was a young one with his alien life still to make, and I would have no stake in it. I sent him on his way to the dark heights on the far side of Waverley Station.

Then I turned my steps towards Morningside, hoping to God that Aunt Madge would by now be oblivious in her soft bed and that I could enter without encountering her.

I came back to London filled with that generalized discomfort that the Anglo-Saxon races call 'guilt'.

I remembered that long-ago conversation with Jacquou, in which he had pointed out to me that the French language does not encourage its speakers to label their unease 'guilt' – that the French are more apt to diagnose grief, pain, nausea, boredom, or simply to evoke 'the human condition'. Yes. But, being English after all, in spite of everything, a multiform guilt is what I felt as my train trundled, late and grubby, into Kings Cross.

Who did I imagine I was, to sit in judgement on everyone else's subterfuges for coping with the human lot, and what did I expect? I had sided with Jeffrey in despising my old friend whose life seemed to have become so silly and self-indulgent; but I had been no better pleased, had I, by my aunt's impulse toward Something Beyond All This? If my own standards were so exacting, what had I better to offer?

I remembered confusedly that I had had a disagreement recently with Lewis Greenfield too, nagging him to divulge facts I had originally said I did not want to know: Lewis, for whose combination of high principles and decent cynicism I had always had regard. Then, worse, had been my row with Ann about Melvyn Baines.

I was conscious of having said awful things to her about the wretched man. I did not exactly think that the charges I had made were unfounded, but I knew that in condemning Baines, and what he stood for, I had been making an oblique attack on some of Ann's own values. So I wanted to indict Ann as well, did I? For what – for naïvety, for lack of stringency, for being the product of an unfortunate era of teacher training and popular sociology? . . . For not, for God's sake, being brilliant? Just for not being my own generation?

I knew Ann to be one of the kindest, most reasonable, painstaking people there are. What more could I decently expect or want, now? It wasn't her fault she was not Simone. Or Marigold. Or Marigold.

I resolved that at least I would be kinder to Ann. Or at any rate less unkind.

As if in some telepathic response to this, Melvyn himself called to see me at my office a few days later. He was not wearing the studied jeans-and-jerseys he usually wore to work (and of which I disapproved, because I don't think that teachers, doctors, psychologists and similar power figures should try to fool their customers by dressing down to them). He was, for once, in a suit; his small beard was neatly trimmed and his manner was quiet and polite, almost diffident. As a matter of fact his manners in general were rather disarmingly good, a fact which I always forgot from one encounter to the next: the odd result of this was that I always felt more charitable towards him immediately after meeting him face to face than when his name came before me at other times.

He made no mention of the fact that I had refused to endorse his Place of Safety application, though I am sure he had come to know about this. (Perhaps even from Ann, I suddenly thought?) Instead he was ostensibly there to consult me on another matter, an uncontentious one to do with home-tuition for sick children.

After he had left, with enquiries after Ann and expressed hopes that we and he and Birgit would meet again soon, I could not decide whether he was genuinely, amiably unaware of my suspicion of him, or whether he had timed his visit carefully to defuse the lurking enmity he sensed coming from me. If so, I had to give him better marks for duplicitous tact and caution than I would have expected to.

Then, for the rest of the winter, work consumed me again. Or I thankfully allowed myself to be consumed by it, visiting schools near and far, going from one committee meeting or day-conference to another, fulfilling my expected rôle on a Government working party. I abandoned, temporarily, that blind, intuitive search for something quite other that I could not yet define – that sense of impending obligation which had preoccupied me recently and of which I had spoken obscurely to the boy Jeffrey. When the uneasy shadow of it crossed my mind, I told myself that it was all part of an anxiety-syndrome of seeking trouble where it did not really exist. I thought I might perhaps be judging the world, and even myself, too hardly, in the vain attempt to reach some certainty, some stripped down core of meaning which, at my stage in life, I really knew to be unreachable.

In brief, for no particular reason that I could tell, I got a bit better again.

I also told myself that to see plots and mysteries in life's chronically unplanned course is a sign of paranoia or religious obsession or both.

Then, in the late spring, I went to a conference in Geneva –

PART IV

Then, in the late spring, I went to a conference in Geneva about prisoners of conscience. I went because I was asked and it seemed churlish to refuse, because I hoped to meet a couple of other people who were also interested in the fate of Piotr Mihailovitch Malenko. And because five days away by a Swiss lake in April seemed an attractive prospect.

The conference was (as we said to each other) very jolly, more so than I had expected it to be; and since it was being conducted bilingually in French and English I was able to make myself useful to the organizers. In the five-and-a-half years since Marigold's death my French, through lack of use, had atrophied, and, with it, my sense of having another identity across the Channel. Now both of these expanded again. I listened to everyone's complaints about each other's national failings, and did a great deal of extempore interpreting, some of it diplomatic. As I say, I enjoyed myself and, for the moment, forgot about everything else. The temporary stage-set of lake, mountains, Old Town, hotels, cafés, flower baskets and *jette d'eau* might have been a brand new life into which I and my companions of fortune had escaped for a timeless eternity. If Aunt Madge's Other Side was supposed to be like this, I could see the appeal.

My chief companions were the President of the historical association I too was representing, who was a wistful history lecturer of White Russian parentage, together with the paid Secretary to the much larger organization which had sponsored the conference. She was one of those lynch-pins on whom such gatherings depend: I had not met her before, but sought her out on the second morning in the conference office, needing her to arbitrate in a brewing Anglo-French dispute about speakers overrunning their time. The International President, a Frenchman given to high-flown oratory himself, was for letting them have their head; James

– the history don – felt that in this case the timetable would disintegrate, but 'couldn't face being the chief frog-offender'. I was inclined myself to the hard line that every speaker knew in advance he had twenty minutes only, and should abide by that. I did not mind, I said, climbing onto the platform myself like Old Father Time to snatch the papers bodily, if necessary, from the hands of over-garrulous Distinguished Contributors, but if I was to do this I felt I wanted a back-up authority. I hoped that the Secretary, Annie-something, would provide this, and she did.

'Of *course* they've got to keep to time. What on earth are Serge and James thinking of? If you don't bully people on these occasions they become impossible.' I was not sure if it was the President and James or the horde of Distinguished Contributors that needed to be bullied, but I warmed to Annie. I learnt later that she was about thirty, but something about her – her complexion, perhaps, her rather awkward movements, her slight plumpness – suggested a younger woman, almost a schoolgirl. She was no schoolgirl however but a natural organizer, and source of information on prisoners round the world.

'You tell Serge and James I say so,' she said, pushing long, curly hair out of her eyes. It was nice hair, I thought, but for some reason it was a deep reddish-purple. This crude signal of a desire to outrage combined oddly with her intelligent but rather pasty face and her brisk Home Counties accent.

'Tell them I said that if the session overruns each day like it did yesterday we'll find ourselves charged thousands of pounds extra for keeping the staff and the cleaners over-time. That'll shake Serge, anyway. He pretends he's a great man of letters and above such considerations, but actually he was wetting himself last Christmas when we weren't sure if we'd costed the Conference right.'

'And have you?'

'Yes, thank goodness. There'll be a surplus. I'm awfully pleased actually. We were going to have to launch a huge appeal to get our legal fund up again after all those African cases, but now we may not have to . . . But don't ask me if it's true about the cleaners. Let's just say it is.'

'I won't ask,' I said, entertained, and wondering at the back of my mind whom she reminded me of: another woman – a man? A child? It was hard to say. I would have liked to linger in the office and talk to her, suddenly bored by the thought of going back into the hall to listen politely to people making speeches in tongues that were often not their own, but she was already attacking her typewriter with an angry vigour: she must get through ribbons quickly, I thought.

'Fuck!' she said. 'Oh not *again*.'

'Trouble?'

'Mmm. It's me really, not the machine, but I'm furious. The professional organizer here said we needn't bring any typewriters, that it would all be laid on, and so it is – but these machines say Awertz, not Qwerty.'

'Awertz?' I was lost. It sounded like computer-speak, something I had recently decided I was too far on in life to bother to learn.

'Yes, Awertz.' Impatiently. '*You* know. There's a Z where the Y ought to be and an A for the Q because it's a silly frog machine – as James would say. Oh dear! Conferences do make one childish, don't they? James says it's because it's like being back at prep school, all rules and prefects and compulsory fun together. Jolly luxurious prep school *he* must have been at if the hotel reminds him of it.'

'Where were you at school?' I was still vaguely thinking that I knew her face because she might have passed through one of my schools years ago. She put on an expression of grotesque disgust.

'Oh-h-h- Cheltenham. But I wasn't much of a success there. I rebelled, and so forth.'

Hence the accent, I thought. And, now, the deliberately shocking purple hair.

After that I began to gravitate towards Annie, as I still believed her to be called, at the parties which were held every evening in hotel bedrooms ('Bring your toothglass'). It really was, as James said with enthusiastic nostalgia, rather like dormitory feasts; except that afterwards we would go out, in fours and fives and sixes, to restaurants overlooking the light-pricked lake, where we ate expensive and delicious Swiss food and felt extravagant but carefree, and glad to be there and not at home.

It was not till the last evening, when the party was a formal reception in a grandiose public building, with waiters, and the Mayor, and an old and famous novelist from a nearby mountain, that I discovered that Annie was not called that.

'Yes, it's really Ammy,' she said resignedly when someone had corrected me. 'I didn't tell you earlier because lots of people mishear it as you did, and it really doesn't matter. I don't like my name anyway.'

'What's Ammy short for, then?'

'Amanda. Amanda Goring.' She made her disgusted face. 'Now you see why I don't mind when people get it wrong.'

Another man joined us, and the conversation moved on. It was several minutes before the notion that I had learnt something momentous began to surface in me. My mind went back over the months to that day in Court when another Amanda-Something, criminal and profoundly alienated from her adoptive family, had stood briefly before me and I had begun to remember. Now I felt as if that non-event had, after all, been the beginning of things, some sort of unfocused preview for this.

'You must excuse my asking,' I said, as soon as I could get her alone in a corner. 'It is a very presumptuous question – but are you by any chance adopted?'

Yes, was the answer, of course, yes. It did not even seem revelatory. Perhaps, at some point long ago, I had heard the name 'Goring' and it had lodged unrecognized within me, in that vast obscure filing system of the memory we hardly consult – except under some strange pressure of circumstances.

Amanda looked fearful. It was as if she, too, had at some level long foreseen this day, and her own emotion was not so much surprise as the tension of expectation realized. She gazed at me, her puffy face a little pale, and nibbled at her already well-gnawed nails. In inappropriate contrast, her stubby fingers were ornamented with silver rings.

'Yes, I'm adopted. How did you know?'

'I think I knew your parents.'

'I thought you'd say that.' She sounded resigned, but devastated also under the impact of something that always might happen and now had. It did not occur to me till afterwards that she might have wondered for a moment if I, I myself –

'Let's get out of here,' I said, as if I were a young man and she desirable to me. 'Let's go and eat somewhere on our own.'

Outside, the week's shining weather had broken and the temperature had dropped many degrees: a fine, cold rain blew across the lake. Huddled in inadequate coats, we made our way a couple of hundred yards along the quay, and then took refuge in the first eating house on offer, a garishly lit brasserie. The neon strips made her hair more virulently purple, her face paler. She was wearing some sort of double-breasted pseudo-male gear, I think, and dangling earrings, but I knew now why I had, all the week, subconsciously expected her to appear in the dusty black of the Left Bank in the 1950s.

On the wet quay, while she clutched my arm, I had established corroborative facts, places and dates. Now I said:

'I remember your parents well.'

'I've met my mother,' she said, surprising me. I think I sensed even then from her tone that it was her father she really wished to meet.

'Met her – how?'

'I wanted to. Once I was grown up. Well, you know the Law's been changed. You're allowed to look for your parents now.'

'I'd forgotten that.' Although of course I knew about changing ideas, the Law changing to suit, I had gone on unthinkingly believing that some impenetrable barrier still separated *now* and *then*. I must have stared at this overweight, uneasy, half-attractive young woman with amazement, for she said defensively:

'Perhaps you think I shouldn't have?'

'No – oh no. On the contrary. *I* would have wanted to, in your place.'

'For a while I didn't,' she said. 'Or at least, I did years ago when I was younger – fourteen or fifteen. You know how you are at that age . . . And I didn't really get on with my parents. I mean Mummy and Daddy, the ones who adopted me. We've always been uncomfortable with each other. I think they were disappointed in me. They'd wanted a dear little girl, I expect, and I didn't fit . . . Oh don't say "Often born children feel like that about their parents too", I shall vomit if you do. I'm so *sick* of that well-meaning line.'

'Yes. I can understand that. I wasn't going to.'

'Then, later,' she said, 'I was at Art School and having a good time, and I forgot all about my real parents for a bit. But then later again, after other things had happened . . . Ideas hang about in your mind and come back to you, don't they?'

'They do.'

'It was quite difficult,' she said, more matter-of-fact now, 'to trace my real parents.'

'I can't quite think how you did?'

'Well, I knew Mummy and Daddy would go into a frightful after-all-we've-done-for-you routine if I even mentioned it to them, so I didn't. I mean, I don't see them that often, and it wasn't really their business . . . But they had an old friend who was a lawyer and who'd been my godfather, wouldn't you know. A fussy old stick, and gay as they come I rather think – not that Mummy and Daddy would have noticed that – but not a bad old thing. He always gave me money at Christmas, proper cheques, I liked that. He's dead now . . . My family'd always stayed stuck in East Grinstead and never gone anywhere or done anything, so I was pretty sure Uncle Stanley (that's what I called this old boy) would know something about my adoption, and I turned out to be right. Oh, he huffed and puffed a lot and said I ought to "leave well alone" and

153

"might turn up some distressing facts" but in the end he told me where I could look up my original birth certificate and even told me the name of this social worker who'd been my *Guardian ad litem*. My parents hadn't gone through a proper adoption society or the Council or anyone. I suppose they thought that was "only for the working classes, my dear". I mean – *honestly*.'

'People didn't have to go through formal channels in those days. Did you meet the social worker too?'

'Yes. I tracked her down. It was quite difficult because she'd just retired. It was by a fluke really that I found her – a friend of mine turned out to have worked with her. Anyway she wasn't awfully pleased to see me, at first. But then she sort of changed and was all over me. I thought she was a bit peculiar, actually. She'd got some fancy religion, and kept talking about taking me to her church . . . I managed to get out of that one. She was kind, really, as if she did want to help, but there seemed to be some emotional agenda to it that turned me off, like with some dykey old mistress at boarding school. I don't think she was a dyke, though. She kept talking about redressing the balance of the past and living with one's mistakes and "facing reality" and I began to feel that *I* might count as one of her mistakes.'

'This was Shirley Gilchrist?'

'Yes – that *was* her name. How did you know?'

'I'll tell you by and by. I'm glad she helped you, anyway.'

'Well it was she who really put me on the track of my mother. I knew what her name had been by then, of course, it was in the records I'd looked up, but Shirley Gilchrist knew that she'd married afterwards and what her new name was. Otherwise I'd probably never have found her, even though I'm very determined when I try. Luckily her married name wasn't a common one. She hadn't moved far, actually, any more than Mummy and Daddy have. I mean, she was born in Kettering and I eventually found her in the 'phone book in Northampton. I can't think how *I* came to be born in Paris: my birth was first registered at the British Embassy there, it was a real surprise when I discovered that. Oh – but perhaps you can tell me why?'

154

'Perhaps I can. Shall we have that later? You go on now. You met your mother – ?'

'I met her.' Amanda's tone was quite subdued now, as if the momentousness of that encounter had led to inevitable anti-climax, or just was not expressible. 'I wrote to her at the address in the 'phone book, and after a while she wrote back. So I went up to Northampton. A little semi-detached house. Not too bad. But just a bit – dreary. Well, like her, I suppose . . .

'Fat – not that I can talk, I'd better watch it, hadn't I? Oh – *you* know: a middle-aged woman. Just anyone, really. Surprised, and a bit flustered and reticent about my coming to see her. Not *nasty* or anything – I mean, she let me come, and even had a cake for me – but not specially nice either. Not anything really. I – I know it sounds silly, but I was awfully disappointed.'

'I can imagine.'

'I'd expected it – her – to be somehow special to me, I think. After Mummy and Daddy and East Grinstead and everything . . . But it wasn't. Not really.'

I remembered Joyce selling Evan's paintings on the streets of Paris in her picturesque black clothes. I thought of her wistful enquiry to me about Sartre and *Madame Bovary*. Then, for some reason, I thought of Humphrey and Carmen.

'You said she'd married again?' I said, and then corrected myself: 'I mean – she'd married?'

'Oh yes. Only a couple of years after I was born – that's how Shirley Gilchrist knew about it, she was still in touch with her then. But she's a widow now. She and her husband kept a café at first, she said (only she called it a coffee house and went on about how it had been the first one in the Midlands, which sounded daft to me). Then they kept a pub at some point, and then ran some sort of old people's home, but that's gone bankrupt or been shut down, I think. And then her husband had died. Of drink, I rather gathered, although she didn't spell it out. Just talked about "bad luck" and everyone having their "weaknesses". She was fearfully sort of respectable, genteel I think it's called –

a bit self-consciously so, I thought afterwards – but there was something about her rather . . . I don't know exactly how to say it. Not as strong as "shifty", but . . .'

'Marginal?' I suggested.

'Would that be it, what a funny word, it sounds French? Yes, perhaps it *would* be the word: on the margins of life, I see what you mean. Oh dear. My mother. Does it sound awful to be talking about her like this?'

'No. Not at all. Or rather . . . Yes, perhaps, but I understand.' How easy it is to say that.

'She was all right, I think,' said Amanda, flushing suddenly. 'I mean – she didn't *want* anything from me, money or anything. She kept making that clear, although it hadn't so much as occurred to me beforehand that she might. I did find that rather embarrassing, I must say . . . That's a sign of the background I grew up in, I suppose. She wasn't on her own anyway, she had two big sons. My half-brothers! I kept thinking about them for a bit afterwards – I'd always wanted a brother – but of course there was nothing to think, really. Like I said: after all that, just nothing really there.'

'You didn't meet these boys – young men, I should say?'

'No. She took good care I didn't. She was keen to get me out of the house before six, kept talking about the best train back. I don't blame her really. They probably didn't know I existed.'

I saw again Joyce, lying weeping in the Paris hospital at the time of giving up her baby, saying that the pain of childbirth had been so awful she did not think she could go through with it again. Then I saw an overweight widow in a Midlands suburb, her life behind her. Emotionally, I could not connect the two, and yet rationally it was all entirely, depressingly convincing: long ago it had been obvious, no doubt even to Joyce, that without Evan's wits to guide her she would just drop back into the world from which she had come. I remembered now her lying in another hospital bed, after he'd ditched her – literally ditched her – in the accident to my Simca, and how she'd talked sadly about his 'creative temperament', saying 'I did try to be what he wanted me to be – '

Yes, she had tried, in every way she could. And later, presumably, that same survival instinct had led her to adapt herself to a different person, different circumstances: a necessary degradation. An unassuageable grief denied?

In a little while I would have to decide whether to tell Ammy about the Joyce of the past, and much more, or whether to leave most of my memories in decent oblivion. But Ammy might not actually ask very much. There had been a faint but persistent self-centredness in her description of her hunt for her origins so far which surprised me a little. I suppose that, illogically, I had expected more from someone who worked for an organization essentially concerned with unknown people and their problems.

'I should think,' I said, 'that it must have been a pretty odd experience for her too, meeting you. I mean, there you were, large as life. And all the time in her mind she must have had that baby you once were. It's odd enough, you know, thinking back even when your child has grown up with you all the time so the transformation has been gradual. But when it happens all at once it must be – inconceivable.'

'Yes. I suppose so. She couldn't cope with it, really. She kept looking sideways at me and saying "What a big girl you are!" I thought that was a bit much, coming from her, since she was much, much fatter herself and it was perfectly clear who I'd got my figure from. Oh, I suppose she was just nervous and didn't know where to pitch it. I was wearing some chains round my neck, like I often wear, and she admired them at one point and said she'd "always been interested in design". She was a bit better dressed than people like that often are, actually. I noticed that as soon as I met her. Black and swirly, with bangles. Touch of showbiz. I suppose she'd put on her best clothes to meet me . . . But – oh, it was really just like talking to someone at a bus stop or in the doctor's waiting room. You know?'

'I can imagine . . . Did you ask her much?' We would have to get onto Evan soon, I thought.

'Well I did ask her if Amanda had been her idea for my name. I wasn't going to be rude about it, if it was. She said no, but wasn't it a lovely name and she'd been pleased when she heard I was called that, through Mandy Rice-Davis had rather spoilt it, hadn't she? Ha, ha. I didn't like the way she said that. She suddenly seemed just a little bit . . . Well, not so respectable after all.'

She glanced at me in a worried way, almost like a child wanting reassurance, but then said robustly:

'Though why *I* should care about that, God knows . . . Oh, she did tell me one thing I thought was a bit sad. Do you want to hear it?'

'If you want to tell me.'

'Well she said she'd had a little name for me herself when I was born, and it was "Penguin" because I flapped my hands around like flippers . . . She was remembering properly then, and I almost thought for a moment she was going to cry. Not that I *wanted* her to, I mean, I'd've been frightfully embarrassed, but I just thought she might . . . I don't really understand what gets women about tiny babies, I don't like them myself.'

I was digesting this piece of information, wondering what lay behind it, when Ammy continued dismissively:

'Oh, but all the rest of her chat was about how she'd let me go for my own *good* and what a wonderful opportunity it had been for me to be brought up by such wonderfully decent, well-off people living in wonderful East Grinstead, rhubarb, rhubarb. Just the sort of guff I got from Uncle Stanley.'

'She felt defensive, I suppose,' I said, 'that you might be going to accuse her of rejecting you . . . And anyway, perhaps she was right. Would you, do you think now, have done better brought up by her? That's the bottom line of the whole question, isn't it?'

Ammy flushed faintly:

'I can't answer that,' she said after a moment. 'Can I? I mean – I might have been different if I'd grown up with her. Mightn't I?'

'Perhaps. And she might have been different too.'

'I never thought of that,' she said in a subdued voice. I began to like her a lot again.

'I think I should tell you,' I said, pompously, 'since I am probably the only person in the world left to do so, that your mother did not want to give you up. She was persuaded into it, rightly or wrongly it's probably not for any of us to say now, but she minded about it very much.'

If I had hoped Ammy would be grateful for this information, I was mistaken. She said she was, and thanked me, but I sensed that at some level it did not please her. Perhaps it did not fit the picture she had formed.

'I wondered about that,' she said hurriedly; 'I thought I might be able to ask her, but then, when I finally met her, I knew I couldn't. I mean – ' her aggressive manner returned: 'she was so full of shit, Tom, she really was. She gave me the impression, actually, that she'd given me up in some splendid sort of renunciation because of my father's Art. Great, I thought; that sort of information makes you feel really important – I don't think.'

'Ah yes, I was wondering if you'd talked much about him?'

'Well no, hardly at all. I was rather sorry, afterwards, when I thought about it, that I hadn't pushed her to tell me more, but she didn't really seem to want to talk about him. She just said he was a painter and a very creative person and that one should never hold an artist back from his Art – using a sort of phoney, special voice that she didn't use most of the time, so I knew that wasn't something she'd thought out for herself, but just an idea she'd picked up somewhere that she thought sounded impressive. I – I didn't feel she was a terribly truthful person, though I had no way of checking up on her.'

'Actually, he *was* a painter, your father.'

'Oh he *was*?' She looked inordinately pleased. 'That's interesting. It said "artist" on my original birth certificate I found, and I was so glad because I'd always wondered where my own painting came from. I mean, I'm quite good at it, though I hardly do any these days, but I went to Art School and had great ambitions at one time. I suppose he was studying art in Paris when I was born? But Shirley Gilchrist didn't seem to think he was much of a painter. She was rather horrid about him, actually . . . Did you think he was any good?'

'Well – in his way.' I was wary of saying much. 'He wasn't a great artist,' I said at last. 'But he certainly had a talent.' I did not elaborate.

'Ever since I discovered his name,' she said wistfully, 'I've been hoping I might see something of his in a gallery. I tried looking him up in *Artists' and Writers' Who's Who* and one or two other lists, but he wasn't there. Shirley Gilchrist told me she thought he might have changed his name.'

'Oh? Why did she think that?'

'Um – I'm not sure. She didn't say. Well I suppose that "Evan Brown" isn't really a name to set the art world alight, is it?'

'Oh I don't know. Proletarian style, and so forth. Kitchen sink. Regional. Roots . . .' I could imagine opportunistic Evan having flourished in the self-conscious egalitarianism of the 1960s. Manufacturing 'Street Art' perhaps. Talking about his good friend John Bratby.

'Shirley said she'd had difficulty tracing him, actually, when she needed a final signature from him for the adoption to go through. She thinks he and my mother were already apart by then. And – I didn't like to put my mother on the spot by asking her too much, but I got the impression from her too that she hadn't stayed with him long after I was born.'

'Or he hadn't stayed with her,' I couldn't resist adding, but she did not seem to hear. Looking away from me across the busy tables under the hard lights, she said softly:

'I even wonder rather if he ever knew she'd given me away, till it was too late to go back on it.'

She could have found out the truth by a simple query to Shirley Gilchrist or to Joyce herself. Presumably she had not asked because she did not want to know. She was not really asking me now; she was telling me what she wished to believe. I saw that she had managed, even out of the umpromising facts she had garnered, to fashion by selection and suppression the classic adopted child's fantasy: *my father was a finer order of being than my mother. He at least really loved me. He did not willingly give me away.*

'I'd love to meet *him* one day,' she said sadly. 'But I don't suppose I ever shall.'

'Probably not,' I said. I hoped very much she never did. She was not a fool. For all that she seemed to have inherited some of Evan's flamboyance and self-absorption, I thought that she would have seen through him.

It occurred to me only late in the evening, when we were talking determinedly about something else, that she had avoided asking me a single question about Evan's personality or how I had come to know him.

In fact she had not wanted me to tell her anything I knew about either of her parents. The opportunity had been there, but she had turned it aside. That, of course, was her right. But our ideas on what we want to know about our own areas of pain can change from one period to another. Might she not regret this missed chance?

Oh well, I told myself, if she does she can find me again, through the Association. She seemed to be good at finding people. We drank quite a lot – she could put it away, for a woman, I thought – and gossiped animatedly about our fellows in Geneva, relaxing back with relief into our old companionship. I even had it vaguely in mind that it would be nice, after all this handling of an emotional subject, if. . . ? This was time out of ordinary life. No form of intimacy between us here need lead anywhere further. But, although she kissed me with warmth in the lobby of our hotel, I understood that this was a goodnight kiss.

I went to my own room, only half regretful, half relieved also. I was rather tired; things might not have gone well, and I would not have liked to end up feeling like a dirty old man. I reminded myself of the last time I had held her in my arms – that red-faced baby with flapping fists on the Gare du Nord.

Later in the night I remembered Ann too. In the morning I felt only half ashamed of myself, not quite believing I had really entertained any clear designs.

161

It did not occur to me then, though it did afterwards, when I thought about it, that Amanda had probably been due to spend the rest of that night with James, another married man old enough to be her father. Evan Brown, I thought, with the vague satisfaction of censure vindicated, really had a great deal to answer for.

'Shirley Gilchrist told me she thought he might have changed his name.'

'Oh? Why did she think that?'

'Um – I'm not sure. She didn't say.'

Eventually, after several weeks during which I suppose I turned the matter over in a submerged way in my mind, I looked Shirley's number up in the book and rang her.

As soon as she grasped who I was she sounded extravagantly pleased, which made me uncomfortable; but, having telephoned on impulse, I could only persist with my intention. She sounded less pleased then, but she answered my query.

Yes, a girl called Amanda Goring had been to see her about two years ago. Yes, she remembered the young couple who had been Amanda's parents and whom she had helped in 1953: 'They were friends of yours, weren't they? Do you see anything of them these days?' There was a hint in her tone that I was the sort of person who 'doesn't bother to keep up with old friends'. I decided to make this call as short as possible.

'No, I haven't seen them for thirty years, actually. But for a quite other reason' (I had no idea myself what I meant) – 'I need to look the man up. His name was Evan Brown, I think . . .' (Sub-text: 'I hardly knew him, so don't blame *me* for him.') 'But Amanda told me you thought he had changed his name.'

There was a pause. Then Shirley said:

'Yes. Well I did get that information.' ('There's a lot more I could say, but I'm standing on my dignity now that I've realized you've rung me up just to find something out.')

'Could I ask where from? Then maybe I could go to the same source.' ('And won't need to ring you up again.')

Another pause, then she said self-consciously:

'Well, it was the police, actually. But I had a good reason at that time to be making enquiries for him – it was when I needed his signature for the adoption to be finalized. I doubt if they'd tell just anyone.'

'Well, we'll see about that.' ('You rude cow.') 'You mean, he was known to the police?'

'So I gathered. In fact, he had quite a record. The police themselves were looking for him at that time. A fraud case, I gathered. Con-trickster stuff. Quite nasty.' A mixture of disdain and relish. 'The detective in charge of the investigations told me about it in confidence, as I was involved in my professional capacity.'

'Oh I see. Did they ever get him, I wonder?' ('You don't surprise or shock me, Shirley. Bad luck.')

'I don't think so. Actually the same policeman got back to me quite a long time after to see if *I'd* traced him because they'd failed to. It was then that he said Evan Brown had probably changed his name – that people like that often do, sometimes several times. Oh, and by the way, he'd had a wife all the time. Back in Wales. I don't think he'd ever told the girl – Joyce – that. Certainly she never mentioned it to me.'

Of course he would be married already. It all fitted. I should have guessed that myself at the time.

'And had you traced him?' I persisted.

'Well . . . Of course if I *had* known where he was I wouldn't have thought it my duty to tell the police. I mean, my professional duty was primarily towards him and Joyce as my clients.'

'Yes, yes, quite.' ('Don't preach to me, you self-important prig.') – 'But *did* you know?'

'Well – not really.'

'And did you ever get that signature you needed? Or was it easier just to forge it?'

There was another pause, during which I could feel her deciding whether or not to be insulted. She apparently decided against it, for she next said, almost affectionately:

'Tom, you always *were* no respecter of rules. Really! I suppose *you* would have done that?'

'Well, why not, in a good cause? I mean, it was just a formality, wasn't it? Everyone concerned was committed to the adoption by then, I take it . . . Even Joyce?'

'Oh yes. Once she'd made the decision. In fact it was Joyce who got the papers passed on to Evan to be signed via some friend who was shielding him. He didn't want *her* to know where he was either, as far as I remember.'

(Or else, I thought, she didn't want to tell *you* where he was, if she knew the police were after him.)

'Did the adopting parents – Whatsernames? Gorings – know about any of this?'

'Oh no. I kept it from them. I thought that best. I mean – nice, middle-class people like that' (she gave the phrase an automatic sneer) 'might have worried about the baby having "bad blood" or something idiotic like that.'

Well, we won't go into *that*, I thought.

' – I did worry about it after, though,' she went on, more confiding now. 'I had sleepless nights about whether I'd done right by Joyce – whether my real duty mightn't have been to help her to keep the child.'

I felt I would rather not go into that either, if for a different reason.

'Well, Shirley,' I said heartily, 'it's all very long ago now, isn't it? Joyce, I gather, married afterwards and had more children. As for Evan, he's probably become a reformed character years ago.' Some obscure impulse warned me to sound as if the whole topic was a matter of little interest or significance to me after all. Shirley Gilchrist I knew to be an obsessional character. Hearing her voice again after all these years had had an odd effect on me, almost nauseating: probably it was mostly my fault that the conversation had been so barbed. I did not want her to start applying her imagination to why I could possibly be interested in Evan Brown now.

I knew why I was. But the notion was so momentous and as yet so unfounded that I hardly dared confront it myself.

Shirley made some ponderously tactful enquiries about my present life and well-being which indicated to me that she'd followed my career, professional and personal,

164

through the years. She knew about Simone and Marigold, she knew I'd remarried. I realized, with a sinking feeling, that she was about to issue a social invitation.

'. . . Only a small flat . . . don't entertain much. I've never cared for cooking . . . And of course it's rather far out of town here for people to get home late at night . . . But a friend who'd be so interested to meet you, she used to work with Melvyn Baines too . . . Of course I know you must be awfully busy these days . . .'

I could imagine it so well. The interminable drive there in the dark. The hesitant search for the address, stopping under street lamps, culminating in one of those roads of semi-detached houses where no numbers are displayed, as if no one expected to be visited. The second unattractive, Baines-struck spinster. The plates of rice salad eaten on our knees. Ann doing her valiant and tactful best to keep the conversation going, glancing at me covertly to see if I were getting depressed . . . The empty reminiscences. The implications: 'Tom and I are *very* old friends . . .' *No*.

When I was younger I used to suppose that if I were invited somewhere I ought to go. Not now, as I tell Ann. Life is at once too short and too long for such pointless, exhausting compliance. I grasped cravenly at the excuse Shirley had handed me:

'. . . Really am up to my eyes, these days . . . A book I'm editing . . . This Government working party . . . And a trip to Canada pending. I'm not sure of the dates, yet . . . Not fixing anything up for the moment. I'm sure you'll understand.'

She did.

'I might have known,' she said, with well-rehearsed, facile bitterness, 'that you'd become far too grand these days to bother with people like me. I was just useful years ago when you needed me, wasn't I? Thanks, Tom. I get the message.' And she made sure she rang off first.

Evidently, I thought ruefully, Evan Brown was not the only person whose actions, decades ago, had left him a certain amount to answer for.

★

165

The Court Sergeant, a grandfatherly figure with a paunch and glasses, was a friend. Once, when he and I had spent a long day in Court, I had run into him afterwards in a nearby pub, subtly different in his tweed off-duty jacket. He had told me then that his youngest had been knocked off his bicycle the previous month and might be permanently brain-damaged. 'It changes your whole view of life, this kind of thing,' he said, looking past me. 'I've been in the force since I was eighteen, including twelve years on the beat. I've seen a lot happen. But I can't feel the same about anything now. Especially drunken driving cases. I just can't trust my own judgement any more. If you see what I mean.'

I did see what he meant, though I did not tell him why. Perhaps I should have, matching his gesture with my own. I excuse myself with the thought that he probably knew about my life anyway, but I suspect that I was really held back by a mixture of social discrimination (encouraged on the Bench) and a lifetime's habit of reticence about my own affairs. Instead I took refuge in a continuing concern for him, inquiring solicitously after his boy whenever the opportunity arose. (To which the answer, by and by, was 'Much better, thank you, Sir. Quite a lot of steady improvement, and the hospital thinks he'll be able to take up his apprenticeship after all. Wonderful really, when you think of it . . . The wife and I can still hardly believe it. That he's been given back to us, I mean.')

After this satisfactory dialogue, I did not hesitate very long before asking Sergeant Pelham if he could do me an unofficial favour. Could he look up someone's criminal record for me? No one, I stressed, who was due to appear in our Court or who, as far as I knew, was ever likely to. I supplied the few details I could, adding that in fact the record might be a very old one, all the convictions long spent – but I would like to know them anyway. Of course I would not mention this to anyone else.

Sergeant Pelham put up a decent show of reluctance – 'Well, it is a bit irregular, Sir' – but I could tell that he was going to do it. It was, after all, easy for him, in his position, and from someone like me the request must have seemed essentially harmless.

A fortnight later, as I was waiting to manoeuvre my car out of the yard of the adjacent police station, he came out to me and handed me a buff envelope, departing again with a professionally non-committal air. Inside was a photocopied 609 form, so familiar to me from Court sittings. How often on the Bench had I looked, with a world-weariness real or assumed, at an identical form, yet another list of a man's misdeeds? Yet this time, as I unfolded the sheet, I found my hands shaking.

Pelham had done as I had asked. Normally very old convictions are simply listed as '12 before 1970' or whatever. However this list detailed them back to the beginning. This man had started his career in Cardiff Juvenile Court ('Theft from a motor vehicle') at the beginning of the war, and on the third such offence had been sent to a 'Reformatory' – the old word, long forgotten, came back to me as I read it, with a musty tang of workhouses and official beatings. The experience had not, it seemed, reformed him. There were a criminal damage and an attempted entry charge in 1943 – his first appearance in the adult Court – then a gap over '44, '45 and '46, which presumably represented his Army service. Then came two charges of handling stolen goods, in Swansea, in 1947. The second of these had earned him a short prison sentence, which seemed to have made him temporarily either more honest or more wary, for nothing else was recorded till 1951, by which time he had apparently moved to London and taken to the more middle-class activity of obtaining money by false pretences.

1951 . . . It was surely in the following year that I had met him in Paris? Presumably his appearance there dated from just after his release from his second spell inside.

Nothing appeared for 1952 or 1953, but then I knew where he had been then: out of England for most of the time. However in 1955 there were several more charges of false pretences and fraud, accumulated together into a star appearance – his first at a Crown Court. Evidently the police

167

force who had been looking for him, at the time when Shirley Gilchrist also needed him, had finally caught up with him. The result was a fairly stiff sentence. It looked as if, by this point, he was slipping over the imperceptible boundary between the delinquent young man, who will eventually settle into more-or-less respectable obscurity, and the lifelong professional crook.

I was therefore rather surprised that these Crown Court convictions were the last ones listed. I even felt in the envelope to see if there was a second sheet of paper, but there was none.

Perhaps he had gone to France again, and, this time, had stayed there?

I had, you will have understood by now, formed an idea. Or not so much formed it as found it lying there, indistinct but complete, in the recesses of my mind. I felt that it had probably been there for some time already, obscurely troubling me, before I had identified it.

I did not yet entirely believe my idea. It was far-fetched. I had no good evidence for it at all. But, compelling and revelatory, it now invaded my mind. And took root there.

On the next suitable opportunity, I thanked Sergeant Pelham for his help, and remarked in what I hoped was a casual tone that Evan Brown seemed to have abandoned his criminal career rather suddenly for one so well launched upon it – 'unless, of course, there were more recent charges under another name?'

'Well, Sir, we had his prints, and anything serious gets checked for that anyway.'

'Oh yes, of course.' I had genuinely forgotten about fingerprints.

'But since you mention it . . . As you know, a 609 form only shows registered convictions. But our police files are a bit more extensive than that, they're all on computer now . . . Well, I don't suppose it matters, in the circumstances, if I tell you that this particular individual was further charged with fraud and drug-dealing at the Crown Court –

in 'fifty-nine, I think it was, but he got off. Then, in the early sixties, there was another warrant for his arrest. Quite a big forgery case it was, something to do with the art world. Several defendants. It went to the Bailey in the end, and the others all got sent down. Well that warrant had him down as Evan Brown plus an alias he was known to be using as well. So, you see, he did go on being a busy lad.'

'And what about that warrant – what happened?'

'It was never executed.'

'You mean, the police never caught up with him then?'

'Looks like it. Of course there may be a clerical error . . . But it certainly seems, from the records, as if he's had the sense to make himself scarce ever since.'

'Early sixties. Twenty years past. Of course he might be anywhere by now?' I said, wondering if there was anything more to hear.

'He might indeed. They've got a lot of that sort in Latin America, I'm told. Or on the Costa del Crime in Spain. Or anywhere really – he wouldn't have to go that far: he wouldn't necessarily get extradited. It wasn't as if he'd committed murder.'

'As far as we know,' I said.

Pelham, a dealer in known facts, looked slightly disapproving.

'Nothing like that on record, Sir.'

'I'm extremely obliged to you,' I said, 'for all you've done. It's been helpful, and in due course I'll explain why.' I hastened on quickly, knowing that no respectable explanation was ever likely to come into my mind: 'Could I ask you one further thing – just to complete the picture, as it were. Could you tell me the other name, the alias, he was using when that warrant was issued?'

Pelham 'couldn't call it to mind'. He said he could look the record up again, but I could tell that this time he really did not want to. I had pushed him far enough – perhaps over the edge of propriety, given both his position of responsibility and mine. It is in fact quite against rules for a police officer to pass on information. I had not let him know

169

that I too knew this, but we avoided each other's eyes and I felt a little guilty towards him.

I did not see him for a few weeks. I was therefore unprepared when, at the end of a stodgy Saturday morning of enquiries into unpaid fines, the usher put a note in front of me. I expected it to say 'Mrs Ferrier rang to say she would pick you up', or 'Will one of the Bench take a sworn statement before you leave?' Instead it said, in an elderly policeman's clerkly hand:

'Memo from Sgt. Pelham.
The name you were enquiring after was Daffyd Huws.'

For a couple of seconds I looked at the message uncomprehendingly. I needed to adjust my mind to its import, but in any case the name seemed so strange that it conveyed nothing to me: it might as well have been Hungarian or Thai.

Then, suddenly, as if indeed my slow eyes had penetrated a foreign script and made sense of it, I understood it.

I crumpled the paper in my fist before shoving it into my pocket.

'Will you tell Sergeant Pelham,' I said, 'that I'm very much obliged to him?'

Then I believe I made a show of signing each page of the Means Register. God knows if I wrote my own name. I suppose I did, as no one queried it. But it might as well have been Daffyd Huws I signed, for all I know.

'Tell me,' I said to Lewis Greenfield, 'how does someone set about changing their name?'

One of Lewis's virtues is that he never looks surprised at a question. He did not say 'Why do you want to know?' but merely:

'In this country?'

'Well, yes. For a start.'

'OK. Britain, and the United States, are the odd-countries-out in that they make it very easy. We don't, as you will have noticed, have identity cards, and so we don't

170

have any formalized notion of unalterable identity. That's an interesting example, by the way, of people's concepts following outward signs such as a word or a symbol, rather than the other way round.'

'Very interesting, Lewis. You know I like these intellectual excursions too. But let's have the facts first, shall we, then the dialectic?'

'There aren't many facts, I told you. You want to be called by another name? So, you call yourself by it. You have a basic right to. It really is as simple as that.' Triumphantly unhelpful.

'Isn't there something called changing your name by Deed Poll?' I suggested, conciliatory now.

'There is – mainly resorted to by long-term lady friends wanting respectability and by people hoping to inherit the family fortune from childless uncles. It's a bit old-fashioned, and it doesn't make any essential difference anyway. Your name, in Britain, is the one by which you are commonly known. That doesn't mean you can decide from one week to another that you're called something different. But it means that, if you live in a community and people get to know you under the name you use there, you can, for instance, establish identity sufficient to open a bank account in that name. Of course, earning the money to put in it may be more tricky.'

'You mean, with National Insurance contributions?'

'And tax, yes. Oh, you can still do it, of course, but you'd have to explain to the DHSS and the Inland Revenue what you were up to. You couldn't do it clandestinely.'

'What would happen if you tried?'

'Well unless you confined yourself to cash-in-hand labouring jobs or illegal street trading anyone who employed you would want your card. And even if you managed to get a new one, the DHSS would say, "Very funny thing, this man of forty-two, or whatever, never seems to have worked before. In fact, he doesn't seem to have existed before. Can we have a few more facts about you, dear Sir, and where is your birth certificate?" '

'Suppose you went abroad. Could they check your employment record abroad?'

'Probably not. But how would you get abroad without a passport?'

'You'd get one in your new name,' I said promptly, as if this had become a contest between us.

'Oh, you are a sharp one, Sir . . . And how would you do that without a birth certificate?'

'Ah, hum, yes, you may have a point . . . So it keeps coming back to the birth certificate, doesn't it?'

'It does indeed. In other words, your hypothetical character will get on peacefully under his new name provided he confines himself entirely to the black economy and never tries to go out of the UK. Bit of a limited life, I'd say . . . Of course, he might get on better if he was a woman. It's easier for a woman to explain away great gulfs in her employment record, and she'll probably find some punter to keep her and call herself by his name anyway . . . But she still can't get on his passport without a birth certificate. At least, I don't think so.'

'I see.' This last bit of information didn't interest me, but I had let Lewis talk on, not wanting my concern to seem specific. 'And what about other countries?' I said, though I felt I already knew the answer. Countries like France that run on formal identity papers would make the adoption of a new name far more difficult. I myself had had to carry a *carte de sejour* in the days when I had lived there. I remembered being interviewed for it at a Parisian police station and subsequently queueing at the Town Hall of the Eighth Arrondissement.

I tried to remember what its issue had depended on, apart from a signed note from my Sorbonne tutor. My passport, certainly.

' – No, don't bother to answer that,' I said, as I saw Lewis marshalling his forces to give me a comprehensive lecture. 'I see the problems.'

'Quite. In most European countries your hypothetical man will have to take to forgery in order to have the required papers.'

'Well, there's always that, I suppose.' I thought of Jacquou's tales of the home-industry of forged IDs, passes and food cards that had been run in Resistance circles. Because of these associations, forgery had previously seemed to me a pursuit more ingenious than intrinsically wicked, a minor art form. I also thought of the warrant from the 1960s the police had never been able to execute. That had been on a charge of forgery.

'Yes, but for documents forgery isn't all that satisfactory except to cover a random check,' said Lewis.

'Why?'

'Because, numbskull, the forgery doesn't correlate to anything in a register. So if a central check is made it is obvious at once that it's false. In other words, it isn't really a clever thing to do. Not for someone who's hoping to develop a solid second identity for himself without much danger of being rumbled . . . Is he clever, your chap?'

What, if anything, did Lewis mean by the remark? Nothing much, probably – but, as in Court when Sergeant Pelham's note was handed to me, I felt my heart beginning to beat perceptibly. As if it had a life and an idea of its own. I answered as casually as I could:

'I'm not sure yet. I haven't decided.'

'Thinking of writing a best-selling detective story, are we?'

'Something like that.'

'But you don't read detective stories. I remember that you don't. I'm the one with low tastes who devours crime novels in the middle of the night.'

'Well I'm thinking of trying it.' (Blast Lewis, he was being deviously inquisitive, after all.)

'Because I was going to say, if you did read detective stories like I do, you might know the answer to the next question, which is how do you begin to establish a solid second identity?'

'As I've understood it from you,' I said, 'it all comes back to a birth certificate.'

'Yes. Do you want to know how to get one in a name not your own that will still be a real one? As I say, nothing like fiction, I've found, for teaching me what Law School didn't teach.'

'You tell me,' I said, imitating Lewis's own manner. 'I know you're longing to.'

'OK. Well anyone can go along to Somerset House – no, it's St Catherines House in Kingsway now, but it's the same thing – pay a few quid and get a copy of any birth certificate, it doesn't have to be your own. And you don't have to give a reason. But if you're trying to pinch someone else's identity, it's not much use picking one at random because he'll almost certainly have been using his identity himself, so to speak. I mean, he'll have a National Insurance card and very likely, these days, a passport as well, so if you try to use his birth certificate to get either of those you're likely to get found out.'

'Yes, I can see that . . . So what do you do?'

'You visit a graveyard,' said Lewis.

I looked questioning.

'A graveyard,' he said firmly.

Some people, since Simone's death and much more since Marigold's, have tried to avoid, in my company, any flippant mention of the trappings of death. I have watched them blundering near the subject and then retreating from it with awkward tact. Lewis had more sense than that.

'You look for the grave,' he said, 'of someone the same sex as yourself.'

'Ah – and the same sort of age?' I began to see.

'You're getting it – but not your present age, not a recent grave. Because, in that case, you'd be likely just to run into the same trouble – I mean that the DHSS would come back to you smartly saying that they were paying a pension to your widow and what were you doing still alive and wanting a new card or whatever? No, you have to find the grave of someone born about the same time as you who died before he could reasonably be expected to have had identity documents beyond his birth certificate. A child's grave, in other words.'

'So then you've got a name, and a date of birth – '

'Exactly. It's then that you go to St Catherines House and you order up his birth certificate. And you use *this* to get a passport in his name, which won't be queried because, if he

174

was pretty young when he died and that was many years ago, he's most unlikely ever to have had a passport.'

'The Passport Office won't check that he isn't still alive?'

'I hardly think so, unless their suspicions were aroused. There wouldn't be any simple way of their doing so, and when you think how many routine applications for first-time passports they receive . . . You'd have to forge the counter-signature by a JP, doctor or whoever, but that'd be no problem. Like that, you'd have a valid birth certificate and a valid passport. That's the basic kit for all other documents. Easy, once you know.'

'If a bit ruthless,' I said.

An image came into my mind, clear but small as if seen from some distance away, of a man wandering alone in a hillside cemetery, trampling the rank grasses round old gravestones, sole evidence of brief existences, long-extinct griefs. He was scrutinizing this headstone and that, kicking aside an empty jam-jar, then finally stopping in one place and noting something down with an air of achievement.

'Yes. Taking the name of the dead in vain, you might say,' said Lewis heavily.

There was a short silence in which we probably both thought the same thing. I had never envisaged the dead as being vulnerable in this way before. The offence, however obscure, struck me as abhorrent.

'Is it done much?' I asked.

'Probably not – but if it's done successfully then by definition it wouldn't come to light. Oh I suppose a certain number of people know about the trick now because it's been used by a couple of well-known crime writers. So I'm afraid it's not an original idea I've given you – for your own best-seller, I mean.'

'I'll bear that in mind,' I said, finding this fantasy of myself as a writer useful. 'Let me just clear up another point, though. You did say the DHSS would be surprised if they got a request for a card from a grown man who never seemed to have had one?'

'Yes. I'm not sure of the answer to that myself. Maybe your chap'll have to kid them he's been abroad since he was

175

eighteen, herding sheep in Australia or something.'

' – Or maybe,' I said, 'having got his passport, he *goes* abroad. Maybe that's what the passport was for – to set up a new life abroad with a clean record. Especially if he was known to foreign police as well under his own name.'

'Yeah, maybe . . . I can see you're getting quite into the swing of it.'

'Yes. Thank you, Lewis.'

'You must let me know,' he said, fixing me with his mock-fierce bushy-browed look, 'when you've worked out a bit more about your chap. I'd be glad to help.'

'I will.'

'Mmm . . . How's the insomnia, anyway?'

'The what?' I genuinely had not heard.

'Insomnia – I thought you were planning to use your spare hours in the middle of the night to write this tale.'

After a moment I said: 'It's you that puts his mind to crime stories in the middle of the night. Not me.'

Lewis said promptly:

'You told me you wake in the night and think about what's-his-name, your Russian. I recommended reading as a more productive alternative. I thought you'd decided that writing would be more productive still – '

'Oh yes, that reminds me, I wanted to speak to you about Piotr Mihailovitch,' I said, grabbing with relief at a new topic of conversation.

Lewis let me. But I don't think he was fooled. At any rate, several times in the next few weeks he rang me, always late at night. He would chat companionably, apparently inconsequentially. But when, on one occasion, I asked him what he had actually rung for, he said:

'Just checking up on your insomnia, Tom.'

It is, I suppose, a measure of my preoccupation with my own idea that it did not occur to me till long after what form Lewis's anxiety about me had taken. From my questions – and perhaps from endemic strains within his own life – it had crossed his mind that I might be planning to disappear. Or at least that I might be playing with the fantasy of doing so. He evidently sensed that something odd was working in me these days, and there I have to say that he was right.

He felt that he ought to keep an eye on me. I was not a bit grateful.

It was July before I got to St Catherines House. I had taken the day off work for this venture, which turned out to be just as well.

It was as Lewis had said: there was no problem about my consulting the registers; they were all available, year by year. It was simply that there seemed to have been many more people born, even in one country within a defined period, than I had ever graphically envisaged. This was foolish of me, but historians tend to deal either in population millions or in recognizable individuals, and do not make the great leap of imagination necessary to bridge the two. At the lists of closely printed names, the births of so many unique human creatures, a sense of claustrophobia came over me. Not on my own behalf, but on theirs, confined as they were into column upon column, reduced to hieroglyphs: no means of knowing anything about any of them but the mere record of their being.

Before coming to St Catherines House, I had wondered if Lewis's information might be out of date – if perhaps everything would now be on microfilm and cross-referenced, henceforth forestalling illegal tricks and making my own work of detection easy. Now I could see, however, that all this material, growing inexorably in volume year by year for ever, would never be put on computer: it could not possibly be cost-effective to do so. The vast majority of the names, once listed, would never be looked up at all for any reason. No wonder the lists, passing barely read under my seeking eyes, exuded an insistent, hopeless appeal: *Notice us; we existed, as you; we were made and went into the world and suffered and worked and made other human beings in turn and went into the void – and you? And you too? By what special claim or act will you make yourself visible? Want to justify your existence, do you? Well, well.*

I did not make my job easier by having to hunt down a relatively common name. 'Daffyd Huws' may seem exotic when it is placed before you in London, but Wales has known a great many of them, even – I soon established – in the 1920s, when ethnic or chauvinistic names seem to have been less in favour than in recent decades.

Had I looked for the name under its still commoner anglicized spelling, probably I would have given up before the great, replicatory multitude, an anonymity of sheer numbers. But, thinking about the matter beforehand, I had decided that it was the name in its Welsh form that I had initially to seek.

Births are listed by years, and the place of birth is given. By and by I compiled a shortlist of Daffyd Huwses born in Cardiff between 1923 and 1927: memory, and my own age, suggested that these years would be the appropriate span. Few imposters would willingly adopt as their own a birth date more than a year or two different from their real one, because of the risk of betraying inappropriate knowledge or the equally inappropriate lack of it in some casual mention of childhood events: one should have been old enough for Army service when one did in fact do it, and have left school in a feasible year.

I initially began to list all those born in those years from other parts of Wales too, but numbers soon made me limit my plan. I would have to work within the most likely scenario, even if I thus risked missing what I was after.

Then I turned to the Deaths, and here my problem was greater. I needed now to find a Daffyd Huws dying, probably still in Cardiff, as a child. Fortunately the Death Registers for the inter-war period also gave the date of birth, otherwise my task would have been impossible: as it was, however, I might hope to establish a reasonable link of probability between a deceased Daffyd and one or more of the births I had already noted down. In fact, as I laboriously realized, I need not have looked at the Birth Registers at all to find my likely candidate, but I was feeling my way not just toward a dead child but to one whose whole brief life would have been comprehended within one place.

But how brief? Childhood lasts many years. A dead baby or a dead fourteen-year-old could equally have been the basis for an assumed identity. Logically, I should look through all the Death Registers from 1923 to the late 1930s. However it seemed to me that if one was attempting to steal an identity, the risks of discovery would be the less the briefer the life of the original owner: I therefore concentrated my search on the late 1920s.

I knew, after all, that I was not following in the footsteps of a fool, but of a calculating, imaginative man. I was trying to use my own guile, my own imagination, to reason as he would have reasoned.

For what else, at this stage, was I doing but attempting to follow in his footsteps to see if the potential steps were in fact there? And I had had to start at a different point in his itinerary, working backwards from the unknown to the known. By these means, I eventually settled, arbitrarily – it seemed the most suitable candidate – on a boy born in Cardiff in 1925 who died in the same town at the age of two, in the year of my own birth. My imposter could even have known of him, this sickly, transient child, through family or street tradition.

I left St Catherines House with a sense of achievement, as if my detective work had really brought something to light. But in fact what I had done was no more than an academic exercise. I had established to my own satisfaction that Evan Brown could have purloined the brief existence and name of a real Daffyd Huws. I had not proved that he did: at best, what I had located was a suggestive coincidence.

Nor had I yet even embarked on the far greater task of exploring what further logical evolution in identity might have taken place over the years. Though this, of course, was the heart of my idea. My Idea. Originally a mere grain of irritant, random fact, it was now slowly accreting like a black pearl in an oyster: the Idea, to which I was now giving the status of a theory. At this point, I believe it had still to develop into anything resembling a plan.

It needed more substance on which to feed. For the time being, nothing further was forthcoming. Yet, oddly, I do not think I felt frustrated. I believe that I was getting used to my Idea, handling it mentally, even deriving some obscure, perhaps perverse strength from it. I was, you might say with hindsight, biding my time, even if I did not yet know it.

Ann and I went on holiday to the United States, to Massachusetts where she has cousins. Then, in the late autumn, I crossed the Atlantic again on my trip to Canada: a conference, lectures to give, meetings with my equivalents in the Canadian Department of Education. In Quebec, a city where I had never been before, my French was called into action again. Perhaps it was this, combined with the oddness, to me, of the setting – the familiar, vivid phrases in flat, unfamiliar accents, the dislocating combination of the Gallic and the Transatlantic – that caused something to shift in the speculative depths of my mind. At all events, I woke one morning in my hermetically sealed hotel room high above the city, and knew that I had dreamed, for the first time in many years, of Jacquou.

He told me, casually, while moving about the mill-house kitchen, that one can look things up in France too – 'Our French police have their uses. After all, many of them are not bad lads at heart. Matters must take their course. Justice needs to be seen to be done.'

Ostensibly his remark referred to the aftermath of the Resistance – to the need to track down a former colleague, as in the story he had once told me about the *maquisard* he suspected of having killed a British agent entrusted to his care. But as I shaved, in the brilliantly lit cell of a bathroom, the essence of the dream still enveloped me. Presently I understood that it had another, more specific meaning.

I stopped shaving for a bit and looked at myself in the mirror. Myself looked back: only a little wary, in spite of everything; lined, solid, greying, apparently dependable. Not, you would say, paranoid, not a man given to unwarranted assumptions or rash campaigns. Jacquou himself was the same sort of age, and with much the same

180

build, when he first talked to me, a young man in his house, about rough justice.

I think now that it was during those few minutes in front of an irrelevant looking-glass in Quebec that I came to understand much more about the Idea that was developing within me and its possible outcome.

In the unreal space between Christmas Eve 1983 and January 1984, the dark but artificially illuminated turn of the year, another year, Ann and I went to Paris. We had not been there together before.

Paul and Hermione had hospitably suggested the visit, perhaps without any great expectation that their offer would be taken up. However, I turned it over in my mind for a while before mentioning it to Ann and it finally seemed to me a good idea.

She was, I knew, wary of Paris: it was 'my' place, one of those locales of my past in which she feels an intruder. But I found I had become tired of her thin-skinned tact on the matter (perhaps my hidden Idea was now making me braver or merely more reckless), and in any case the prospect of our both spending the rest of our life avoiding ever passing through the nearest European capital together struck me as tedious and impracticable.

She, poor love, took my sudden enthusiasm for a week in Paris with her as a sign that I was 'better' from whatever had been wrong with me, unmentioned, the previous winter. She was also encouraged by the information – which, with my usual crass uncommunicativeness about the past, I had apparently failed to impart before – that Hermione was American: she, Ann, would not therefore be expected to talk in French. I forbore to tell her that Hermione, so intelligent and adaptable and with Paul now for so many years, had long since shed most signs of her original identity, including almost every trace of her gritty New York accent. I trusted that this same adaptability and perception would lead Hermione to realize that Ann needed emotional nursing in Paris. Sure enough, Ann was further emboldened by a charming note from Hermione telling her

181

how much she and Paul were looking forward to our visit and advising her, sisterly, to bring a warm coat – 'Paris is often *freezing* in the winter, and damp with it. Don't believe its PR image: it's worse than London!'

Of course there were other good reasons, spoken and unspoken, for our trip. Neither Ann nor I had any relations in London for whom we felt we must perform Christmas rituals (though Ann would willingly have done so), and the fact is that, for those who have no child, small or grown, the long British Christmas holiday is a desolate one. (It also held, for me, an anniversary, though I don't think Ann knew that.) Far more fun, we said to each other, to be in a city where shops and restaurants remain open and the public transport runs as usual.

Perhaps I should add another, private reason of my own: I had something now to pursue in Paris, my further investigations. But I did not think directly about this till we were on the 'plane on Christmas Eve, enjoying two free glasses of British Airways champagne 'with the compliments of the season' from a hostess unreassuringly dressed as a Christmas clown.

At some point in the last five years Paul and Hermione –who had remained childless for reasons they never discussed, or at any rate not with me – had inherited a sizeable apartment in Passy, to the west of Paris. They were not poor: Hermione probably did not earn much as an editor with an historical journal, but Paul was employed by an international organization; they could certainly have afforded to have the flat redecorated and refurnished. However, true to the French tradition that was Paul's by birth and Hermione's by adoption, they had simply moved into the place as it was, casually inhabiting a repository of family history, even as Jacquou had taken over the cluttered mill-house. They had imported a few opulently modern objects – a new shower in the bathroom, a freezer cabinet in the hall disguised with a tapestry, tape-deck, turntables and speakers among the Louis Seize furnishings of the double living room – but otherwise they conducted their blithe and busy existence apparently unaffected by the family presses full of books and linen, and the family portraits looking down on them.

It was not that they were mean. They spent money without seeming to count it: on meals in restaurants, on a good car, on skiing holidays and trips to New York. Their clothes were elegant and expensive – not that I had noticed this myself, but Ann did, silently pointing out to me that Hermione's coat had the name of a famous couture house in it. And of course they spent money readily on my mill-house, whose ancient roofs constantly required attention and whose river meadow had recently needed new ditches cut for drainage.

'I ought to contribute,' I said inadequately to Hermione. We were on our own, dawdling over breakfast coffee in the flat's austere but serviceable Parisian kitchen, all exposed gas-pipes, oil-cloth and traditional iron pans. It was the Saturday after Christmas, and Paul had taken Ann to see the Centre Beaubourg, mainly (I realized) to give Hermione and myself a chance for a chat on our own.

'Nonsense, Tom,' she said firmly. 'Absolute nonsense. That was the deal – that we should take the mill-house off your hands for the time being and keep it in good order in return. We love going there, you know . . . Oh dear, does that sound thoughtless?'

'Not at all. I'm just glad someone's getting pleasure from it.' It sounded mechanical, but I did mean it.

'I was going to say "we love going there in spite of everything" – but of course it's really because of everything too. I mean that there were many, many good years before that awful accident, when we used to come on visits and you and Simone and Marigold were happy there. Those years were – are – *there*. Nothing can take them away or alter them. Somehow I don't want to abandon them.' She added quickly, 'Of course, that's just how *I* perceive it, for myself,' as if afraid I might hear in her words an implied criticism of my own flight.

I pushed a sugar lump around the oil-cloth that was faintly ringed by a palimpsest of hot pans. 'The trouble is,' I said presently, 'What you say is a truth that works both ways. Horror – evil – are there for ever too as well as happiness. Like the marks on this cloth. Even God, as they say, can't undo the past. For good *or* ill. Though some people, I've noticed, turn somersaults trying to pretend that He can.'

'Like who?'

I had difficulty in explaining. For some reason I had been thinking of Humphrey and his panic-stricken retreat into the Deadly Embrace of Carmen, but as soon as I focused the thought more I realized this did not quite fit. Nor, really, did my Aunt Madge, though she was closer . . . 'It isn't really the same, I suppose,' I said, 'but a silly old aunt of mine wants to believe that the dead are still alive. Messages from the Beyond and so on. But then a lot of people much less silly than her have that weakness. Isn't that one of the basic tenets of Christianity, that through belief we overcome death?'

'I wouldn't know,' said Hermione equably. 'My family are Jewish – were, I should say. They've all gone now.'

'Oh.' I'd never thought of Hermione having any particular background lying behind her New York one, but of course it fitted. 'Isn't it much the same set of beliefs, though?'

'No. Jews don't believe in personal survival. Not in an afterlife in which you see Granny and Cousin Ruth again, anyway. It's this life that counts. There are no promises that anyone will meet up again.'

'I didn't realize that.' I wondered if Lewis knew that. But of course, he must.

'Lots of people don't realize,' she said. 'Paul didn't, till I happened to mention it one day. People reared in even a vaguely Christian ethos tend to assume that it's the proto-religion and that all other cults must be a version of it – give or take the odd Virgin Birth and such dispensables.'

'I imagine my aunt does.'

'Yes, I should think she would . . . I'll tell you one thing I've noticed, though: a fervent belief in personal survival is actually a rotten preparation for dying. You might think it

184

would be a strengthener, but it isn't. Too much at stake, perhaps. And too essentially incongruous. I've seen one or two of Paul's elderly relations die in a blue funk *muni des sacraments de la Sainte Église* etc., etc. . . . I'm willing to have a small bet with you that when your aunt's time comes she won't take kindly to the reality of death either.'

'Interesting. She seems in good form at the moment. But I'll let you know.'

'Yes do, I should like to know.' Hermione spoke briskly, as if I had offered her some useful statistics that she needed for a scholarly article.

'Did Paul's family mind him marrying you?' I said, wondering a little that I'd never thought to ask her this before.

'If they did,' she said, smiling at me with her cat's eyes, which still seemed screwed up against the wreathing smoke of the cigarettes she had long since abandoned, 'they were all, including Paul, too polite to tell me so. And I was too self-centred and pleased with myself in those days to notice.'

She got up to fetch us more coffee from the swan-necked enamel pot. I did not say anything, for I could feel her thinking. As soon as she sat down again she said:

'Now that most of his old people are dead and gone I'm rather sorry that I didn't ask them more questions about their beliefs. They wouldn't really have minded, as they'd got me classified as *une originale* anyway, like some sort of precocious child, and it might have been interesting. I don't know about you, but I find I get more interested in these things – the theories, I mean, no yearnings or anything like that – as I get older.'

'You don't hope for anything in particular?'

'Nope. Nor in this life either, come to that. I mean – we've *had* a lot, and what else is there?' Her eyes met mine again, half mocking and half, I thought, in boundless commiseration. 'The less I expect of anything or anyone, though, the more fascinated I find I get by other people's structures. I mean – well, just look at the Christian attitude to the body. The full-strength Catholic version of it,

185

anyway: "That which is sown in corruption is raised in incorruption, and we shall be changed". – See, I do know something of the Christian cult, after all.'

'Quite. I knew you were lying in your usual way when you said you didn't.'

She put out her cat's tongue at me, but continued determinedly:

'What I'm trying to say is that there's the most extraordinary paradox there. The Christians seem to have no doubt that the body is – is not made to last.' (I heard her substitute this for the more graphic phrase she must have had in her mind.) 'Scripture even emphasizes the body's transience to teach us not to be vain. But at the same time they – and all of us, come to that – go on respecting a dead body as if it remained the – the temple of the soul. Or however we like to phrase it. The lasting symbol of the loved spirit, anyway. Well I do think that's rather interesting. Don't you?'

I did, as a matter of fact, but I probably looked as if I was wrestling with unwieldy thoughts of my own (which I was) for Hermione apparently decided she had said more than enough on this subject. She became brisk, and bustled about and asked me if I wanted to go to the local street market with her to pick out vegetables and fruit for the weekend? Hermione, who had yearned loquaciously for unobtainable hamburgers and liverwurst-on-rye in the Paris of the 1950s, had, with the passage of the years, become a skilled and scrupulous French cook.

Markets always lift my spirits; there seems something brave and also vulnerable about them: the cold air, the good, perishable things to eat, the wrapped-up stall holders, the racks of flimsy underclothes and cut-price sweaters . . . But that morning I made an excuse not to accompany her. I wanted a little time in the flat on my own. In the bottom of one of the family tallboys, I had noticed a stack of telephone directories a few years old. Two had fallen out when Hermione had been extracting her winter boots and she had shoved them back again, apparently not reflecting that it might be more convenient to get rid of

186

them. At the time, I had thought this amusing. Then my mind had got to work on the matter, and I felt glad the directories were there. I wanted to look something up, and I had already established that the current directory was no use to me.

'. . . it was his own car, or so I understood. Paris-registered. I suppose he lived there.'

1977. September 25th 1977.
I found, in Paul and Hermione's cupboard, three directories for 1975.

French telephone directories are not quite like British ones. Subscribers are listed under their names, but many also under professional categories and occupations; and some, from the over-developed French sense of privacy, are only listed thus. This complicated double-entry system, which had sometimes irritated me in the past, now turned out to be a blessing. For of the fat books for 1975, two were professional listings; the only one that was the straight list of subscribers was for the latter part of the alphabet.

Strung out between frustration and qualified hope, I began to turn the pages of the first occupational tome: *Abattoirs, acrobates, acuponcture, apiculture* (in Paris?), *aquafortistes, arboristes, architectes* . . . I had hardly dared hope that there would be a section of people proclaiming themselves *Artistes-peintres* – surely there would be just too many of them? – but there they turned out to be. Or a selection of them, at any rate. Vaguely speculating on what formally codified French basis such a selection might be made (Income tax status? Long establishment? Proof – submitted in triplicate – of having had exhibitions of work?) I was only beginning to run my eye down the column when the name I sought stood out, as a known name sometimes will. After all, I reflected in weak triumph and surprise, this particular step really was as easy as that. I could have taken it any time in the last six years.

'*Hughes, David, artiste-peintre; commissions, encadrements. 18 bis Rue Vieille du Temple, 75004.*

There was a telephone number too, of course. But it was the address I wanted.

The Fourth Arrondissement of Paris includes most of the old quarter of the Marais, the district in which Simone and I had first lived together. By one of those pointless but poignant operations of chance, the Rue Vieille du Temple had been a very little way from our own hideout off the Place des Vosges. But, thinking about it, I realized that something other than chance was operating. When Simone and I had found our two cheap rooms above a bakery in the 1950s the district had still been poor, its great sixteenth- and seventeenth-century mansions blotched by damp, defaced by sign-writing, divided up into printing shops and garment-trade warehouses. Indeed, since the war and the enforced exodus of many of its inhabitants, the area had been particularly run down; in our street, near the junction with the Rue des Rosiers, a barber's shop and a one-time kosher restaurant had stood derelict, and boards covered the windows of a small synagogue. But I knew that by the 1960s and '70s the Marais had become first a district where those with foresight quarried new apartments out of spacious, rat-frequented attics, and then a place where it was smart to live, the bakers and grocers giving way to sellers of antiques, new art and newer clothes. If David Hughes had been living in the Marais within the last ten years, I thought, he must have been doing nicely, in spite of the apparently modest, workmanlike claim in the directory to be a craftsman who accepted commissions and also undertook framing.

I found some excuse to set out for the Marais on my own. Since Ann believed me to be constantly in the grip of nostalgia that week, it was not difficult. In fact she was wrong: cumulative passages through Paris over three decades had all but obliterated for me my own earliest traces. Wherever Simone was for me, she was not here, in this city of traffic and neon lights. But it was true that I had hardly been in the Marais for many years, though I was aware in a general way of its changing face.

The Place des Vosges particularly impressed me.

Remembering it as a patchwork of façades, mostly nineteenth-century reconstructions subsequently decayed, I was unprepared for the newly restored homogeneity of pink brick with stone dressings which now met my tourist's eyes. The spacious public garden in the centre of the square was unchanged, merely tidied up a little – but I remembered only now (how could I ever have forgotten it?) the sculptured horse and rider near one end. Louis XIII? The horse's belly was, for prosaic reasons, supported on a stone tree-stump; crossing the square to my destination in the Rue Vieille du Temple, I suddenly recalled, in a blurred way as through many waters, a joke between Simone and me, a lovers' joke, about that phallic trunk.

I also recalled – though I do not believe I had ever shared this with Simone – that during that first winter we had together, crossing the square on my hike home from the school on the south side of the city where I still taught, I used to watch the muffled children at play with their hoops and balls and little carts on strings, and fantasize the child that, through our love, would one day become a living creature in the light. That was more than two years before Marigold was born, in England. We never, as it turned out, had a child who played like a real, storybook French child in the Place des Vosges, watched over by a Breton nursemaid in a cap with streamers. But just as, even now, I catch myself day-dreaming consolingly, vainly, about the grandchildren, Marigold's children, whom I will never see, as if they really existed somewhere in that alternative time-scheme which even God cannot now implement, so, before her birth, I kept her place warm for her with a child of air.

The baker's shop above which we had lodged had become a purveyor of expensive objects announced in gilt letters as 'Gifts': phrenological china heads, Art Deco tea-cosies, pre-war telephones, toy steam trains, moneyboxes, dolls in Victorian dress, consciously Naïvist pictures of sheep . . . In keeping with what I recognized from French newspaper features as '*la mode retro*', the flyblown painted glass panels of the baker's, showing cows and a few inches of miniature central French landscape, had been preserved and restored.

The cobbler's next door had become part of a photocopy and instant print shop. The defunct barber's at the corner of the Rue des Rosiers had gone, but new kosher establishments had appeared: evidently Jews from North Africa had infused fresh life into the district's old identity. I was glad to see that.

At number 18 *bis* I rang the bell marked '*Concierge*'. With the double vision, past and present, that the Marais had induced, I really did not know what I expected. A traditional French female dragon in bombazine, impregnated with perspiration and garlic? Surely not. But I was faintly disconcerted all the same when there appeared at the adjacent small window a young black girl, clutching a toy black baby to her breast.

Monsieur Euze? I gave the name the kind of sound, like a distant French river, that a French speaker would give it.

The girl was uncertain, pleasantly dithery, sexually responsive to me. She had not been here that long, *voyez-vous, Monsieur*. She would ask her aunt.

The aunt, an even blacker lady but of a different vintage, now joined her in the window, which was beginning to resemble a Punch and Judy stage. I was reassured by the aunt. There was about her the old-fashioned air of a colonial French subject firmly aspiring to be *du metropole*. Yes, one remembered Monsieur Euze quite well. An artist he had been. But he had gone away. Three or more years ago now. In '79 or '80, perhaps.

I heard myself embark, for reasons that were not entirely clear even to me, on a rambling explanation: I believed I had known Monsieur Euze when we were both young, but I was not quite certain that this would be the same Monsieur Euze: Euze was a common name in our country, *voyez-vous . . .*

My vague trial balloon (for so the French call such overtures) seemed to strike my listeners as plausible. At any rate they did not tell me that their Monsieur Euze had been far too young to be a companion of my youth. Instead, the

190

older lady nodded sagaciously and confirmed that their Monsieur Euze had been a compatriot of mine but 'dark haired, for an Englishman. With a little beard, you know – ah, but perhaps not in your day, Monsieur?'

It was indeed many years since we had met, I assured her. It would be so good to talk over old times. Perhaps, if the ladies had a forwarding address – ?

They regretted. There *had* been a forwarding address, no doubt of it, the older informed the younger, who was now inclined to coy, disclaiming smiles. But letters sent on to it had eventually been returned undelivered.

A faint embarrassment now hovered in the air. A reticence that suggested, to my over-attentive senses, that more might be suspected of Monsieur Euze than I was going to be told. At length the older lady ventured that she had intended to take the ownerless letters round to the local police station. After all, the police would know where he was. The police had everyone on record, not a doubt. Domiciles, after all, had to be registered . . . But somehow she had never taken the letters. It hadn't quite seemed her place to do so . . . *Voyez-vous monsieur.*

'Perhaps I will call at the police station,' I said, 'and see if they can help me.'

The ladies beamed. This was obviously the most satisfactory solution to their obscure, half-admitted problem. They had been waiting for several years for someone like me to appear, and here I was. *Voilà tout.*

As I left, the young girl with the baby called after me:

'Come back and tell us if you find out where he is – ' And then, reproved by her aunt, relapsed into childish giggles.

I hastened on my way to meet Ann outside the Musée Carnavalet which was not far away. I did not go to the police station in the Marais after all, that day. I was already a little late for Ann. Was that why I did not go?

Not really. For on none of the remaining days in Paris did I go. My long-term campaign of action (for so, in retrospect, I now see it) was not consistently sustained, being punctuated by prolonged lapses during which I stayed quiet, gathering my forces for the next oblique assault. It was also punctuated by fits of cowardice.

Better stop here. Better not know any more.

'You said at the time that you didn't want to know anything about the man.' Lewis's voice, superficially reasonable but with a hint of panic in it.

I know I did. But I've changed my mind. Only, I need to wait. Two lines of approach, I have. But do they really join as they appear to? Is the pattern of which I am now convinced, in both hope and dread, actually there or is some mocking, stupid coincidence at work?

Is there a meaning to events after all?

Whether I would ever have taken the matter further if another piece of information had not precipitately intervened, I hardly now know. I like to think that I would.

Of course I would. The information, and its source, were merely another of those chances, like the coincidence of location in the Marais, which are not really chances at all but the working through of a sequence of links. By one route or another, these links were likely to bring me, sooner or later, to the same point. It was all, simply, a matter of time.

On our last evening in Paris we talked of what Hermione, with an abrupt vestige of her native speech, referred to as the 'gussying up' of parts of Paris such as the Marais. Ann responded eagerly with the wharves in Boston, round which her cousins had escorted us in the summer. We all spoke inconclusively of Camden Lock in London, and of fashionable nostalgia. I could tell that the subject had no particular fascination for Paul or Hermione any more than it had for me – partly because, once stated, it is a boring subject anyway, but also no doubt because the outdated objects tended to look, to the three of us, merely ordinary, part of our own past lives. But by this stage in the visit, we were beginning to run out of topics that could rewardingly be discussed by all four together. The Marais seemed safe, at least.

192

However the conversation progressed to the commercial exploitation of tradition in general and hence to regional arts and crafts now self-consciously mass-produced. Hermione described a shop behind the Madeleine, in central Paris, currently selling for thousands of francs a-piece small items of wooden furniture decorated with 'peasant' paintings.

'Like Maryk's chests?' I couldn't resist saying. Ann would not know what I meant, and anyway I suddenly wanted quite badly to know that Maryk's chests were still in the mill-house for me to find again if – when . . . No doubt one of them still contained the more innocuous of Jacquou's Resistance papers, stacked at random as when I had last seen them. Paul and Hermione would not have done any clearing.

'Yes, just like that!' Paul agreed. Worth a fortune now, probably, those chests. And that reminded him – he and Hermione'd gone looking for old Maryk, he'd meant to tell me.

Hermione gave him a slightly anxious glance but, seeing that he and I were both careless with an excess of food and wine and that Ann too looked quite cheerful, she let us be. Paul's rapid English was good, but it was of the kind which is like a tightrope off which the very slightly drunk performer must not fall. He launched unstoppably into his story – one of those set-pieces in which, according to him, he had been forced by Hermione into an unwanted or grotesque excursion. Since Hermione knew that, in marrying Paul, she had willingly subordinated her future, career, identity and even nationality to his, she always listened placidly to these dependent diatribes.

' – *She* took it into her head that she'd like to find out if he was still alive, this implausible Pole or whoever. Said you'd taken her to visit his workshop once, long ago, and that she was sure that it and he would still be there. "Time passes, my girl," I told her. "Time passes. Your Maryk has probably gone now to some Slav heaven full of valuable old gold ikons where everyone is peacefully drunk on schnapps all the time." But would Madame have it? Hell, no.

'*She* said it was just in the next village but one. But we drove miles. I think she got lost and we went round in rings. We kept on crossing and re-crossing small bits of the Creuse. "So much for you knowing this part like your native land," I said. And then when we finally got there, to this damned Holy Sepulchre, it wasn't the famous Maryk any more at all.'

'So he *is* dead?' I said. I felt a brief, sad emptiness inside me.

'I don't think so,' said Hermione equably. 'They didn't say so. I got the impression he was just out for the day. Or putting his old feet up.'

'Most of the paintings were by someone else,' Paul forged on. 'His successor, it seemed. As soon as we got there and took one look my heart ran out into my boots – I'd known it all along. Phoney. To the core. They almost always *are*, now, these so-called local artists. *De la grande bogue . . .*' ('Bogue' is not in fact a French word, but the phrase was part of Paul's complex joke Franglais, like the way he and Hermione used to describe things as being '*un peu beaucoup*').

'Anyway he wasn't a local man either,' said Hermione. 'Like Maryk, he'd settled in the area.'

'So much the worse! They always are – the worst, those types. Anyway, as soon as we located the place and got to the door we were sucked in – yes, really – by two female acolytes of very certain age, who treated us as if we were the Three Wise Men who'd actually found our way to the stable. We were supposed to Admire. And Adore. *Le Grand Maître*. Let us worship at the shrine of creativity. Oh dear, oh dear – ' A pantomine of head shaking . . .

'Rustic nostalgia turned out by the metre. The kind of Naïvism that is compromised at source by its own consciousness of being naïve. *Des paysages de folklore*. In sweet – nice – pretty colours!' Paul gave these classically English words a particularly venomous emphasis.

'God knows what Maryk thinks of his successor,' said Hermione dryly. 'You can only hope that, being such a one-off artist himself, he just hasn't much perception of other people's talent, or the lack of it. Real, genuine naïvety, you might say . . . Now what was the name of this imposter? Not a French name either. I'm trying to remember it.'

'It was one of those names that are deliberately constructed to be unpronounceable in France,' said Paul promptly. 'Like an English Prime Minister. You know – Heath – or Thatcher – or perhaps with a g-h in the middle . . . Th-th – fff – '

'I don't think it was an English name, though,' said Hermione. 'We saw it on a poster. It was very odd.'

'Dahrvid Euze,' I said.

'What's that you say?' Paul really had not quite heard.

'David Hughes, in English. But spelt the Welsh way. Ffs and u-us. Was that it? I – I vaguely remember it. From before.'

I expected the skies to fall, I think. But they did not, not really. It is only afterwards that you know that they have irretrievably fallen.

'Yes, that's it,' said Paul readily. 'Quite right.'

Hermione wasn't sure. Or she wouldn't commit herself. I could see she thought Paul, his story told, was talking at random now. She got up to make some coffee.

Neither of them asked me any questions about my knowledge of the name. Why should they? It wasn't important to them. And I might have been mistaken anyway – it didn't matter. By the time Hermione returned from the kitchen with the fragrant enamel pot, the talk had moved on.

PART V

Before going away at the end of the year I had sent a card and a letter to Piotr Mihailovitch. These contained carefully anodyne and non-religious wishes for the season, in the weak but always viable hope that they would, through frontiers and censors, reach him. For people to have given you up, for lack of a sign, when you were still alive and in more need of them than ever, would, I thought, be the worst thing of all.

Then, one evening in January, I had a telephone call.

'Tom? . . . It's Amanda here.' She must have felt me hesitate, for she added rather sharply: 'Amanda Goring. We met in Geneva.'

I should at once have realized she might have some news from Russia. But at the sound of her name my other preoccupation sprang to the fore – my Idea, now became a theory, which had, since Paul's revelation, developed coherent form and substance. Had Amanda another piece of confirmation for me?

'It's Malenko,' she said. 'He's dead. He died in Perm camp of a kidney complaint, at the beginning of the year. That's what they say, anyway. We've just heard in the office, through eastern Germany.'

Malenko, Piotr Mihailovitch. So, after all, my efforts to reach him had been like Aunt Madge's, useless messages sent to someone beyond receiving them.

Amanda and I had an unsatisfactory conversation, during which I tried to express my regrets in words that turned to clichés in my mouth, and she responded monosyllabically. I had the feeling that she expected something more of me, some effort of imagination or will or intuition, but I did not know what. What was there to say? The dead man in Russia, reduced by hunger and cold and neglect to a mere flake, a shell of a man, whom I would now never meet, lay

196

across our conversation and across my inner life like a shadow. But it was a shadow that did not express anything beyond itself. The sense of a link with myself, some sort of parallel however distant, was severed. I could not dream of avenging Piotr Mihailovitch. I could do nothing further for him, and perhaps never had. The very fact that he had been allowed to die seemed to indicate that I had not made anyone in power care enough about him. My efforts had therefore been in vain.

But he, I now found, had done something for me. Now, in the following weeks, as his wasted, featherlight absence gradually gathered weight, and a few indignant mentions of his case, some of them engineered by me, appeared in the serious newspapers, I found that with his going, my shadow-twin, something else had gone as well. I had lost a model of endurance, a personal guardian of Christian concepts for which, through the years, I had retained an unreflecting, agnostic respect-in-spite-of-myself – a moral brake, perhaps. Moral brakes are out of fashion today, but I do not know how else to express it.

'But *he* may not have felt he died in vain,' said Lewis, when I spoke to him of Piotr Mihailovitch. 'He was a practising Christian, wasn't he? And hasn't Christianity a long tradition of martyrs? Gold medallist stuff, with people getting extra points for being flayed or grilled? Such a cruel religion, it's always seemed to me.'

'Christians don't think so,' I said argumentatively, though I at once felt him to be right. 'Look at your Old Testament and your "I the Lord thy God am a jealous God". The God of the New Testament, with the Christian ethic of love and forgiveness, is much kinder.'

'But the Old Testament doesn't have a tortured man as its central symbol. I tell you, the first time I ever went in a church I was disgusted – appalled. I was a kid, evacuated to Somerset, and I remember it to this day. That poor, poor man. I cried about him afterwards in bed, and the woman we were boarded with got annoyed with me – not that I blame her exactly. When I wasn't crying I was wetting the bed or throwing fits of temper and wanting to walk home to East Ham. And then, later, when she took me to a service to try to convince me it was nice, it was all so dreary and sad and no one greeting each other when they came in. Quite unlike a synagogue. To be honest, I think Christianity is a repellent faith. Can't understand why it's done such good business for the last two thousand years.'

'Oh well . . . "A thousand ages in Thy sight are but an evening gone" etc. A mere flash in the pan, you might say. A passing vogue, now rapidly nearing its end, you'll be glad to hear.'

'Think so? Oh good, you reassure me. Always did say our lot would do better in the end. More realistic, see.'

But under the jokes, with which we hastily forestalled any deeper involvement in the subject, I knew that meanings had hovered between Lewis and me.

'God is Love,' we were taught in childhood: even I was taught it, in a tentative, non-denominational way, as a sop to the feelings of older relations and as an insurance policy – in case the modified Socialist millennium for which my good, decent parents confidently hoped, did not arrive soon enough? But the Love of God has no convincing logo and precious little evidence to support it. The more direct message of the ubiquitous figure on the cross is that sadism is a central impulse in both God and man. Very clever of the Christians, I thought now with a sudden surge of anger, to have dressed up this unpleasant truth in the doctrine of Redemption, thus allowing themselves to contemplate their tortured man and regard his suffering as being necessary while yet paying lip-service to the idea of their own 'guilt'. Sadistic and masochistic tastes catered for together. What a potent mixture. No wonder Christianity had been so successful.

This, of course, was the way I sometimes talked to Simone, who infuriated and eluded me by refusing (rightly) to talk back at this level on the subject. I suppose I had learnt the tone from my own father who, while not jettisoning quite everything, had emancipated himself far enough from his Methodist upbringing to be roundly contemptuous of phrases like 'miserable sinners' and 'the

Blood of the Lamb' – phrases that spoke to him of yellow gaslight in ugly chapels, of tight blue suits and cold brawn suppers and aching, pleasureless Sundays. He was not, I think, interested in the exact nature of the dogma, merely in emphasizing to me its 'Victorian' unattractiveness. Taking my cue from him, I had not made much distinction in my mind between the distasteful idea of being Saved, and the God of the Old Testament with His threats of something worse. It only now occurred to me, at my advanced age, that the Christian doctrine of the Redemption was a way of trying to sidestep a more basic human need – the demand for justice to be seen to be done. Avenging hosts. Wrath visited even down the generations, because the past must not be forgotten. People getting what they deserve, reaping as they have sown – the pattern of meaning working itself out inexorably over the years. A true moral constancy.

Psychoanalysts, I thought, might do well to take a harder look at the human need for retribution. So should the horde of teachers, social workers, therapists, counsellors and all the other 'caring' professionals who are, today, so imbued with the diluted essences of Christianity and Freudianism that they are complacently unaware of the provenance of their own convictions, taking them for inalienable fact. By this vast, soft establishment, guilt and love are persistently over-emphasized, whereas the primary instinct towards revenge is hardly examined, treated as 'pathological' or 'a neurosis'. They attempt to belittle it, perhaps, because they are afraid of it. They sense its power, and look away.

I tried to say something of this to Ann, but the conversation became unfortunately and confusedly side-tracked into a further attack on Melvyn Baines from me (or rather, on 'people like him') and a further hurt defensiveness from Ann.

All my fault as usual, and I apologized. But how could I explain? Too much was going on in my head these days that I could not possibly impart.

My theory was continuing its secret life. In fact it was no longer an intellectual theory; it was solidifying into a plan. My dark pearl, taking shape inside me.

Some people, I realize now when it is all over, might have seen what was forming within me in a different guise. They might have diagnosed it as something to be cast out, an otiose construction, a monstrous growth. A delusion, even. But I prized it. I nurtured it, with much thought and with exercises of the imagination. In the years since Marigold's death I had felt – empty. Like an empty shell. There is really no better way to describe it. Now I felt as if something new, however different, had come to occupy that space.

There were days, a good many of them still, when this presence seemed to me an absorbing conjecture but as yet no more. Like a story being worked out in a writer's mind before he gives it substance in words. Or like the preoccupation of a lover before he takes steps to make his dream come true. Or of a man or woman wishing a child into life before it is yet conceived. In other words, a fantasy. Intricate, life-transforming – but as yet only potential. Not totally real.

Then there were other days, an increasing number of them, in which I knew with a heavy clarity which I did not even relish that my conjecture had acquired such significance that I now had no alternative but to go on pursuing it. I think that at this point the campaign of enquiry had become necessary to me. Still, for the moment, I did not take an irrevocable decision.

Once, some years ago, there was an odd murder in rural France. A British father and son had been camping on holiday in a wood; I think it was somewhere in the south. The father was murdered. The son maintained that he had simply found the body. He told the French police that his father had been in Intelligence during the war, had Resistance contacts in France, and that the murder might be the paying-off of an old score. The French authorities, however, took the view that the war was too long over (it was the 1970s, I believe) for such a tale to be likely, and that they were dealing, rather, with a commonplace patricide.

Since there was no firm evidence either way, I rather think that the police let the son get away to England and then demanded his extradition – to which imperious Gallic request, of course, the Home Office did not accede. There, in an atmosphere of mutual, self-righteous recrimination, the matter was allowed to rest. It remains, as far as I know, unresolved in the annals of justice, a small monument to an incompatibility of assumptions and fantasies on different sides of the Channel.

Its only relevance here is that, after Lewis had told me that Marigold's killer appeared to have been an Englishman, this other case came sporadically to my mind. When both the protagonists are English no wonder, as I remarked bleakly to Lewis, the French don't exert themselves much to find out what really happened.

The notion of a Resistance reprisal had also struck a chord in me. Not in direct relation to Marigold: that would have been too far-fetched even in my current state of theory-construction. But I had long surmised that Jacquou, during the years after the war when, as he told me, 'wounds were opening again', had had a lurking anxiety for his own safety and Simone's. What, after all, of the family of the man he had himself shot in the river meadow, or of that boy from a tobacconist's in Argenton? Or indeed that other, whom he had sought out after the war to persuade to make a confession to the authorities about the death of an SOE man?

In the event, nothing more had happened. Time had passed and Jacquou had ended his life in peace many years afterwards. But the image of a figure coming out of the past – any past – exacting a revenge for things gone by, had settled, it seems, into the tissue of my imagination.

It was also, although I did not see it like that at the time, an image that could work in two ways.

So was this image that started it all, the piece of grit round which my theory grew and grew: an insistent conviction, at first quite unsubstantiated, that Marigold's killer was known to me and that the death might not have been an accident at all? So it seems, so it seems.

Evan Brown had adopted the name Daffyd Huws in the

early 1960s. Perhaps permanently, but of that I could not be sure.

In 1977 my Marigold had been killed in the region of the Creuse, thrown from a Paris-registered car driven by an Englishman whose identity papers styled him David Hughes.

At the same period a David Hughes, painter, had been living in Paris, a man of about my age who had gone again without leaving a proper forwarding address.

Much more recently a bogus painter whose name might – but it was not certain – be written Daffyd Huws, was reported to be operating from Maryk's old workshop, also in the Creuse.

The facts, in connection, were highly suggestive. But they were no more than that. Even in my obsessed state, I could see that I had no conclusive proof. But when I reminded myself of this I was not admonishing myself to keep what is called 'an open mind', I was driving myself on to further efforts of proof.

One thing has always puzzled me. If I say too that it had saddened me, that may sound foolishly redundant in context, but it had added a precise extra sadness on top of all the rest. How had Marigold – Marigold who had been so sensible to the point of wariness, a little shy also – how had she ever, ever come to accept a casual lift from a stranger?

She might have accepted one from the Post van. Or from the local Mayor or the baker or from some other known person. But not, not, I had cried out inside myself, from some Paris-numbered car driven by a man she had never seen before.

The eventual conclusion from this was that perhaps the man had not been a stranger to her after all?

After a good deal of thought along these lines, I wrote a careful letter to Sophie.

Sophie was the girl who had stayed on with Marigold at the mill-house when I took my leave, that bright morning when Marigold had eleven more days to live. Now aged twenty-seven (I knew that, as she and Marigold were the

202

same age), Sophie was married to a man in the British Council and was on the other side of the world, in Malaysia. In the past few years, she and I had kept in rueful, symbolic contact, mainly through Christmas cards, so I had her address. I took my time about writing to her but, having done so, became restlessly impatient for her answer.

It was a long while coming, and meanwhile I fantasized about it with morbid precision. 'Funny you should ask,' she would write, 'because, yes, there *was* this man who used to come to the mill-house. A dark man, middle-aged, with a little beard. Welsh, I think. He used to call quite often that summer, always when you were out, and he told us not to tell you because, he said, he was a very old friend of yours and was preparing something that would be a surprise for you . . .' ('*It was a sort of secret. He wanted it that way, said it was better . . .*' Simone's voice, so long ago, thin and wretched, tainted by the degraded act of another.)

'He seemed very keen on being friends with us, a bit treacly, I didn't really like him. I didn't like to say at the time, but it's been worrying me ever since . . .'

However, when Sophie's reply at last came, it was full of enthusiastic news of the birth of her first child. I felt that my awkward enquiry must have arrived at exactly the wrong moment. She wanted to rejoice, and here I was driving her back into the past, asking her to re-live something she had once, with bitten lips and tears, been inclined to believe had been partly her fault (– 'If only I hadn't left Marigold on her own because I was going to Paris.' Unspoken – *if only I hadn't agreed to meet that boyfriend there, I knew that was a bad idea at the time* . . . 'Then everything might have been different.')

But Sophie was a good little soul, and having got the excitement of the first and second stages of labour and the personality of her baby off her chest, she finally got down to answering my question.

'. . . I really can't tell you much about that last week because, although of course I remember masses about Marigold and will never forget her, what we did wasn't all that different from what we'd always done at the mill-house. I know we went swimming and for bike rides and played our guitars together. She taught me *The Four Maries* (which now always reminds me of her; it seems so dreadfully appropriate) – and she was learning a new setting to *Thomas the Rhymer* which was quite difficult because it had chords in antithesis to the main melody – I expect you remember it? What else – well, we ate up the rest of the food left in the fridge and Marigold made some sorrel soup and I made a cake. She went for walks sometimes on her own, but she'd always liked to do that. I don't remember anyone else calling, though of course they might have.

'There is just one thing I can think of. On the last day I was there, Marigold got a letter (in English) from an old friend of her mother's. This friend said she was passing through the area and heard Marigold was there and might call and see her. I remember Marigold saying it was a bit difficult because she didn't know at all who this woman was – Daphne Something, I think. We couldn't read the signature properly.

'After the awful accident, I never thought to mention this because it just didn't seem relevant. I only really remembered it now, years later, when your letter came. You ask if anyone called at the mill-house while I was there, but apart from the postman and the baker this is really the only possible person I can think of. I hope it is some help.

'Well, I must close now. John and I are due to move into our new flat on the 24th. I am so pleased, as it will make life with Baby much easier and there will be room for Amah to live in . . .'

Sophie, as I have said, was a good little girl: her daring Parisian excursion had been untypical. That was one reason among several why I had felt fairly tranquil leaving her and Marigold alone to keep each other company. No doubt, now, she was busy being a good wife to her John, intrepidly facing a lifetime of arbitrary moves round foreign lands, a succession of new flats, amahs, ayahs, mammies and local languages. It was evident that it simply had not occurred to her now, any more than it had at the time, that Marigold's mother's old friend might not have been a woman.

It is intoxicating to have your obsessional fantasies reinforced, even partially and uncertainly. It becomes addictive. Six years before, if Sophie had suddenly seen fit to tell me that she thought a person who might have had a name like Daphne had been due to call on Marigold at the mill-house, I too would have thought little of it, brushing the detail aside in impatient misery. But now, in connection with other things, the information seemed like startling corroborative evidence. Up till then I had recognized the logical fallacy in taking such evidence for proof when the first premise has been a wild one. Now, evidently, I had passed some psychological frontier.

I had left behind the life in which I believed Marigold's death to have been a brutal but meaningless happening. Because the indications that the driver of the car had been Evan Brown now seemed to me so strong, it literally did not occur to me that this in itself might have been a bizarre coincidence, even as almost all accidental deaths and many murderous ones depend upon a chain of coincidence.

It did not occur to me to think that Evan, after all, might have had no dark plan of his own: that he might simply have picked up by the roadside a girl appearing to need a lift – a missed bus? A non-appearing taxi? – without having the least idea who she was. Instead, I could see now only a dreadful symmetry. All those years before, I had ordered Evan and Joyce out of my car and told them to find their own way back to Paris. Then, after Simone's revelation, I had threatened Evan with the police and had told him that, if he ever showed his face at the mill-house again, it would be the worse for him.

'You bastard,' he had said. 'I'll get even with you. You wait.'

And I had waited, but not for long, since the showiness of the remark seemed to me patently shallow. After he had stolen my Simca and landed it in a ditch the police *had* come . . . In my youthful innocence, my attempted reasonableness, I had believed that that would be the end of the matter. Or wanted to.

If I had looked harder into my own heart, even then, at

my own sense of wordless, physical, male vengefulness, I might have come to a different conclusion. Not necessarily the right one. But one more in keeping with the present time.

Now I could see with telescopic clarity Evan, hitchhiking his way back to Paris: the young, dark man at a distance, once again alone, whom I had already seen wandering over a graveyard on a Welsh hillside. On the roads to Paris, he must have believed I had set the police on his trail. He had alienated another group of useful friends, ditched another compliant girl: the murderous justification of resentment must have been fermenting within him.

Or so I, from the depths of my own concentrated emotion, surmised.

Opportunists like Evan do not let anything go to waste, including, I reasoned, hatred. The determination to turn defeat into victory would be Evan's own form of morality. It looked now to me as if, in spite of his initial defeat in the Creuse at my hands, he had returned there years later under a different identity, cultivated old Maryk – he whose carved bird he had once stolen and then broken . . . If I was right in this supposition, all my suppositions, then how wonderfully neat and satisfying it must have seemed to him, covertly observing the mill-house from afar, when the long-deferred opportunity at last came, planning the casual geniality with which he would introduce himself, an old family friend. ('*It was a sort of secret. He wanted it that way. Said it was better.*') Perhaps, I fantasized, he had crouched inconspicuous in some heathery eyrie above the river, had watched for my departure, had seen me, had heard the echo of my voice as I kissed the girls goodbye and drove off, a man alone . . .

This time round, he was the one there, with a car, readily offering a lift – to the bus, to Argenton, to Châteauroux even. And the person needing a lift was Marigold, my daughter, my bird, the one he would break in two.

First my Simone. Then, a lifetime later, my Marigold. Bastard. Foul-hearted, filthy, desecrating bastard.

★

So, I attributed to Evan my own inexorably growing sense of purpose. So, somewhere along the line of investigation, perhaps quite recently, I had ceased to regard Marigold's death as chance. Like Jacquou long ago, I had to make an on-balance assumption either of guilt or innocence. I made the huge assumption of guilt, and the rest followed. Rough justice, but the best that, in the circumstances, I could offer.

A car door can be opened on a crucial bend. A passenger can be hit and pushed out. If no assiduous pathologist thinks to look for the evidences of assault, they may not be noted. The incredulity and then the terror as the attack takes place, the horrified struggle of the last few moments of life, may leave no identifiable traces.

You bastard. I'll get even with you. You wait.

Thirty years had passed, the heart of a lifetime. During it, certain things had taken root in me. And grown. And therefore in Evan too, I assumed, in Evan too.

I had to establish and verify the link with Maryk, since, without it, Evan-David's presence in the Creuse in recent years became purely conjectural. But I too waited. I could afford to. Whatever it was, exactly, that was evolving inside me, with a life of its own, seemed to be doing so now without my conscious volition. I had a strong feeling that I must not force this process, must not be impatient. So, I bided my time, waiting simply for another natural opportunity for me to revisit France. At the end of the summer, Marigold would have been dead seven years.

Meanwhile, in that late winter and spring of 1984, I contemplated one or two other moves which, even if I did not regard them as essential, might be useful. One day I nerved myself to ask Lewis if he still had a copy of the post-mortem report on Marigold.

From his immediate expression, I expected him to say that he did not. I thought in that instant, 'I shall tell him I don't believe him – that I know well he keeps documents for ever. I shall tell him he's been cowardly all along in this business – that he never pushed the French authorities as he

207

should have done, asked the questions he should have asked – '

But I was saved from making this manic onslaught by Lewis's honesty. He said heavily: 'Yes, I've still got it – somewhere. But I wish you wouldn't, Tom. I do wish, for your sake, you wouldn't.'

'I know you do,' I said, my ready anger against him suddenly evaporating into reciprocated tenderness. 'But I must, Lewis, I must.'

'Mmm . . . Well must you this afternoon? Because I'd have to turn the attic upside down to get at the old files.'

'No. Not this afternoon. But you must promise me you'll look it out for me when I ask again.'

On one level I flinched as much as ever at the thought of flat, irrefutable words the report would contain. Contusions and fractures and cranial haemorrhages . . . The language of a broken body. No, I was in no hurry that afternoon. But it calmed me to have extracted from Lewis a promise that I could look at it when I wanted to. I told him so.

'Well I haven't much choice, have I?' he said grumpily. 'Since, if I refuse, you could no doubt write off yourself to the French police records for a copy. You're hardly one of my more helpless clients, Tom.'

This idea had also occurred to me. I had turned it over in my mind, but had, after some further meditation, rejected it. In the same way, though less consciously, I had rejected in Paris the idea of calling at the police station in the Marais to see what they could tell me of Monsieur Euze. Evidently I had developed, along with my preoccupation, some sense of circumspection, even cunning.

As the winter ebbed, two things began to happen, both of which, by coincidence, reinforced my opinion of my own insight and prescience. One event was to do with my Aunt Madge and the other with Melvyn Baines.

I say 'my' insight and prescience, but the idea that Auntie might take very badly to death when it came to the point had originated with Hermione rather than with me. However I had adopted it, and it had settled like a jigsaw piece into my current view of things. So that when I received a distracted letter from Edinburgh in February, speaking of going into the Royal Infirmary for 'tests', it felt to me like something always known which had long cast its distortion backwards on her life. Why, after all, should anyone go to such lengths to convince themselves the dead are alive unless death inspires in them a particular terror?

In April, during Ann's school holidays, we flew up together on the shuttle to see Aunt Madge. It meant that we could go there and back in one day. I have enough nights in hotels travelling in the way of work; in any case Aunt Madge might have been hurt had she known we were staying in one, but Ann did not think that we ought to burden our elderly invalid by staying with her. I was not going to suggest that we stay with Humphrey and Carmen.

In the event, however, I don't believe it occurred to Aunt Madge to wonder if or where we were staying. She had lost a great deal of weight: both her clothes and her skin sagged on her, and the plump rouged and powdered mask I had known for years seemed to have slipped, revealing underneath the cranium of a shrivelled old woman. But it wasn't the weight-loss that shocked me but the horror in the eyesockets. By a cruel but logical irony, she who had wanted so much to believe that beyond death lay a cosy pleasure park now apparently found herself already, in this life, in hell at the prospect.

'It's *It*, you know,' she said, staring at me. Her appalled, squeamish tone suggested cholera or syphilis. Another analysis might have indicated that the core of the affliction was fear itself.

'You mean, it's cancer? Well yes, we supposed so.' In fact I had already spoken on the 'phone to her consultant, a brisk Scot who, no doubt rightly, regarded the case as an everyday one and extensive treatments as inappropriate.

She flinched from the taboo word.

'Don't *say* it, Tom. I can't bear it. You don't understand.'

I knew I was not really being kind, not as many people, including Ann, would have been: Auntie should have chosen to speak to her, not me. However I was her nephew and she had picked, presumably deliberately, a moment when Ann was out in the kitchen washing up the lunch. I felt mutinously that too much was being expected of me. Simone had been not quite forty when she had died of cancer. Aunt Madge was in her late seventies. Not from me would she milk any response of shocked horror.

Trying to find some meeting-ground, some acceptable basis for commiseration – the supportive, efficient male – I said: 'Are you worried about having a lot of pain? Because I don't think you should be. They're much better these days at controlling it, and there's no reason why, when the time comes, you shouldn't have all the dope you want. Would you like me to speak to your doctor about that?'

But it wasn't pain that was worrying her. To my surprise (I have always been rather afraid of pain and bodily weakness myself, mainly because I have so little real experience of it) she hardly seemed to have envisaged the later stages of her illness, and was unresponsive to further queries I tried regarding nursing homes or hospices. Her face crumpled, tears spilling like a child's from the puckered lids.

'I don't want to die, Tommy. I just don't want to die.'

'We all die,' I said crossly, after a pause.

I should have moved across and put my arm round her. I could not bear to touch her. It was no longer just a lack of sympathy I felt for her but a disgust, almost a kind of squeamish horror on my own side. No doubt there were complicated reasons for this. As Ann knows, I am not good when faced with emotional demands. But what I thought consciously was that Aunt Madge's present mental state, near the end of her life, was, after all, a sickening indictment of that life. It was disillusioning.

Ann had come back into the room and may have heard my unhelpful remark. She looked from one to another of us. I got up and retreated to the kitchen in turn, leaving them to it.

We sat in the airport café, too early, waiting for our 'plane to be called. Ann said, with the nearest to a tone of reproach she ever uses towards me:

'Of course she minds dying, Tom. It's only natural.'

'Is it? It doesn't seem so to me.'

It was Ann's turn to look distressed. I could see her busy equating my professed equanimity in the face of death with depression or general dissatisfaction with life, which of course was not what I had meant. Furthermore, she tends to take my state of mind as a comment on herself, and though I tried to explain to her once or twice when we were first married that I do not see marriage in those terms – that the notion of the married being responsible for 'making each other happy' has always seemed to me fatuous – she persists in her idea.

I made an effort, and took her small hand, with its little round nails, in mine.

'People who've had a fair chunk of life,' I said patiently, 'shouldn't make a song and dance about it ending. That's greedy.'

'Of course in theory I know what you mean . . . When I was a little girl, the sort of age I am now seemed quite old.' (She was approaching forty.) 'And when I count it up I see I *have* lived years and years already and done quite a lot of things and travelled and so on, and been with you . . . But I still feel I want to do and see a lot more – oh, masses – and I have the feeling I still shall even when I'm an old lady.'

Because I could not share this, I went on holding her hand without saying anything. It felt, irrationally, almost as if I were saying goodbye to her, as if I, not my aunt, were the one looking on the end. With Aunt Madge's departure, my last traditional spectator would be gone: the last of that audience of elders we carry from youth, even when far removed from them, the essential ones for whom we mount our life's performance.

After a bit Ann said: 'Of course if we had' – corrected herself bravely and went on – 'if we'd had a child, I expect I might feel differently – more as if I'd had something solid to show for my life. But then I'd want to go on living anyway, to see him or her grow up and see the grandchildren . . .'

After a moment more she squeezed my hand hard. I did not need to look at her, I knew her eyes would be shiny with tears – for herself, for me, for the ever-unmentionable Simone? At the stage I had reached myself, both openly, so to speak, and within my heart, incapable as I was then of love, I was an appalling burden and brake on her natural happiness, poor dear girl, but I do not think that this view of our marriage ever once occurred to her.

I wanted to say something nice to her that would yet be true. At last I said:

'I'm glad you came up here with me today.'

I was still incubating my Theory. Or did I now mean my Plan? Perhaps, by then, it had turned conclusively into a plan. Or, at least, an intention. I know that, a night or two afterwards, it came to me that, in spite of what I had said to Ann, I was now less indifferent to my own future than I had been for several years. I wanted actively to go on living for the moment, for a particular reason. I had a mission to accomplish.

I needed to get back to France. Alone.

But meanwhile, that summer, I had to make several more visits to Edinburgh, till my aunt, back in the Infirmary, faded on waves of morphine into a state in which the Other Side no longer even interested her. At the last, life becomes very tiny: a mattress, sheets, walls, a few hovering faces, a cup and spoon. Such shrinkage is perhaps rather a betrayal of all those human passions, convictions and yearnings by which we set so much store, but when it comes to us we do not see it like that.

I found that not only was I glad that I was alive, I was glad still to be in possession of my own passion and purpose.

In between these journeys north, and interwoven with them now in my memory so that they are no longer quite distinct but seem like two counterpointed dramas of dissolution, the Melvyn Baines saga continued.

During the past year life had been exciting for Melvyn. My refusal to rubber-stamp his allegations of sexual abuse and my subsequent letter to him had not perceptibly daunted him; indeed, within a few months of that occasion, his views had spread beyond the professional circles in which he moved and had attracted enthusiastic media notice. He became something of a celebrity: television producers invited him to discuss this Hidden Evil in our midst; a newspaper published a eulogistic profile of him in which the word 'fearless' several times occurred. I have noticed that people are only described as 'fearless' when they are in fact saying something that many people are currently avid to hear. My unkind one-time remark to Ann, that Melvyn had a highly developed sense of the mood of the moment, seemed to be validated.

'The moment' continued for the best part of a year. However the acclaim of his colleagues was less uncritical. What I had been accustomed to refer to as the Melvyn Baines Fan Club began to be paralleled by another loosely constituted body which I christened the Get-Baines Group. You might suppose that I would myself be a leading conspirator in this movement, but you would be wrong. With sufficient doctors, teachers, psychologists and social workers already muttering in corners that Dr Baines was too big for his boots and wrong-headed anyway, it was unnecessary for me (as I told Ann) to say a word more. I sat back and waited for it all to pass. I hoped, with vague malevolence, that something would occur to make Melvyn look a fool, but since life does not normally work so obligingly I did not really expect it. I was therefore on the public level 'not surprised', but on the private one taken aback and gratified, when something did.

In the early summer I had just returned from another visit to Edinburgh, when Ann said that there was a rumour running round her staff room: a complaint had been brought against Dr Baines himself. A mother, whose daughter was being seen at his Centre for disruptive behaviour in school, claimed that Dr Baines had cuddled this daughter and made 'an improper suggestion' to her.

At first I did not take this allegation seriously. That is to say, I could believe the mother had made it, but such charges are not uncommon: educational and medical authorities get a steady trickle of them, usually unsubstantiated. Melvyn, with his own over-wrought views, must have been aware of the chronic risk he ran. I suspected that he had stirred both mother and daughter up emotionally simply by being as he was, asking the questions that he did, but I did not want to say so publicly since the man was obviously now in need of protection. I assumed that the other staff of the Centre would close ranks and support him.

But it appeared that they were not doing so. At any rate, the allegation did not evaporate but hung in the air, thickening slightly. The police had a look at it, but were disinclined to bring a charge; perhaps they had no firm evidence. But the tale broke sensationally in the press all the same when a busybodying MP took advantage of Parliamentary privilege to name Melvyn at House of Commons question time. It began to look very much, I said to Ann, as if it had abruptly become Melvyn's own turn to be the Hidden Evil in our midst. Ann said it wasn't funny. Quite right, I said cheerfully.

Two days later I had a visit in my office from Birgit, Melvyn's wife. Her normally pink-and-white Nordic complexion today bore a resemblance to an albino rabbit: she must have been crying much of the night. Since I had never seen any sign of emotion in her before, merely a flaccid smile as she chewed the cud at Melvyn's side, I now warmed to her a little. After all – poor girl. I made gentlemanly efforts, sitting her down in a chair, patting her shoulder, offering coffee, telling my secretary we were not to be disturbed. I believe I even lent her my handkerchief.

Would I stand up for Melvyn publicly? Life had become awful: journalists were camping on their doorstep and photographing her and the children going in and out. The police had been round again –

Fresh burst of tears. More pattings, more nose-blowings. I fetched her a glass of water. Finally she burst out, almost accusingly:

'He *needs* someone like you to speak for him. Someone with a good reputation who will be believed. People have le

214

him down. He seems to have no one who is any use on his side – '

The appeal was a flattering one. I said as kindly as I could:

'But what would you want me to say?'

'Well, that Melvyn would never, never have done that thing, what they say he's done.' Her English fracturing under the strain, she stared at me as if amazed I needed to be told.

'My dear, I can't say that.'

'*Oh.*' She clenched my wet handkerchief to her. I expected her to shred it. 'So you too are in league against him. I am sorry for coming! I did not know.'

'Don't be silly,' I said tetchily, wishing after all that she would revert to her usual unresponsive manner: 'It isn't a matter of *for* or *against* – ' (It was, of course, but it should not have been.) 'I mean that I can't possibly say what you want because I'm not in a position to have any views on the matter. I don't work with Melvyn; I've never worked with him. I know nothing in detail about his methods. It isn't my field. How can I say what might or might not have gone on one morning at the Centre months ago? I mean – ' I added quickly, for she was now glaring at me, 'how can I say what words or gestures Mrs Whatsit and her kid may or may not have misinterpreted? Do try to see it from my point of view.'

Of course I was asking too much. Why should she see it from my point of view? But she calmed down to the extent of saying wretchedly:

'But couldn't you just say in a general sort of way that Melvyn isn't someone who'd ever do anything – not nice?'

Not nice. Dear God. I wondered what fuzzed echo I was hearing of some Swedish genteelism for depravity. I said sadly – I found that after all I felt sad, not triumphant or retributive:

'You know, Birgit, one should never presume to say that about anyone. Even someone one knows really well, much better than I know Melvyn. Oh, I don't mean I suspect him' – I did of course, vaguely, but hastened on – 'Don't run away with that idea. But I just think one can't make such a confident statement about something so complicated as – as human nature.'

I had been going to say 'as sexual desire' but, inhibited by the sniffing, salt-mucus-smelling rabbit in the chair, I substituted the more anodyne phrase. As it happened, I had for some reason always found Birgit herself sexually off-putting. 'You see,' I added, defending myself against the mute criticism coming from her, 'very often when something like this happens – or when a man goes berserk and knifes someone, or simply disappears, leaving his family in the lurch – all his friends and relatives tell the police they're sure there must be another explanation, that they "know" Joe couldn't have done such a thing. But they're wrong. Just wrong. We *can't* know these things about other people, so we shouldn't pretend to . . . I'm sorry, Birgit, I really am.'

She left, soon after, sourly resenting me. I did not blame her.

No, we can't know what others just might or might not do. We can't even necessarily know that about ourselves.

Everyone, I suppose, has fantasies they would feel embarrassed to share. To assume that we would all like, given the right circumstances and provocation, to act these fantasies out, has always seemed to me facile: half-baked psychiatry. Most fantasies, I suspect, *can* only exist where they are, in the comfort and privacy of the imagination. Exposed to reality, they would instantly wilt. But it does seem that some fantasies carry within them the potential to become real, and that one cannot tell which they are or who may be harbouring them. You cannot necessarily even know till the moment comes if your own fantasies carry this extra coding.

Nor, if you pull back at the last minute, aborting action and driving the fantasy back within its own realm, do you know afterwards, in your weak relief and confusion, whether you really were about to go ahead and transpose day-dream fully into reality or whether this too was just part of the dream.

*
216

I had dismissed Birgit's cry about people being 'in league' against Melvyn as paranoia either on her part or his. However it was not far wrong after all. The following Sunday a newspaper ran a front-page story about 'revelations' from a retired social worker regarding 'the Director of a Child Guidance Centre in the Greater London area' and previous 'irregularities known to colleagues'. In deference to the libel laws, the piece was couched in rather confusing, allusive terms and Melvyn was not named – but, thanks to the vociferous MP, his name was well-known already.

The social worker was not named either, but her identity at once became an open secret in Melvyn's world, since she was quite happy to identify herself off the record. It was Shirley Gilchrist.

'Hell,' a cynical colleague remarked to me, 'hath no fury like a woman scorned.' Evidently the detail of Shirley's long-term passion for Melvyn was more widely known than I had realized.

'Do you think she's made it all up?' I asked. I wasn't so much interested in what he thought of Shirley as in what further light his reply might cast on Melvyn.

'You mean – was there really any laying on of hands? Dunno. But I wouldn't be surprised. I always thought he was a bit of a barmy bugger under all that smooth chat. Got no common sense. If you know what I mean?'

I did know.

'It's typical, isn't it?' he said, cheerfully ruminative, 'that this Gilchrist woman used to be all over Baines when they were working together and now she dishes the dirt on him. Spiteful, I'd say, whether it's true *or* false . . . I think Baines'll have a real problem on his hands now.'

'So do I.'

Evidently the police and the Director of Public Prosecutions had been thinking too. Four days, and another insinuatory newspaper article later, Melvyn was arrested. He was charged with various offences of indecency toward juveniles. There were headlines, and his picture on the front page of the evening paper.

I was surprised when Birgit telephoned me that evening. She must have been desperate indeed if she came back to me.

When I'd finished talking to her, to Melvyn, to the police and to Melvyn's lawyer, I came back into the room where Ann was correcting fifth-form essays on *Romeo and Juliet* and told her I had agreed to stand as bail surety for Melvyn.

'How much?' said Ann, after a pregnant pause.

'Five thousand. He's on bail in his own recognition for a much larger sum, as I understand. His house must be worth a bit, so I suppose that's all right. But the Court wanted a separate surety – someone to keep an eye on him, in other words. Exert moral pressure on him to stop him doing a bunk.'

Ann said, shocked:

'But how can you do that?'

'Just by being there, I suppose . . . The police and the lawyer think that Melvyn won't skip off to the South Sea Islands if he knows that would land me with a bill for five thousand pounds, and, who knows, they may be right? I think Melvyn does have his principles, such as they are. And, on a more cynical view, if he did that he really would have cooked his goose with everybody, and that isn't what he wants. He thinks he's going to prove his innocence, you see.'

'But do *you* think he's innocent?' said Ann.

She was right, the question ought to have been the heart of the matter. But I had not really wanted to ask myself.

'I don't know,' I said after a while. 'And I'm not sure Melvyn knows any longer either.'

'How did he sound?' said Ann after a pause.

'Oh – a bit manic. Odd, anyway. Over-talkative but distracted. Not surprising in the circumstances. And then, when I said OK I would put up the surety for him, desperately, embarrassingly grateful. I don't think he'd really expected I would.'

'Actually,' said Ann, rather distantly, 'why have you?'

'Ho, hum, I thought *you* were the one who liked Melvyn,' I said unfairly.

218

'Well I used to think you were rather mean about him, before all this happened . . . But – after all, Tom. Five thousand.'

'We won't have to pay it. Not that it'd break us if we did.' Between our two salaries, Ann and I are quite comfortably off. And what is all the money for in the end anyway these days? But Ann doesn't think like that.

'Well I hope you're right,' she said. 'But you still haven't told me why it has to be you. Couldn't someone else – ?'

'Ann, that was my first thought too, and apparently there isn't anyone else. No colleague now prepared to come forward – people have turned against him in a big way, you know, because they're afraid his mistakes will rub off on them, and he's made them feel foolish for being taken in by him. And no friends, apparently, or none with any money. And of course all Birgit's family are in Sweden. But as a matter of fact I don't get the feeling Melvyn's ever had many friends anyway. Certainly he and Birgit now seem very much on their own. And bloody pathetic . . . It was really that that made me agree to do it. If someone hadn't, you see, Melvyn would stay in custody, and that miserable wife of his would just have had to go back home tonight to their house and be there for weeks and weeks alone with the kids. She had them with her at the police station, I could hear one of them yelling in the background. No one to leave them with, I imagine. Well, in all the circumstances . . .'

'You're too good-hearted Tom,' said Ann warmly, if still reproachfully. 'You really are.'

Melvyn's lawyer would soon be at the door with the bail papers for my signature. I went to make some coffee, feeling a fraud.

All right, why? Showing off, patronizing Melvyn when he's down, playing Decent Elder Brother (a favourite rôle, since I never had the opportunity to try it in childhood), playing the system (another favourite occupation of mine), keeping faith with my own self-image, my own self-esteem – but then a lot of being 'good-hearted' must come into this category.

Yes. All this, no doubt, as well as the more presentable

reasons I had already given to Ann. But I was confusedly aware, as I waited for the kettle to begin to whisper and then sing, of another layer in all this, a more specific one, knotted and dark. Something unadmitted that I wanted to placate? Something that was a memory but also like something that had not quite happened: a fear, a possibility, perhaps a threat. As when you surface from a troubling dream, and struggle for a few minutes with the knowledge both that it was only a dream and that it announced a truth that has previously been buried . . .

I saw it now in the same hallucinatory, distanced way that I had seen Evan-David wandering in a Welsh graveyard, far off but clear; and had known his purpose as if I were also within him. Only, this time, it was myself I saw, and I was both within and without this self. I was walking in the river meadow by the mill-house.

Other people had been there in the days before, but they had left. Marigold and I had been swimming in the river, and I had gone briefly back to the house wearing my wet shorts with a shirt pulled over them. I was returning now across the meadows: the remains of an exotic sunset lit one end of the sky, but elsewhere the dark had almost come. Much of the summer had been wet, the river was high for the season and the grass long as it brushed against my legs; but that day had been hot and even now, when the temperature had dropped, the air reverberated with the creatures of heat: dragonflies, may-bugs, cicadas. A late bird was still calling from the big elm; I stopped a moment to listen and to breathe the dank scent of the river.

Marigold's voice called from below the bank:

'*There* you are, Daddy. I'm just getting cold.'

I approached to the edge. She was standing on the sandspit rubbing one foot with a towel, reduced by the coming-on of night to little more than a silhouette, a pale line of shoulder and back, silvery planes of limb. She still wore, I suppose, the miniature bikini she had bought that year in Argenton. She was not quite fifteen but as tall, now, as her mother had been, and the same slight build. It was the summer after Simone's death.

220

'You should have followed me up to the house if you were cold,' I said. I jumped heavily down beside her.

'I wanted you to dry me.'

Her tone was matter-of-fact and childish. So was the request. I had been ritualistically bear-hugging and rubbing her dry after swims since always. Not, however, this year.

Did I say, this time, as I had perhaps before, 'Dry yourself, you big baby!' Did I, an indulgent but prudent father, remove myself to the bank again, telling her to pick up her clothes before the dew descended on them? I don't know. I don't know.

What I see in my mind, separate from myself, now in long shot, now in close-up, is myself with my arms round Marigold in a violent embrace, her small shape crumpled by my strength and weight, my fingers brown and time-worn against her whiteness, her face a pale blur in the dark below my chest. And what I feel within myself – can feel now, years after – is the known yet never entirely known scent of her skin, her damp hair, herself, herself.

No. I do not think anything very terrible happened. Not terrible. Desperately I prod at memory and imagination takes over – but I do not think that anything happened. I know I was suddenly consumed with feeling and – must I call it desire? Carnal desire I suppose it must have been too, since that had lain almost dormant within me since Simone's dying, and no doubt the mindless springs of life were now inexorably renewing themselves in me. But for a few seconds my desire to possess her went beyond that, into a dimension where I wanted to absorb her, smother her, take her into me, destroy her even, if that would keep her mine for ever.

Then, with a cry of protest, she escaped. Or did I, terrified by the strength of my own feeling, put her abruptly from me?

– Or did we never really quite reach this point of conflict except in my dark subsequent fantasy, but each retrieved ourselves, shocked, from the brink of emotion, gathered our clothes and made our way in sedate, self-conscious

221

Indian file across the darkening meadow to the lighted house?

The most extraordinary paradox, said Hermione. The body's corruption, she said. It is the temple of the soul, the only thing we have to venerate and which must not be desecrated. Yet the body is not made to last, she said. She meant: it can rot. Be rotted.

She was talking Christianity, not human love. But I interpreted it on that level too. And she saw, and changed the conversation.

Marigold's body. Flesh of my flesh. The thing I loved more than I could love anything else. The thing I most needed to possess yet needed, even more, in shrinking horror, not to possess, not to desecrate. Not to corrupt.

. . . *It cometh up like a flower and like a flower is cut down.* My Marigold.

'*All flesh is grass,*' the Preacher says. Yes, in the end. But she is not grass. She lies in a wet vault in Limoges, unviewable and by now unrecognizable. A thing. Like the dead girl in 'Jacquou le Croquant' – '. . . *perdant toute forme humaine, tombant en décomposition* . . .' Possessed and destroyed by corruption. This world's corruption. An act of man. Did he desire her too? Lay hands on her, as he did with Simone before her, try –. Was that originally to be his long-prepared revenge, and only when she thrust him away did killing replace it? Did he?

Or was the repetition in my own heart? In my own darkest, most agonized dreams, Simone and Marigold are the same person.

Enough. No more.

PART VI

After we had spent part of our summer holiday clearing up my aunt's house in Edinburgh, we drove further north for a few days, into the highlands. It seemed a good opportunity, for I had an idea that I, at any rate, would never have a reason to return to those parts. We did not stay away very long, however, as I was planning to take some time off again in October to go to France. An international conference in Lyon on language teaching had provided me with the pretext I needed.

When we came back at the end of August to our hot, quiet house in London, the police appeared on our doorstep within a few hours. I was disconcerted. Melvyn's case was not due to come to Court till November.

But Melvyn, it seemed, had lost confidence, one empty summer day, in his own power to prove his innocence. He had persuaded Birgit to take the children away for a holiday with her family in Sweden, and then had efficiently killed himself in his kitchen. The police were kindly coming to tell me – perhaps even to assure me, in case I was about to ask them irritable questions, that his action had been nothing to do with them. *Please Sir, it wasn't our fault, Sir. We didn't do anything* . . . These days all police, except for the Sergeant Pelhams, are young. The echoes of a lifetime of schoolboys rose in my mind.

When they had left, Ann said to me, embarrassed and subdued:

'It sounds awfully callous to ask – but will we lose our five thousand now?'

I laughed aloud.

'Good God – you don't think I'd have talked so sympathetically about him to the police if that had been the case? No, no – it wasn't part of my duty to stop Melvyn from killing himself. That's the end of it. We all get let off the hook now: the police, the local education authority, Melvyn too, in a sense. Though not much of a let-off, for him.'

Ann said sadly:

'Everyone will think he was guilty now. Won't they?'

'Oh, he must have known that, poor sod,' I said easily; though in fact I do not believe one can tell what suicides really know about the message of their own action and its finality.

I felt light. It was as if I too had been working obliquely toward some crisis, some fate – and now Melvyn had sprung the trap for me. Had acted for me. Or had freed me for some action of my own.

So, in late October, I drove in a hired French car across the autumn fields of central France. I had duly put in an appearance at the conference in Lyon. Now I was making my way westwards to the Creuse.

I had seldom approached the area from this direction. But all the same, as I neared it, the small towns and villages became ghostly familiar: either I had driven through all of them before, one way or another, on excursions over the last thirty years, or they had finally all become for me one, an irreducible rural habitat, place of zero summer and every other season. A curving street lined with irregular, low, pitched-roof buildings opening out into some sort of square; a cracked church bell chiming, flowers in pots, a war-memorial, a garish poster for a local event, a whiff of woodsmoke, a café bright with plastic chairs . . . And a shop or two, these days with newish façades papering the old stone, but still as ever advertising *Vin fou* – 'Mad Wine' – and *Laines de Pingouin* – 'Penguin Wool'. When Marigold was small, Simone and I used to joke with her that it really did come from penguins.

Penguin. Ah, Penguin! I had meant to contact Amanda Goring again; out of friendship, or desire to make efforts for other prisoners on her list, or perhaps in vague masculine intent – whatever that means. She could easily have been my daughter.

Yes. Anyway . . . I had not contacted her. I regretted this

a little, now, when it was too late. But perhaps it was better so.

I stopped in one village at random to buy some provisions and to drink a glass of Mad Wine – thin red stuff imported from Algeria, nothing like Jacquou's purplish local brew which we called the Real Wine. But I knew from the hilly roads lined with oaks and Spanish chestnuts through which I had been passing, and the pinkish light that was now, in the late afternoon, clothing the landscape, that I was in the right countryside. I was home.

And there, on the wall of the café, as if in travesty of what I had found again, was an eye-catching poster: a rendition of an autumn wood, all lush reds and golds and mauves, advertising an exhibition of the work of 'local artists'.

I was disconcerted by the phrase. Gripped as I was by the past, it had not occurred to me that there might, by now, be more than one man appropriating to himself the local artist rôle. The café proprietor assured me that there were a number of them, that the Creuse was becoming 'quite a little centre'.

It looked as peaceful and unenterprising as ever, to me. I pointed out that the dates of the exhibition were long past.

Yes, but his wife liked the picture, so he had left the poster up. Beautiful, wasn't it? Real, you might say.

Did the proprietor recall a Polish painter called Maryk who had worked in the area for many years. Was he still alive?

The man became vague. He thought he recalled the name, but there were a number of painters now, like he said. Anyway he and his wife had only been in these parts for five years. But there was a man had a studio several villages away that attracted visitors in the summer, like, though not much now in the off-season. Might that be the one? He named the place.

It was indeed where Maryk had had his workshop, in the old barn that Jacquou had found for him.

I tried another name on the man, but it meant nothing to him. A lot of these painters seemed to be foreigners, he said

225

tolerantly. Perhaps a lot of people painted in my country, did they? Indeed perhaps I was an artist myself?

Yes, I agreed, yes actually I was. This satisfied both of us.

Covering my tracks.

By the time I reached the mill-house, it was getting dark. I had not written to Paul and Hermione to tell them I was going there; I was counting on avoiding the unlikely chance of them being there at that time themselves, and it was all right. No vehicle stood in the yard, where the autumn grass had pushed up undisturbed. In the beds at the side, flowers, which Hermione must have gone on planting out there each year, had grown tall and tangled. The shutters were drawn at the windows. All the doors were locked. With my set of keys I unfastened the big outhouse; someone had tidied it since I had last seen it and there were some tiles, re-roofing spares, at one end. Contrary to old custom, I put my hired car away inside it. Then I let myself into the silent kitchen.

The next day I drove to the village I had known as Maryk's, but I avoided his barn which stood by itself on the edge of a wood. Instead I sought out the local Mayor; Mayors are numerous in France, as every village has one. The Mairie, of course, was shut; I was directed by a notice to a relentlessly modern bungalow. The Mayor wore a cap indoors, and looked as if he would have been more comfortable in a plainer home without mock-leather chairs chosen by his wife and daughter. I think I caught him just as he was contemplating an after-lunch nap. He was not especially pleased to see me, but resigned himself to answering my queries.

Yes, he knew Monsieur Maryk. Everyone did. But he was old and ill now, in the hospital. The Mayor doubted if he would ever come out. Not too good in the head any longer, see.

I had been told he still had his workshop, though?

Yes, but it had been taken over by his apprentice. (Evidently it seemed quite in order to the Mayor that an artist should hand on his business, like a plumber or a garage-owner.)

Yes, the apprentice was a foreigner, like Maryk, but the Mayor thought that he too had lived in France for years. No, he couldn't call his name to mind right now. It might be written down in the Mairie but he wasn't sure of that either. It would depend who was paying the rates now, see.

I hinted that it might perhaps be possible to go round the corner to the Mairie and look this up, but the Mayor replied that Thursday afternoons were when the Mairie was open. 'Today's Friday, Monsieur.'

He stared firmly past me, an elderly peasant farmer who was not going to be pushed around by a stranger. I gazed at the bought-from-a-catalogue tapestry, an Alpine scene which dominated the small sitting room, and decided to take a chance.

'But if this apprentice has been here a long time he must have a *carte de séjour?*'

The Mayor resented me more openly:

'I didn't say he'd been here a long time. He comes and goes. We don't see much of him here in the village. And as for a *carte de séjour*, yes, I daresay he has one, but I wouldn't be knowing about that. You'd have to ask the police that, down at Gueret. I don't meddle in other people's affairs.'

An enthusiastic interest in other people's affairs is really the only requirement for being a French Mayor, besides basic literacy. This Mayor seemed to be fulfilling his rôle only minimally, if that, but, re-running the conversation in my mind after I had driven off again, I thought that his general lack of interest was perhaps just as well.

He had at least told me the whereabouts of the hospital where I would find Maryk. It was, I realized only as I arrived there, the place where we had visited Joyce after Evan's disappearance.

It was just the same. But also quite different. A new country hospital in the glass-and-concrete idiom of the 1970s had risen airily nearby; the ancient building, cleaned up and garnished with neat lawns and flower beds, had become an old people's home. This still seemed to be run by a religious order, but the crowding and squalor I recalled had been abolished. Pastel floor tiles lapped the

227

seventeenth-century pillars, partitions divided the echoing wards into tidy, four-bedded suites. I was shown into one of these by a portly teenage boy in an overall, who remarked with middle-aged kindness that it would be nice for Le Père Maryk to have a visitor for once.

As I approached the indicated bed, I thought that the Maryk I remembered would have felt more at home in the old place as it had been before. But the ruffian-like character in a dirty undershirt I expected to see rearing up like a bear from the pillows seemed to be no more either. The Maryk whose bony hand, extended to me automatically in vague bewilderment, I now shook, was much diminished: a shrunken old man in respectable pyjamas, more or less shaven, his sparse white hair neatly clipped. If he had not been pointed out to me I should not have known him. Only by looking into his remarkable eyes, faded by age to a baby blue, could I perceive the man I had once known.

I was a stranger to him of course. Even when I mentioned Jacquou's name, and Simone's, I elicited only the uncertain response of someone who wishes to be helpful but cannot call to mind the necessary information just at present, though he feels it to be lurking somewhere. Because I mentioned the painted chests – trying vainly to stir the deep waters of his memory – he decided that I must be a prospective customer, and attempted a brisk manner.

'I don't take on commissions any more, Monsieur. I've retired now – been ill, you see. But that's all right, I worked hard in my time, I made my pile . . .' He seemed to be saying more, but the old voice rambled off into a mutter.

'I'd like to show you some of my work, though,' he said suddenly, loudly, like a radio set coming back on station again. 'Nice things, I make, I take a lot of trouble. Birds and that . . . People like them. People like my pictures too.'

'I know. I like them very much.' I wished I could get this fact at least through to him, but his attention seemed to have drifted away again. In the opposite bed a corpulent old man lay, like a contented baby, while several female visitors gossiped in subdued voices above and around him.

'I don't have any materials here today,' said Maryk,

228

returning mentally to me again. 'If I had, I could show you . . .' He began to look restlessly around, leaning his fragile body perilously far over the edges of the bed. I was afraid he would fall out, and tried to settle him back against the pillows. He became distressed, and called a woman's name. The gossipers stopped momentarily to stare, and then the teenage boy reappeared. With a practised manner he soothed Maryk down, promising him: 'You shall go and get your materials tomorrow. Or Anya shall bring them tomorrow, if you're tired.'

'Tired . . .' agreed the old man obediently. 'Yes, I *am* tired and that's a fact. I've done my bit.' He shut his blue eyes. I said to the boy:

'Who's Anya?'

He shrugged. 'We don't know. He calls for her sometimes, but no one knows anybody of that name round here. We think perhaps it was someone once in his own country. A girl – a sister perhaps – or a servant . . . No one knows.'

He went away again. With eyes still shut, Maryk said distinctly:

'I should like to go out to the café.'

'I am very sorry,' I said, meaning it, 'that I can't take you out there.'

He opened his eyes, and looked candidly into mine.

'They don't like me saying I want to go to the café. They say I've got everything I want here. Of course that's true. But I still should like . . .' His voice petered out once more but then returned, with his stronger, more boastful tone:

'I can't complain,' he said. 'I've made my pile.'

'I hear,' I said, 'that you have a partner now to carry on the business.'

My voice sounded intense in my own ears, but of course Maryk did not notice.

'My partner . . .' he echoed vaguely, as if searching for the meaning of the word. Then suddenly, with a grin he found it. 'Ah-ha, yes, my partner! Well, I've taught him everything I know, you see. So now he can make the money.'

'That's good,' I said.

'And he's selling our stuff like hot cakes . . . I could say, like something else! But I won't offend your ears, Monsieur – ' The reedy voice collapsed again in weak chuckles. Senile tears poured from his child's eyes. I felt glad he could still produce even this travesty of his old manner.

'What is your partner called?' I asked.

'Who?' Maryk seemed suddenly lost again.

'Your partner – the one who's making all this money for you.'

'Oh, him . . . You know him, do you?'

'No,' I said carefully. 'I don't know him. But I should like to. Please will you tell me some more about him?'

'Wonderfully gifted young man . . . Mind you, I've taught him all I know. And now he's working for both of us.'

'That's good. I'm pleased for you . . . What did you say his name was?'

But Maryk had dropped into a mutter again. I studied the wrinkled, sun-dried old face, the sagging mouth, and thought that, on the other side of Europe, on the far side of his life, there had been someone called Anya, who had come when he called.

'Very dear!' he shouted suddenly.

'What?' He had made me jump.

'This place. Very dear. Kept in the lap of luxury, I am, as you see. Everything I want. So it's just as well, isn't it, that that partner of mine is making a fortune for us?'

I tried to steer him back to the topic of carved wood and pictures but, like an old gramophone sticking in one groove of the record, he would not be shifted.

'He seems to be destitute. It's the State that is paying for him here, or that's what I understand. I suppose the matter will be settled one way or another when he dies. If he does leave anything, the State will have a claim on it in payment for his time here. That's the system, you see.'

I had sought out the sister-in-charge in her office, where Saint Somebody presided, with moon-faced resignation, over filing cabinets. Sister spoke placidly enough; the financing of the hospital was not her affair anyway. I sensed some constraint there all the same, perhaps something she wanted to ask *me*. After a pause, she did.

'Are you by any chance related to him?'

'No. Just an old friend. I happened to be passing through the area.'

She sighed. 'I thought you weren't family. The poor soul doesn't seem to have anyone at all of his own.'

'Yes, I think that is the case. He used to say that, in fact, long ago. When he was in possession of all his wits, I mean.'

'You're the first visitor he's had in I don't know how long.'

'What about this partner he talks about?' I felt my heartbeat increase with a life of its own, as I thought *Now I'll hear, now* – I hurried on:

'I mean, surely he visits him?'

Sister looked surprised and then faintly sceptical.

'Well I've never seen him. Between you and me, I used to think he might not exist at all. These old people do invent stories, you see, to cheer themselves up. But there's a lay sister here – she's off sick today, or you could have spoken to her – who says the partner *does* exist and that maybe he's – you know – conned the poor old man out of what he had left.'

'I've been wondering that myself.'

'Mind you,' she went on hastily, 'I don't know just what reason Sister Bérénice has for thinking that. She sometimes exaggerates things herself. To be honest, I don't know quite what to think . . . And anyway,' she added more cheerfully, 'it isn't really my business. It's my job to look after them while they're here. We make them as comfortable as we can.'

'I can see you do.' She seemed diffident, a little defensive perhaps, not knowing who I was or if I might be anyone of importance. I wanted to encourage her. But I still had not got what I needed.

'Doesn't anyone else on the staff know more about Monsieur Maryk's affairs?' I asked at last. 'After all – a country area like this: people usually know all about each other.'

Sister wasn't sure. Of course a number of people had told her he'd been an artist, his work was known in the district. but, 'as to money matters, people know things because they hear about them through family connections, you see, but what with Monsieur Maryk being on his own, and an outsider too . . . Someone told me he was of gipsy stock?'

'I don't think so.'

'Well that's what I heard.'

'But he's been in the area – oh, since just after the war. Half a lifetime.' For me, in the past, the Creuse had been such a place of welcome and acceptance: I had never, till now, fully realized the exclusive insularity of French rural society. 'Surely,' I persisted, 'there must be someone else here from his village? Someone who knew how he was living just before he came into hospital?'

Sister did not think so. His village, it happened, was one of the most remote in the hospital's catchment area: 'It's twenty-five kilometres from here, you see. Not really the same bit of country.'

'Yes, I realize that.'

'You know where he was living then?' She sounded faintly reproachful, as if I had been wasting her time.

'Oh yes. It was there that I was told he was in here.'

'Then why not go and make enquiries there?'

'Yes Sister, perhaps I will,' I said submissively.

She clearly wanted me to go away and stop bothering her, so I did. I was already leaving the room, with her behind me, when she said: 'If you find his partner that's supposed to be so rich,' – she suddenly sounded anxious and scornful again – 'you might come back and tell me.'

I said that I would.

'I'd like to meet him,' she said.

Maryk's barn might be twenty-five kilometres from the hospital, but it was only about eight, cross-country, from the mill-house. It was further by road. However I had already decided, some time before, that that Sunday morning I would travel there on foot, by the field paths and trackways that had been Maryk's own favourite routes. In

232

an isolated spot a parked car, even an anonymous hired car, can be a conspicuous object.

I believed that, so far, I had been extremely inconspicuous. Neither to the Mayor of Maryk's village nor to the hospital sister had I identified myself. I had not been up to the village near the mill-house at all, and I thought that no one who had ever known me was aware of my presence there. In the empty house, which was yet not empty to me, of course, but full in every part of the life it had previously sheltered, I had kept the shutters drawn.

It was cold, the night before that morning. I woke several times, under the quilt on the kitchen divan where I was sleeping, and each time the temperature seemed to me to have dropped further. It was not yet dawn, and the alarm I had set had not yet gone off, when my febrile dreams frayed into persistent wakefulness and I knew I would sleep no more. I got up, and relit the stove.

The kitchen was only just getting comfortably warm when I left, but outside a bright morning had come: the first morning of winter, the first of the rest of my life. The dew of the previous evening had turned to hoar frost; each blade of grass, each twig, was sugared white. The late-blooming flowers in the beds by the wall were frosted too. I knew from other mornings, other years in my old life, that though this decoration would melt away as the sun rose, it would have finished off the chrysanthemum flowers: later in the day their extravagant heads would loll and blacken. But the small marigolds were hardier; they usually survived the first frosts.

At first the ruts in the track seemed to jar my legs inside my heavy boots, but when I had been going ten minutes or so I had warmed up and swung along more easily. I wore my own padded jacket and Jacquou's ancient, peaked hunting cap and his game bag. I also carried his shotgun, the one with the silver chasing on the breech. Early on a fine Sunday morning in the autumn, a hunter is the most ordinary and unremarkable figure in the French landscape.

I was not the only one about. Although I saw no others, I heard sporadic shots in the distance as I passed by the woods. Birds called sharp warnings to each other, wheeling in flocks across the stubble fields, and once I disturbed a partridge that ran in panic down a long green alley before me. My breath steamed in the bright air. Later, as the sun rode higher, and I followed it, I became almost too warm; sweat trickled between my shoulder blades. Except in the shadows, the hoar frost had melted away, leaving the autumn leaves wet and brilliant.

My walk seemed to go quickly, the eight kilometres vanishing without effort, as in multiple dreams I had had of it in the preceding weeks. Under my boots it went, hills and descents, stony tracts and muddy ones, grass and bracken and heather, through gates and under wires – and yet I have the impression that I remember every yard of it. I had checked the route carefully the night before on the detailed maps that had lived since ever in a table drawer, and two of the maps were now in the game bag I carried. But they were out of date. At one point I had to retrace my steps where I found a marked track impenetrably blocked by saplings and brambles, and make a wide detour round several fields. And in another place, where I distinctly remembered once picnicking by a narrow, rocky stream, a chain of trout pools now spread themselves under the sky, as if not years but decades had passed, and I was Rip Van Winkle returning. I had to by-pass them through a farmyard with a hysterically barking dog. And all the time the sun lay ahead of me on the tops of the trees, a golden coin, dazzling me and drawing me on.

Then, when my walk was almost done, and I calculated that I was nearing the wooded back of the hill on which Maryk's barn stood, I came to another stream and a ford. The wooden footbridge had been half-demolished by a fallen tree, so I waded where the carts and tractors were meant to cross, holding the gun well clear. The water went over my boots, soaking my socks and feet inside, but I was going so fast by this time, as in my dreams, and was so elated at being nearly there, that I hardly cared. I just tramped on in my squelching boots, and a song that had been at the back of my head ever since I had set out broke through to the front of my mind. I began to sing it under my breath in a dirge, since I cannot sing in tune though Simone could and Marigold had perfect pitch . . . It was one of her guitar ballads:

'. . . *It was mirk, mirk night, there was nae starlight*
And they waded through red blude to the knee;
For a' the blude that's shed on earth
Rins through the springs of that countrie . . .'

Thomas the Rhymer, travelling for seven years through a faery land that is also hell, accompanied by the queen of that place.

So, out of hell or faeryland, out of dreams and fantasy and into the day, I came at a great pace, up the wooded rise, through the thinning trees and shafts of sun and shadow, nearer and nearer to the barn till at last I saw it. I stopped, still in the woods' shadow, to get my breath. And also to make one or two final adjustments. Then I walked slowly round to the front.

Cleaner and tidier than it used to be. In the past, there had been bits of Maryk's rubbish and scrap-iron lying about, for he was a dedicated scavenger of anything that might come in useful, and also gruesome piles of bones under the nettles, as if the place were a fox's lair. And when Maryk was at home the door had regularly stood open, to let in the light. This morning, it was shut. But two windows had been made in the long wall that faced the open country; their shutters were open. A new chimney at one end had replaced Maryk's old iron stove pipe; as I watched, smoke drifted from it into the morning air. The dirt track up the hill had been smoothed and gravelled, and by its side was a newly painted notice:

Daffyd Huws – Artiste Peintre.

I stood looking at that notice for quite a long time. I almost felt as if, in spite of all my conviction and purpose, all my rehearsing fantasies, until that moment I had not entirely believed in it. But it also seemed like something known for years, as if everything had long been decided, and this morning was only the final enactment of a long-foregone conclusion.

It appears odd to me now that at no time that morning, or in the preceding days, did I ask myself if he would actually be at home. He might well have been away: the local Mayor had said he came and went. The signs of life in the house might simply have indicated the presence of another person, perhaps one of the 'female acolytes' of whom Paul had spoken.

But I did not think these things as I walked towards the door, and nor did they turn out to be so. I pulled a wrought-iron object that set up a rustic jangling within, then retreated a few paces. After a pause, he opened the door himself.

Fattish. In a track-suit and espadrilles as if he had just got up. Balding. A small dark beard, trimmed. A middle-aged man whom I might have passed in a street without another glance. And yet, as I looked directly at him, he was clearly and unmistakably Evan Brown. Most people do not change essentially over the years, or only do so in predictable and transparent ways, as school reunions testify.

'David Hughes?' I said, making the name neither French nor Welsh but firmly English.

'That's me,' he said, English too, in mild surprise. 'Who are you?' His face was ill-tempered, but he spoke pleasantly as if I might be a prospective customer. The morning sun was in his eyes, he could not see me clearly. He came out, raising a hand against the light.

During my whole journey, I had been carrying the shotgun over my arm, broken at the breech in the approved manner. Now I swung it round, clicked it into place and shifted the safety catch. The sound alerted him.

'Who are you?' he said sharply, a different tone, dodging into a position where he could see me clearly. 'What do you want – ?'

I too moved, into the space between him and his own front door. I also told him my name. But even as I spoke I saw that he had recognized me. I have not changed very much either, less than he had.

His face became fixed, and I saw again the ugly lines I had seen long ago when I had threatened him with the police, when he had told me 'I'll get even with you, you bastard.'

Now that phrase had become mine. No filmic rhetoric, but the literal truth.

'What the hell do you want?' he said. He was frightened now.

I raised Jacquou's gun. We were only about three yards apart.

I have sometimes asked myself since that morning what I would have done if he had remained calm. Just suppose he had said, in his most genial tone: 'Tom, put that down a minute and let's talk.' Or suppose he had come forward, hand advanced, to shake mine. Or, as Jacquou had once imagined, had gone down on his knees before me . . . Even then, at the very last moment, I think my Plan might have been deflected, my fantasy remained inanimate.

But he did not do these things. Instead, like the guilty man Jacquou had been sent to shoot in the river meadow by the mill-house, he turned and ran, ran away from me down the slope, floundering flat-footed in his espadrilles as he went. And so I went after him and shot him in the back at point blank range. And then reloaded and shot again. And left him where he fell, his lungs filling with blood, blood trickling from his back and his neck, beneath his lying signboard.

I don't remember much of the walk back except that, though I hastened, I felt very tired and shivered constantly. I wondered if my wet boots had chilled me so much that I was turning feverish. The bright morning had dimmed: clouds had come up.

I was deeply glad when I came over the brow of the last hill, trudging on newly ploughed soil, and saw the mill-house below, and wisps of smoke from the stove I had lit hours before still rising from the chimney. But I suppose it was then that I began to realize I was not as hidden there as I had thought. Just as I had noted the smoke from the barn

237

chimney as a sign of occupation, so someone in the last few days might have seen mine.

But my idea of the mill-house as a refuge was so strong that it overcame any prudent thoughts I might have had about making a quick departure. I was exhausted now, and easily persuaded myself that it would be an act of greater folly to set out to drive across half France in such a state. Better, surely, to have a wash and something to eat and leave only when I felt rested? For in any case what urgency could there be? Even if Evan had been found already, nothing there, I believed, pointed in my direction. Not yet. And perhaps not ever.

Of course I was mistaken. Absorbed in my own purpose, I had no idea how many people in that apparently empty countryside had noted my presence. Afterwards, I was to learn that as early as Thursday the baker, passing with his van, had told the Mayor of our own village that someone seemed to be in the mill-house with the shutters drawn and he hoped it wasn't an intruder – gipsy or such. The Mayor, a much more energetic functionary than his colleague in Maryk's village, had got into his car the following day and driven down to have a look himself. I must have been visiting the hospital at the time, but he saw the padlock was off the outhouse door and the track-marks of my car, and decided that the visitor was as likely to be someone with a right to be there. Later, I was apparently spotted driving back, which settled the matter.

Still, there would have been nothing at all to link me with the killing five miles away – had I not put in an appearance in that village also. Naturally, when Evan was discovered dead, the old man from the modern bungalow was one of the first to be called to the scene, and even he was eager to tell the police what he could. This must have included information about my visit on Friday, my questions to him about Evan, and a description of myself and the car.

I had, in any case, been noticed with my gun on Sunday morning by an old woman, as I tramped through the farmyard with the noisy dog. And I had been seen wading through the ford by some children, playing in the wood.

Two and two and two were quickly put together, an identification suggested.

Of course, I allowed all this to happen. I do know that really. A 'kamikazi approach' Lewis Greenfield later called it. Yes.

However, as I was to hear later also, it was only in the course of that busy Sunday that a local police officer, excitedly checking records, realized that the artist found shot was a man who had been in a car accident involving a fatality in the neighbouring district seven years before. It seems that no one had made that connection till then. The accident, on the road down to Argenton, had occurred some fifteen miles from Maryk's village. Daffyd Huws, with the fancy spelling more suited to the artistic pose, had only established himself as a permanence in Maryk's workshop several years later.

Whether it was also spotted on Sunday that the family name of someone they now wanted to interview coincided with that of the accident victim, I never heard. I like to think that the discovery was rapidly made: it must have been so satisfying for them.

Some time after, an experienced criminal lawyer said to me in the course of one of our many conversations, that Monsieur Brown-Hughes-Huws had shown a lack of taste and judgement, did I not think, in establishing himself so near the scene of the earlier accident, not to mention the territory of his previous dealings with my family? I said yes indeed, the same thought had occurred to me, but that 'lack of taste and judgement' seemed to me an inadequate diagnosis in the circumstances. Whatever else I believed I had fathomed about the workings of his mind, that particular crass move of his was, to me, inexplicable.

The lawyer remarked then that such apparent tempting of fate was 'not untypical of the habitual wrongdoer'.

'Men like that are often clever, I find, but ultimately they tend to commit some stupid or outrageous act because they literally do not see life in the same terms as most people. At some level, they really do believe that everything they want can be justified.' He paused, and then added: 'Perhaps quite a few people, in certain moods, may be subject to such distortion of view.'

I should have liked to have explored the theme further with this mild, intelligent man, but after a long pause, during which we gazed at one another, he brought our dialogue back firmly to the subject of my own actions.

But that long Sunday I knew nothing of the activity going on elsewhere. I sat quietly in the shadowy, lamplit kitchen. I was tired, weak I suppose, but not unhappy. I had eaten the stale bread that was left and finished the cheese. I had drunk most of the remaining bottle of Mad Wine, wishing only that I had some Real. One further thing I intended to do before I left. I knew that Jacquou had destroyed many of his Resistance papers when he surmised his end was coming, but I wanted to look over what remained and perhaps take some of them away with me. I opened one of Maryk's chests and embarked on this. But, in the strange, vague state I was in, I got side-tracked, coming across some ribbon-tied bundles of letters in an ornate, browning copperplate. They turned out to be decorous but passionate love letters – I think from Jacquou's father, the school teacher, Mayor and finder of the wooden angel, writing to his future wife. She must have kept them all her life, and after her death no one had wanted to throw them away. Jacquou had not; nor did I. I sat reading them, till the afternoon light began to fade again beyond the shutters, reading of emotions long appeased, of intricate daily plans now gone into the void, of vivid hopes for children not yet conceived and now all past and over themselves.

I was still reading when I heard several vehicles coming nosily down the track towards the house and then into the yard. I think I understood already, during that moment, that it was over.

I left the letters lying round the chest and went to open the door. Two police vans were drawn up, engines running, one with a blue light flashing. There was a police motor bike too, its radio babbling. I stood watching and, just as once before, when my Simca had been stolen, gendarmes

240

tumbled from the vans. But this time they hurried to surround me, pistols drawn. One of them even had a submachine-gun.

Ridiculous over-reaction, I thought, in my Anglo-Saxon way. Do they think I'm going to shoot at them?

Note by Lewis Greenfield

I believe that Tom had intended to add a few pages more to complete his account, but never did so. However, I may be mistaken about this.

He was arraigned in France for the 'voluntary homicide' of Evan Brown, alias David Hughes or Huws; but, as both he and the dead man were British subjects, the case was eventually transferred to the British Courts. This caused some unfocused indignation in the French press, the confusion centering on Tom's true nationality. The assumption that he was surely French stemmed partly from his Huguenot name and his family connections in France, but also from the nature of the charge: the French public affected to believe that such a *crime passionel* would be alien to the phlegmatic British temperament. The lack of any noticeable *sub judice* restrictions in France had ensured that the supposed facts of the case, plus a wealth of background information and speculation, had been copiously publicized in advance of any judicial hearing. *Le Père Vengeur* – 'the Avenging Father' – became almost a cult figure in some popular papers, while a more right-wing and intellectual weekly ran an alternative sideshow on the Danger of Anarchy and the folly of pointing the finger at a dead man who, criminal as he might be, could not speak for himself. Everyone else, however, seemed to speak a great deal. The police gave interviews. The examining magistrate for the prosecution gave interviews. So did assorted Mayors, farmers, café proprietors and old ladies. To anyone reared on British legal constraints the whole thing was a farce.

Almost a year after the event, Tom appeared here at the Old Bailey, where (I afterwards learnt) a garrulous and polyglot woman juror did not hesitate to tell her fellows everything she had read in the French papers. I had fixed him up with a QC, a good friend of mine, Harvey Bron. The

242

charge was murder. Harvey induced Tom to plead Not Guilty to this but to offer an alternative plea of Guilty to manslaughter – which, however, the prosecution were disinclined to accept. So matters had to proceed as for a full trial. Harvey had also wanted Tom to plead diminished responsibility, but of course he would not. In fact his evidence was a model of lucidity and reason, almost damningly so, I was afraid. It made Harvey's speech in mitigation, about the extent of Tom's previous suffering and its effect on his mind, seem a little specious. Although I believe myself that what Harvey said was true.

The Judge (who had also read the French papers on his summer holidays) made a meal of telling the jury to consider only what they had heard in Court, a useless request in these or any other circumstances, I'm glad to say. He then went on to talk about 'a measure of sympathy' – but that people must not imagine they can take the Law into their own hands. Especially not well educated, respected citizens with distinguished careers. And especially not a magistrate, 'of all people', who should, rather, set an example. The rule of Law embodies, indeed, the fundamental principle that the execution of justice should not be left to the injured party. Or supposedly injured party . . . hearsay evidence . . . And so on and so forth. 'Oh Jesus' I thought at this point. But then he changed course again, reverted to extenuating factors, directed the jury to accept the Guilty plea to manslaughter only which they obligingly did – and Tom ended up with four years. He could have fared a great deal worse. Another example of rough justice, you might call it.

Tom turned down any suggestion that he might appeal against sentence. He served just under two years, mainly in an open prison, worked in the prison library, wrote a lot. When I visited him there he said how peaceful and decent a life it was on the whole, and that he often thought of Piotr Mihailovitch and how much he must have suffered by comparison. He – Tom – had made friends with the prison chaplain who, he said, was 'a bit of an old woman' but nice, had worked in Africa and was interested in Amnesty

International. I could tell from the way Tom spoke, without him spelling it out, that he had come to regard himself as being in some sense a 'prisoner of conscience'. 'I did what seemed to me right and I had to do it,' he had said to me before the trial. I did not argue with him.

He also became particular friends with a fellow prisoner, a chartered accountant serving a sentence for embezzlement, who was an amateur ornithologist: the prison was in a remote area near the east coast, and there were lots of birds to watch. 'Old Peter taught me a lot, I shall miss him – and the birds,' Tom said to me the morning I came to collect him. He had just been paroled, officially because he had had a slight heart attack but really because everyone concerned wanted to let him out.

He seemed well in himself, a bit withdrawn but cheerful, and more simply affectionate than I have ever known him. Ann, poor girl, took great care of him, but he had another attack and died unexpectedly, at the end of 1987.

Although he died in London, he lies buried in France, in Limoges Protestant cemetery, near his distant ancestors and in the same vault as his father-in-law and his daughter. I arranged this, with Ann's distraught acquiescence. It was one thing I felt I could do for him.

The following year Myra and I and the two younger ones were driving through France to stay with friends in the south. I took the opportunity to visit the cemetery on my own. I had been there once before, on the terrible day of Marigold's burial, but now it seemed a quiet, pleasant enough place under the summer sky. On the stone rim of the grave I left a small round pebble, which I had picked up earlier beside a road in the Creuse. In my faith we do not believe in personal immortality. And we do not say 'forgive', we say 'remember'. An indestructible stone is what we leave to show respect and continuing memory for the loved dead.

BOOK BARN BOOKS

3255638-1.5

£1.50